LONE STAR VIGILANTE

ALSO BY MARK GREATHOUSE

LONE STAR VIGILANTE

JUSTICE TEXAS STYLE

THE TUMBLEWEED SAGAS
BOOK 8

MARK GREATHOUSE

WOLFPACK
PUBLISHING
— EST 2013 —

Dedicated with love to my wife, Carolyn, and to our two sons, Mike and Matt.

COMMEMORATION

August 10, 2023, marked the 200th anniversary of the founding of the Texas Rangers by Stephen Austin.

Luke Dunn, the fictional protagonist in my Tumbleweed Sagas is a composite, a prototypical Texas Ranger delivering justice and redemption. I tip my hat to the likes of my Texas Ranger ancestors: grandfather Horace Charles Greathouse, cousin Rut Evans, and cousins John Beamond "Red John" Dunn and his brother Matthew Dunn. It has been a pleasure to learn the stories of and incorporate in my fiction the adventures of real-life Texas Rangers like John Coffee Jack Hayes, Samuel H. Walker, John Salmon RIP Ford, Ben McCulloch, William Bigfoot Wallace, Leander Harvey McNelly, and so many more who fought for justice on the vast and varied landscape that is Texas.

There's something to be said for the old story of the mayor of a town experiencing a riot and complaining to the Texas Ranger that showed up, "They only sent one Ranger?" And the famous response, "Well, pardner, thar's only one riot ain't ther'?"

I do invite readers to check out Texas Ranger museums in places like Waco, Fredericksburg, San Antonio, Falfurrias, and Austin, as they bring the exploits of the famed lawmen to life.

THE NUECES STRIP

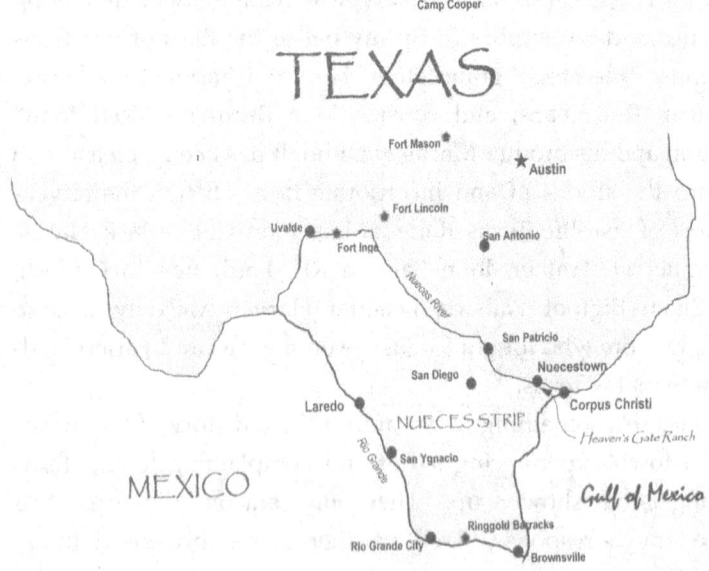

The vast Nueces Strip serves as the primary setting for the
Tumbleweed Sagas. The Strip was also called Wild Horse Desert,
owing to the millions of Mustangs that roamed its prairies. *(Sketch by
Mark Greathouse)*

NUECESTOWN

Nuecestown, Texas, established in 1852 by English and German settlers, was developed by Corpus Christi founder Colonel Henry Kinney along the Nueces River as a ferry crossing. Mostly thanks to the railroad passing it by, it's now a "ghost town" marked only by historical markers. All that remains is a preserved schoolhouse and the old Nuecestown Cemetery. *(Sketch by Mark Greathouse)*

NUGESTOWN

THE CAST

Lucas Dunn, Jr.—*Goes by the nickname "Junior." The proverbial fruit doesn't grow far from the tree, as Junior follows in the lawman footsteps of his legendary Texas Ranger father.*

Cassie McCully Dunn—*Daughter of Grant McCully, who owns a ranch near Heaven's Gate. Cassie is married to Junior. Family ties complicate our story.*

Grant McCully—*Cassie's father. McCully is a successful rancher.*

Bode McCully—*A former Texas Ranger and grandfather to Cassie McCully. Bode falls into a twisted set of circumstances.*

Lucas "Long Luke" Dunn—*Was one of the greatest Texas Ranger Captains ever, having gained repute as an Indian fighter and respected lawman. Comanche called him Ghost-Who-Rides. Luke builds Heaven's Gate Ranch and has eleven children with his wife, Elisa.*

Elisa Corrigan Dunn—*Married Luke Dunn after losing her family to frontier rigors, including fighting off Comanche and hired killers.*

Rex Rucker—*Retired Army general, hero of War Between the States on the Union side, and old acquaintance of Junior.*

Gordon Belknap—*Retired Army officer who built his career fighting Comanche, Apache, Rebels, and bandits on the prairies of the Nueces Strip before turning to journalism.*

Edward Thorpe—*Son of the evil scion Horatio Thorpe. He inherits his father's fortune and fights against evil-doers to achieve legitimate business success.*

Jubal Strong—*Cousin to the outlaw Bad Bart Strong, whom Luke had brought to justice back in 1856 near Laredo. Strong left Wyoming to build a life in Texas.*

Jim "Eagle Eye" Smith—*Half-breed renegade Kiowa warrior conflicted between White man's and Indian's worlds.*

One Arrow—*Aging Comanche chief living on a reservation in Oklahoma while maintaining his friendship with the Dunn family.*

Brad Tyler—*Sheriff of Nueces County.*

Buffalo Watts—*Famous mountain man who lived long enough to retire to Corpus Christi after a life of trapping, buffalo hunting, and stalking Indians for the Army.*

Trey Bolton—*Outlaw with a penchant for robbing banks and trains. Known to kill folks.*

Colt Driscoll—*A malcontent working to build a reputation as a killer and robber.*

Carlos Diaz—*Mexican bandit aiming to carry on the legacy of Cheno Cortina, the Red Robber of the Rio Grande, and to succeed where the bandit Jesus Seguira had failed.*

William "Big Bill" Riordan—*Rustler and murderer who fled the Texas Panhandle and plagued the Nueces Strip.*

Jim Bigcrow—*Renegade half-crazed Apache that escaped Fort Sill and sought vengeance for perceived wrongs inflicted upon his people.*

Cal Pardoe—*A rancher in South Texas who finds himself embroiled in a range war, not of his own making.*

Plug Nichols—*A gunfighter hired to tame a range war and becomes inadvertently involved in more mayhem.*

Hank Johnson—*One of Archer Parr's hired ranch hands working in the midst of a range war.*

HISTORICAL CHARACTERS

Charles Culberson—*Followed Jim Hogg and then Joseph Clay Stiles Blackburn as governor of Texas. He ran afoul of the Democratic Party over his opposition to the Ku Klux Klan.*

Nicholas Dunn—*Legendary Texan who contributed hugely to taming the Nueces Strip as drover, Comanche fighter, rancher, and livestock breeder and speculator. An Irish immigrant at age 15, he marries Andree Ann Goebel and they have nine children in building a life near Alice, Texas.*

John Reynolds Hughes—*Became the longest-serving Texas Ranger Captain. Hughes dealt with Comanche and Apache over his years as rancher and lawman. He was a sergeant in the Frontier Battalion down along the Texas/Mexico border until 1893, when he was promoted to captain.*

John Beamond "Red John" Dunn—*A tough, wiry character who served as a Texas Ranger, was a vigilante, raised dairy cows, and established a museum in Corpus Christi famed for its collection of militaria. In his exploits, he often found himself flirting with being on the wrong side of the law.*

Matthew Dunn—*Rancher brother of Red John Dunn with a spread near Corpus Christi.*

James B. Wells—*Political power broker of Cameron County, having been Brownsville city attorney and state district judge. He was the protégé of Democratic Party boss Stephen Powers in Corpus Christi and was close with Archie Parr, the party boss in Duval County west of Alice, Texas*

Patrick Dunn—*The son of Thomas Dunn, Patrick called himself the Duke of Padre Island, as he successfully raised longhorns on North Padre Island east of Corpus Christi for nearly 50 years (1879-1926) before selling out to a developer. The island now comprises the North Padre Island National Seashore.*

Emilio Forto—*Sheriff of Cameron County.*

Archer Parr—*Known as "Archie," he established a political dynasty in what became Jim Wells County and led to decades of Democratic Party control through means fair and foul.*

Stephen Powers—*Political power broker exercising tight control over goings-on in Corpus Christi. He has close ties with Archie Parr and Jim Wells.*

THEME

VIGILANTE

A member of a volunteer committee organized to suppress and punish crime summarily, also, a self-appointed deliverer of justice.

YOU'RE INVITED

Howdy,

It's been a pleasure to share the first seven Tumbleweed Sagas featuring the exploits of my namesake legendary father, Texas Ranger Lucas Dunn. From here on, I reckon to share my own experiences wearing the Texas Ranger badge. You can call me Junior.

Lone Star Vigilante: Justice Texas Style offers a twisted tale of intrigue as justice goes awry. It's set in 1895 on the Texas Nueces Strip. The Strip could be said to be afire economically, as agriculture, railroads, communications, and black gold spawned ever greater growth. Communications? While the telegraph expanded its reach, it was the soon-to-be-ubiquitous telephone that was beginning to make its presence felt mostly in the larger Texas cities. And black gold? The "Lucas Gusher" at Spindletop Hill in 1901 near Beaumont would usher in the Texas oil era. Gushers of oil became ever more common, creating gushers of money in bank accounts. But I'm ahead of myself.

Barbed wire had made its appearance on the Nueces Strip a decade earlier and was creating a topographical patchwork of pasture and farm. The resulting range wars, fence cuttings, and water rights battles fostered lawbreaking challenges that tested the mettle of many a lawman. Lynching and worse bore evidence to a rise in vigilante justice, as frustrated and fearful citizens took the law into their own hands.

The Nueces Strip could be inhospitable six ways to Sunday. The similarities between natural and human dangers were often striking. Imagine the intense eyes and coils of a rattlesnake on the hunt. A rabbit looks about innocently unaware. The snake's forked tongue picks up vibrations in the air. Patience...of sorts. The moment of attack must be exactly right. Only an infinitesimal twitch of the tip of his rattle-bedecked tail reveals the tension in the beast. He dares not indulge a blink of eyes. Now imagine a lone bushwhacking vigilante, as he peers down the long blue-gray barrel of his 1895 Winchester. The bead at the muzzle is on the target and cradles in the notch of the rear sight. His finger curls around the trigger. Only a slow bead of sweat down the side of his face reveals his intensity. Patience. The moment must be precise. His breathing, his slow squeeze of the trigger. The murderous prey he's hunted looks about cautiously but unaware. A sudden uncoiling, mouth open, fangs exposed, and the rattlesnake is fed. Breath held, trigger squeezed, and a man lies dead. In its vast silence, the Nueces Strip sucks it all in.

Application of the law could too often be horrifically fast or mind-bogglingly slow. The accused lawbreaker could as easily meet his end at an impromptu necktie party as be convicted in a court of law. Vigilance committees or vigilantes had sprung from this environment over the years, especially as normally law-abiding citizens grew impatient with the delivery of justice. My own cousin, Red John Dunn, capped off a ten-year enlistment with the Texas Rangers under Captain Bland Chamberlain and later Captain Leander McNelly with several instances of involvement with vigilante justice. Taking the law into one's own hands was expeditious but illegal and fraught with far too many instances of innocent men being on the wrong end of a rope or bullet. Dunn himself was tried twice for murder and acquitted both times.

In *Lone Star Vigilante*, I'm right pleased to share my story of following in my legendary father's lawman footsteps and seeking to make significant headway in bringing justice to the Nueces Strip. Blood, as shed by both innocent and evil men, colors the Strip. A single vigilante, a stealthy lone wolf operator, presents a huge challenge as I must artfully wreak my brand of justice on the lawbreakers that don't make my efforts any easier. My life is complicated by occasionally tense family relationships. Meanwhile, prairie fires, blizzards, floods, stampedes, desperate killers, rustlers, disease, and savages are part and parcel of my life. Just about anywhere I ride, death could be reaching for my reins. While I possess a natural tendency to emulate my father in building considerable notoriety and creating enemies by virtue of success in bringing lawbreakers to justice, I'm very much my own man and have established my very own reliable allies. It's 1895, and there's an ever-present sense of trouble lingering in the air.

For anyone of a mind that the frontier had been won, they had a second think coming. The wild prairies and hills of Texas were alive and kicking, lawbreaking was very much in abundance, and what one might call the residuals of old wild west justice prevailed. It's in this setting that vigilante justice remained strong for better or worse.

Kindly,
  Lucas Dunn, Jr.

LONE STAR VIGILANTE

PROLOGUE

THE DARK-BLUE STEEL barrel of his rifle had been lovingly rubbed to a matte finish. The lever-action Winchester Model 1895 was the latest creation of the Winchester Repeating Arms Company. The lever fed .405 Winchester cartridges into the receiver as fast as it could be worked and earned it a reputation as an efficient and reliable carbine. His coal-black eyes nestled the fixed post front sight into the sliding ramp of the rear sight. The shooter, dressed fully in black and with charcoal smeared over his face, blended fully into the shadowy shelter of the live oak motte. The range to the target was well within the Winchester's window of accuracy. The crescent moon hung in the night sky like a set of silver longhorns partially covered by clouds, allowing just enough starlight to seep in to enable the hunter to distinguish his prey from the enveloping darkness. The night air was still and unusually dry, the bullet ready to perform its deadly mischief.

Concealed in the shadows, he breathed slowly, ever-so-easily, as he watched his target silhouetted on horseback against the night sky. Patience. His prey was drawing close. Just a little closer would do just fine. The target's blackness drew near enough to block out the very tip of the moon behind him. He could hear the horse's hooves clicking on the rocky trail.

The shooter breathed in, held his breath...his finger flexed against the trigger. He squeezed. An explosion, a flash, and the crack of a bullet splitting the air on its way to its target. The silhouetted head disappeared in an atomized spray of blood and bone. The riderless horse looked about panic-stricken before galloping off, lighting the darkness with a trail of sparks.

A satisfied smile spread across the deep lines and crannies of the shooter's face. He stood and stared out toward where his prey had fallen as if to confirm the kill. He shrugged. He never missed. As clouds blocked the moonlight, he found his way to his horse, slid the Winchester into its scabbard, mounted up, and quickly rode away. Somewhere, a victim could rest easy. Justice had been served.

ONE
DARK PERIL

THREE BUZZARDS HOVERED in descending circles over the broad, dry prairie nearly a day's ride west from Corpus Christi. They were cautiously eyeing a pair of coyotes that, in turn, were pacing about warily, observing a mountain lion chawing at the haunches of her breakfast. Two lion cubs played nearby. It was altogether a quiet scene save for the gnawing sound of tooth on bone.

A lone riderless horse moved in circles ever further from the scene.

The coyotes suddenly yipped and scattered, and the lion's ears perked up. She let out a low growl at the approaching sound of hooves and the interruption of her meal. Listening guardedly, she reluctantly gathered her cubs and slinked off into the grasses. The buzzards broke off their circling and found a roost a safe distance away in a lone live oak. None of them cared to deal with a live human.

The rider approached with great care. His horse's ears shot up at the distant growl and nostrils flared at the faint smell of mountain lion. The rider nudged his heels ever-so-slightly into the cayuse's sides and kept him heading toward whatever held all these varmints' interest. Sheriff Brad Tyler was dreading what he might find. The riderless horse had been an all-too-obvious clue even from a distance.

Sure enough, the aroma of death reached him just about the time he came upon the mostly intact victim. He gazed down from his saddle. Other than a goodly chunk of the victim's head having been blown away and a substantial chunk of flesh torn from his butt by the mountain lion, there was pretty much just enough remaining to warrant burial.

Tyler dismounted, covered his nose with his bandana, and began to search the pockets of the dead man. "Damn," he muttered to himself. He knew of the victim. Bad to the bone, and a bounty hunter to boot. He considered how ironic the man's end had been, and yet it was decidedly just but unjust.

It took the sheriff nearly an hour to calm the victim's horse and coax him to the murder site and nearly half again that time to load and tie the blanket-wrapped body over the skittish animal's saddle.

The mountain lion looked longingly at the goings on from afar before licking her chops and nudging her hungry cubs away. She rightly sensed that it wouldn't be a suitable day to take on a human. The coyotes? Well, they were only brave from a distance in their whimpering and yipping. They likely avoided a tussle with the lion and buzzards in any case. And the buzzards would sit and wait patiently for the next opportunity. Perhaps, they held out hope that the lion would take out her frustration on a coyote.

"Dang, Bode. You lookin' like you ain't slept a wink."

Bode looked up through sleep-deprived eyes. "Grab a seat, Slim. Have some coffee." The deep gravel in his voice bore little hint of an energy that belied his early morning condition, not to mention his advanced years.

Slim poured himself a cup of brew and plopped himself

down across from his friend. "So, when did you take up wrestling polecats?" He watched Bode scoop a generous forkful of eggs into his mouth and wince as he chomped down on a broken tooth.

"Lot on my mind these days, Slim. The whole damn world's gone to hell in a handbasket. Too many folks getting away with all sorts of lawbreaking, and there aren't enough lawmen to corral 'em."

"You been sayin' that since before you retired from the Texas Rangers, Bode. Ain't nothing gonna change. It's just the way it is."

"It should change, Slim. It's got to change."

"You did your best."

"And I'd still be doin' it, if they hadn't aged me out. I can still shoot the hair off a gnat's ass."

"Not gonna argue 'bout your marksmanship, Bode. You've always been right handy with just 'bout any firearm ever made." Not said was Bode's tendency to shoot first and ask questions later. He'd more than once been hard-pressed to convince a judge of his innocence, be it charges of manslaughter or murder. At least the Texas Ranger honchos appreciated his dedication enough to supply witnesses that would absolve him. Slim looked enviously at his friend's breakfast, then motioned to the server. "Hey, Mabel, how 'bout getting' me a plateful of this fine breakfast like Bode's eatin' afore I drown in my own spit." He licked his lips for emphasis.

Mabel walked over and refilled both men's coffee cups. "You like your eggs as usual, Slim?"

Slim smiled broadly. "Dropped fresh from a hen would be just fine, Mabel darlin'." He turned back to Bode.

"Speakin' of marksmanship, how you likin' that Winchester 1895? .38-72 ain't it?"

The deep wrinkles around Bode's eyes scrunched up as he grinned. ".405, Slim. Pretty much destroy anything I hit." Bode made like he was squinting down the barrel of the rifle, aimed toward Mabel, and pulled an imaginary trigger. "Bam!"

Mabel doubled over playfully. "You got me, Mr. McCully. I'm a dead goner for sure." She nearly spilled Slim's breakfast as she laughed.

Slim turned to Bode. "What you fixin' to do this fine day, Bode? You doin' much of anything' in yer old age these days?"

"Figure to take a nap." Bode offered a wry grin. "My granddaughter is fixing to visit later on."

"She's a looker, she is."

"Not for you, Slim. She's already got herself hitched to that young buck Luke Dunn, Jr. Now, there's a young man with the smarts and energy to keep that wild filly tamed." Bode chuckled to himself at the thought of it.

"Hear tell the kid's signing up with the Rangers. Guess the fruit doesn't fall far from the tree."

"Likely you're right. Legendary wouldn't do justice to describing the boy's father. He was far and away one of the best Texas Rangers that ever rode the Strip."

"Junior's a big man, too. I'd guess he's taller than his father and 'bout as broad of shoulder. The kid can shoot. They say he can shoot the eye out of a rattlesnake while it's in mid-strike."

Bode sighed longingly. "I used to shoot like that."

"Hell, Bode. You were good, but…"

"I suppose you're right. I could hold my own with the best, though."

Slim smiled and nodded.

I sat thoughtfully astride Tornado, striking a pose not unlike my famous lawman father. The big horse swished his tail about, patiently awaiting my next command. The Appaloosa had a sort of sixth sense as horses go. Whatever was on my mind, it was as though Tornado sensed my thoughts. Maybe, it was thanks to the tornado that ripped through the countryside the night Tornado was foaled. Some folks were convinced that me and my horse communicated telepathically, as I gave him no discernible voice commands and it took a practiced eye to catch any movement of my heels or knees in the cayuse's sides or any telltale shifting of my big frame. The big stallion had been sired by way of Twister, the Appaloosa my father had ridden across the vast prairies of the Nueces Strip on the final missions of his legendary Texas Ranger career.

If I had a mustache like my father had cultivated, I'd likely have been stroking it while in deep thought. Somewhere out there lurked a killer, and I was fully stumped as to whom it might be. "Let's head home, Tornado." Concern gripped pretty much everyone that a bushwhacker was in our midst.

I'd ridden but a couple of hundred yards when I heard the sound of shod hooves on hard-packed gravel. I felt Tornado's legs tighten, and his ears went erect in anticipation of a command. I looked back over my shoulder, relaxed, and turned the big horse toward the approaching rider. "Dang, Gordon Belknap! Well, I'll be!" I called out. "Where you headed in such an all-fired hurry?"

Belknap pulled up. "Catching up with you. I hear there's news brewin'."

"You think I've got a story for that rag you call a newspaper?" I laughed.

"Hear tell there was a shootin' last night. Also rumor that some old Texas Ranger's son was putting on the badge."

"Well, you're wrong about me knowing about any shooting, but right about the rumor. Don't look like my dad's ready to give up ranching just yet, and he doesn't want to carve out another parcel. I need to make a living for Cassie and me." The fifty beeves given me and Cassie as a wedding gift had been appreciated, but I figured I'd need a lot more to make a serious go of ranching. Given that I was exceptional at tracking most anything that walked or slithered, was a fine marksman, and pretty much had my father's passion for justice, the very idea of becoming a Texas Ranger was hardly far-fetched. Me and Cassie surely needed steady income, and while I appreciated her efforts at sewing and altering garments to earn extra money, I felt stressed that I wasn't contributing more. Fact was, I sensed that the stress was likely part of the reason Cassie had yet to become pregnant. It surely wasn't for lack of us trying.

"Mind if I ride along with you?"

Belknap snapped me back from my momentary dream state. I nodded distractedly. "Er...just heading back to Nueces-town. Was figuring to catch up with the sheriff."

Belknap pulled up alongside and rode along for a moment before speaking. "You won't find Sheriff Tyler in Nuecestown. He's bringing back some bounty hunter's body that a cowboy discovered early this morning. Don't know who the dead man is, but early word has it that he was as much outlaw as bounty hunter."

I glanced over at Belknap and patted Tornado's neck. "Seems that's how most bounty hunters are. My dad said that he survived on bounties as a lawman early on, but he told me that most bounty hunters led dual lives as you say. There's a lot of folks out there living on the edge between lawful and lawless."

"I recall you have a Texas Ranger cousin named Red John that's been known to take up with vigilantes. He's been tried for murder at least once that I know of. Gotta believe that's no better than bounty hunting. Shoot, I heard that your Cassie's grand..." Belknap caught himself. Cassie McCully Dunn's grandfather, Bode McCully's unsavory reputation for delivering rough justice wasn't an appropriate matter to discuss.

"You've been getting around, Gordon. Army retirement pay not enough?"

Belknap forced a laugh. "I'll take that as a joke."

"To your earlier point about me joining the Texas Rangers,

I'll be heading off tomorrow to sign on with Captain John Hughes."

"You're right capable, Junior, but I hope they don't expect you to fill your father's shoes...at least not right away." Belknap rightly recognized the pressure that might bring.

"Have to deal with that when and if it happens." I brought Tornado to a halt and thought a moment. "Now, you've got me curious." He had me thinking about Sheriff Tyler bringing in a shooting victim. "I think I'll double back to Corpus and see what Sheriff Tyler has found."

"Mind if I ride along?"

"Suit yourself, my friend. Just spell my name right in your newspaper."

"I thought Junior was stopping by today." Elisa looked concerned as she sipped her coffee.

Luke looked distractedly at the gallery railing where the rowels on his spurs had worn a deep notch over many years. He had his hands locked behind his head as he stretched back and gave a knowing sideways glance at Elisa. "Must have gotten himself distracted."

"You're not worried?"

He shook his head. "No cause to be. He pretty much can handle himself."

"I heard from the ladies in Nuecestown saying that there's a cold-blooded killer ranging around Nueces County who's exacting some version of justice. Word has it that he struck again the other night."

Luke stroked his mustache. His red hair had turned a nearly white shade of gray, silver some might say. He was wont to stroke his mustache when seriously thinking on anything. "I understand your concern, Lisa, but Junior is an adult and wise to the ways of the Strip. I've about taught him all I know." The implication was that Junior was, in fact, quite teachable, absorbing information like a sponge. Importantly to Luke's thinking, the young man exhibited that rare combination of book-learned intelligence and innate prairie smarts. Luke thought appreciatively on that. He smiled lovingly at her. "He may pull in late." Luke made a final serious stroke of his mustache. "Did he tell you about figuring to join the Rangers?"

Elisa was silent. She and Luke had raised eleven children and been blessed to have only lost two during their life and times around the rough environs of Nueces County. A son had fallen prey to the bullets of a Mexican rustler about ten years back, and a daughter was lost to a bout with yellow fever. "I feel as I felt when you'd go riding off on one of your missions. It's like sending loved ones off for battle...you can never be certain they'll return."

"You really felt that way when I'd leave?" Luke knew that, but he always asked whenever she brought it up.

Elisa sighed. "You men are clueless." She smiled lovingly. "My favorite sound used to be the pounding of your horse's hooves coming up the trail to our house and you singing one of those Irish airs." She turned and looked lovingly up at him. "Of course, you'd have your way with me and leave me pregnant before you rode off to deliver Texas Ranger justice again. Cassie must be beside herself with worry about Junior's choice." Elisa couldn't help but wonder whether Cassie supported her husband's decision. The girl's grandfather had been a Texas Ranger.

"Guess I was clueless." Luke offered a sheepish smile and wrapped an arm around her.

"I am proud of all you did, Lucas. I knew better than to hold you back." She looked deep into his eyes. She'd got him to quit once, but she didn't like what it did to his spirit, so she released him from his promise. Still, she'd had to nurse him back from one near-mortal wound, and that was one too many.

She prayed such a fate might never befall Cassie. She blinked, then smiled.

Luke felt her gaze penetrate his very soul. Dang, but she was still a beautiful woman. His face took on an all-too-familiar expression, as his eyes sought to penetrate her very essence. His hand moved to caress the softness of her breast.

"Oh no...at this time of day?" She removed his hand, kissed it, smiled fetchingly, and gently led him back inside the house.

As Sheriff Tyler came into sight, I reined in and turned to Gordon Belknap. "I'd like some private words with the sheriff, if you don't mind, Gordon."

The newspaperman didn't have to be asked twice. "I look forward to hearing about Luke Dunn's namesake," he said with a laugh, as he rode off.

I shook my head, nudged Tornado forward, and approached the sheriff. "Sheriff Tyler. I see you've had a busy day." I nodded toward the horse with the blanketed and quite aromatic body draped over its saddle.

The sheriff anticipated my next question. "Big caliber like an old Sharps is my guess. Maybe one of them new 1895 Winchesters. He's been dead maybe a day and a half. Wasn't robbed. Found his horse wandering nearby. Varmints hadn't done him too much."

"You know his name?"

"Bounty hunter and sometime killer named Dawson Smith. He was hanging at one of our local watering holes last I'd heard." Tyler was feeling just a tad annoyed at my questions. He likely only tolerated them out of respect for my father.

I stroked my chin. "Guess some frontier justice up and bit him."

Tyler guffawed. "This bite near blew his head clean off.

Somebody out there is right handy with a rifle." The sheriff paused. "Smith is the third man of dubious reputation to meet his end in Nueces County in the past couple of months. I'm of a mind that it's the same shooter."

"So I hear. Do you know of any vigilance committees being called up to find the bushwhacker, sheriff?"

"Nope. I suspect that's because the victims have been men that folks figured got their just desserts. Been nothing to get anyone emotionally riled up over. Still, murder is murder, and I expect it's my job to find the killer."

"I'm heading off to see Captain Hughes tomorrow. Maybe a Texas Ranger would be of some help."

The sheriff stiffened a bit. "I'm of a mind to handle this myself, Junior. Don't be telling Captain Hughes about this. None of his business."

I paused. I could sense the obvious resistance. "Well, I would be surprised if he didn't know. Do let me know if you'd care for any help." I nodded by way of a goodbye and turned Tornado eastward. "You know where to find me. Good luck, Sheriff." I urged the big Appaloosa forward with nary a glance back.

I pulled up to my folks' Heaven's Gate ranch house, slid easily from the saddle, and draped the reins across the hitching rail. I vaulted up the stairs and crossed the gallery to the door in what might seem to some like a single fluid motion. As I grasped the latch, the door swung open, caught me off balance, and pretty much catapulted me into my mother's arms.

"We thought you might not get here," she said, brought to near breathlessness by my hug.

I stood back and stole a glance at my father. "I do need to

get over to the McCully place right quick. Cassie is fixin' a dinner and promised something special."

Elisa nodded knowingly. Dunns always seemed in a hurry to get somewhere or do something right away. "Well, we won't keep you," she said with just a hint of sarcasm.

"Aww, you know what I mean, Mom."

Luke stepped up and took my hand. "Hear tell your joining up. I'm proud of you, son."

"The weather hasn't been kind to the ranch lately, Dad, and we need the money. We're not fixin' to borrow."

Elisa nodded. Heaven's Gate had been barely getting by, thanks to the drought. Their management of business magnate Edward Thorpe's extensive southern Texas ranch holdings pretty much kept them solvent. She handed me a bag filled with cookies. "Do take these to the McCully's."

I hugged her again and them, in an unusual move, gave my father a hug. "Love you, Dad."

Luke was momentarily taken aback. "Love you, too, Junior." He gave a perplexed, slack-jawed shrug followed by a grin. In the rough and tumble atmosphere of the west, family loyalty was a given, but affection often overlooked.

I turned, and after waving the bag of cookies high as though it was some sort of trophy, mounted up, threw a wave at my folks, and gave the Appaloosa its head for a quick stop at Cassie's and my place before heading to the McCully spread.

Cassie Dunn had followed to the letter the cornbread recipe Elisa had given her. Her family was going to be gathering for Saturday evening dinner, and she was determined to cook up something a little special. A couple of blueberry pies were already cooling on the windowsill, but Elisa's cornbread would be an extra treat. It wasn't going as great as she'd hoped.

"What's troubling you, Cassie?" Her mother seemed always to be around in times of crisis.

"Lucas is joining us for dinner, and I so wanted to impress him." Her lower lip pouted with just a touch of disappointment. She gently tucked her strawberry-blonde curls back behind her ears. She frustratingly released a short burst of air through puckered lips.

"I think the heat was just a tad high, sweetie." Her mother examined the burned edges of the cornbread. She smiled. "We just might have time to try again."

Cassie sighed and rolled her eyes resignedly.

"You're worried about him, aren't you?"

"What is it about men? What does he have to prove?"

"It's in his blood, sweetie. His destiny is wrapped up with his father."

"I mean…being a Texas Ranger…it's…well…he could get himself killed."

"What burned?" Grant McCully walked into the kitchen, his nose raised to better sniff the air.

"Cassie's cornbread got burned. Pay it no never mind."

"Well, what you lookin' so down in the mouth fer, young lady?"

"Leave her be, Grant. Its woman worries."

Cassie went to work mixing up a new batch of cornbread batter. She so wanted to make a great impression on me. We'd been trying for five years now to have children, but the stresses of working their new ranch seemed to be making that difficult. She longed to bring some sanity and relaxation into our, at times, frenetic existence. Now, she was dealing with the added stress of mr following in my father's footsteps and joining the Texas Rangers. Ranching had been rough owing to especially dry weather, and we needed steady income. Prolonged drought could do that.

Her father shrugged sheepishly and left the kitchen.

The cat was frozen in place. Not a muscle moved. His pointy ears were on full alert. Only a slight twitch of his bobtail and ever-so-slight flaring of his nostrils distinguished him from a taxidermist's masterpiece. His spotted coat blended perfectly with the surrounding brush and rocky terrain. The rabbit certainly had no idea that the lynx lurked but ten feet away. He sheared off a luscious green shoot of grass. It was his final life morsel.

The dark figure watched from afar as the theater of nature unfolded. He'd been sweeping the scene with his spyglass when he came upon victim and hunter by sheer chance. Some sort of magnetism drew him to witness the play. He felt an instant kinship with the lynx. The only difference was that the rabbit had done no wrong. He smiled and then shrugged as he collapsed the telescope. Poor rabbit.

He arose for a moment but quickly kneeled back down with one hand gently stroking his horse's nose to keep the cayuse still. A rider was approaching and not far off. He wasn't but fifty yards away. Only a live oak motte shielded the watcher from view. His hobbled mount stood silently beside him. Nary a sound. As Sheriff Tyler rode off into the distance, he stood back up and urged his horse to stand. He allowed himself an ironic smile and slipped the telescope into his saddlebag before mounting. Watcher indeed. Observer. More like vigilante, deliverer of justice? He found himself murmuring under his breath. "Damned worthless lawman."

As the vigilante turned his horse back toward Corpus Christi, a second rider appeared in the distance. He retrieved the spyglass and peered through it. He watched the traveler for a few moments in the fading light as though memorizing its features. He collapsed the telescope and drew a folded paper from his breast pocket. He opened it and read it for the umpteenth time in the dim light for perhaps the twentieth time. Blond beard...handlebar mustache...broad-brimmed brown hat...bay gelding...yep, the distant rider fit the description. It had been what he'd been looking for, when the lynx caught his attention. He turned and looked off to where Sheriff Tyler had ridden. The sheriff was still much too close. A gunshot on the broad level reaches of the Nueces Strip at this moment simply wouldn't do. The echo would travel for miles. Trey Bolton would blithely ride on to live and to break the law for at least another day.

The vigilante, for that's whom he was, patted the 1895 Winchester as though consoling a dear friend, stuffed the spyglass back into his saddlebag, and resumed his ride toward Corpus Christi.

After making the brief stop at my folks' place and making the short ride from our modest cabin on the 5,000-acre spread that Cassie's father had gifted us as a wedding present from the McCully ranch, the ride to the McCully place was brief. The dim light of evening had begun to settle in, as the moon and stars began to ask their silvery shadows in the nooks and crannies of the rough plank walls of the main house. It was rustic and exceedingly comfortable. I slipped from the saddle and hitched Tornado. I eased through the front door, slipped off my gun belt, and hung it on the post as I entered the McCully foyer. I felt Cassie's eyes on me and smiled inwardly. Her father had already greeted me out by the gate and shaken my hand with his typical bone-crushing grip. I had learned to retaliate in kind, though not so strong as to diminish the man's ego.

"Dinner's just about ready, Lucas. Come grab a seat." I could see that Cassie was experiencing a raging urge to wrap herself around me in a huge hug but found herself having to be satisfied with my hand placed behind her back, as I escorted her to the table. She was perhaps overly sensitive to her father's tendency to be uncomfortable with any public displays of affection even between married couples.

I politely pulled the chair out for Cassie to sit. The table was a veritable cornucopia of culinary delights. The aromas were near overwhelming. It didn't take a mental giant to figure that Cassie had gone all out for me. It was surprising that I managed to stay fit and trim with her fine cooking. "I stopped by at Heaven's Gate on my way here. My folks send their best." I pulled the chair up to the table, nodded toward Cassie's folks, and handed Mrs. McCully the bag of cookies. I scanned the table. "Jake's not joining us?" Jake was Cassie's younger brother and was a cattleman through and through.

"Have a seat, sweetheart. Jake's on some business up Victoria way and won't return for a day or two."

"Is your pa enjoying retirement?" Mrs. McCully was already up to making small talk.

I half smiled. "If you call managing 300,000 acres plus ranching our own 30,000 retirement. But to your question, ma'am, I think my father misses his work as a lawman."

"Well, do you recall that Cassie's grandfather was a Texas Ranger? Bode rode with Leander McNelly."

"I think I do recall that, ma'am."

"Are you still joining the Rangers, Lucas?" Mrs. McCully was full of questions.

"Mother!" exclaimed Cassie in mock chastisement. She knew the answer before her mother had even mouthed the words, though she was ever hopeful that I'd change my mind.

"Be seeing Captain Hughes in the morning." I figured it wouldn't do to mince words. It was my destiny. I sensed that my answer wasn't what Mrs. McCully or Cassie wanted to hear. I desperately sought a diversion. "Dang, but this cornbread is nearly as good as my mother's."

Cassie perked up. "It should. It's her recipe."

"Do you know about her secret ingredient?"

"Secret ingredient? What is it?"

"Wouldn't be a secret if I told you." Now, I had her hooked. "I'll give you a hint, though." He chuckled a bit. "It has to do with the firewood."

"Firewood? Oak? Cypress? Mesquite?"

"You'll have to ask my father. Even my mother doesn't know."

McCully laughed as he enjoyed the dialog between Cassie and me. It made for a light dinner during heavy times. Drought had not been especially kind, and occasions that warranted festive dinners were welcome toward relieving the drudge and grind of carving a life on the vast, mostly grassy prairies of Nueces Strip.

"Care for a smoke, Junior?" McCully offered me a cigar.

I appreciated the cigar as it confirmed recognition of my welcome into the McCully household, but like my father, I'd never cottoned to the smoking habit. "Thanks, but I'll pass, Mr. McCully." I always turned down the invitation.

McCully shrugged. "Hear there's been talk of another railroad." McCully floated the comment out like a random puff of smoke from the cigar he'd just lit.

I welcomed the shift from firewood secrets. "Mostly rumored from what I've heard, Mr. McCully. I understand Bob Kleberg is looking to get a fellow named Ben Yoakum to finance the project. When it happens, the chosen route will have a huge impact on folks around these parts. Nuecestown ought to take care lest it become another Collins." I glanced at Cassie who was duly impressed with my thinking. I continued, "Collins is barely surviving after the railroad gave notice that it was bypassing the town."

McCully was pleasantly surprised at my interest in the prospect of a railroad nearby. "How about that Kleberg? From lawyer to being part of the biggest ranch in the country. I understand he's managing more than a million acres."

I smiled. "Keeps us all humble doesn't it, Mr. McCully?"

McCully took an extra-long drag on the cigar and smiled. He was enjoying what he was hearing.

"Seems to be a lot of concern about vigilantes. Sheriff Tyler says three men have been bushwhacked recently. He's of a mind that it's one or more vigilantes taking the law into their own hands."

"Wasn't one of you cousins building a reputation as a vigilante?" McCully pressed the line of thought.

Cassie gave a concerned look as though her father seemed to be turning earth not in need of planting.

But I wasn't fazed. "You mean my cousin Red John?" I said with a chuckle. "He did manage to stir things up a while back as Texas Ranger and get into some trouble on his own. Seems he walked the fine line between legal and illegal. I suppose you could call him a vigilante...but I hear he's out of that business these days. He's got that museum of militaria he loves and watches over a passel of dairy cows. I doubt he's even on the sheriff's mind."

Mrs. McCully took the opportunity to chime in. "Seems every family has at least one black sheep in its lineage. Just look at what a wild Texas Ranger your daddy was, Grant."

Grant McCully couldn't deny his father's errant ways. He well knew that Bode McCully would as soon shoot a lawbreaker as put manacles on him. "I suppose you've got me there, Martha. But he was favored by McNelly." He took a long, satisfying drag on the cigar.

I saw an opportunity to defuse the tension. "I'll help Sheriff Tyler so far as I can, Mr. McCully." I knew that any assignment would be at the discretion of my soon-to-be boss, Captain John Hughes.

"You're likely the man for it, son." McCully seemed to have appreciated my honest assessment.

Soon enough, dinner and dinner conversation ended. I waved off McCully's second offer of a cigar.

I caught Mrs. McCully offering a not-so-subtle nod to Cassie to take me outside.

"Where you headed, Junior." McCully was clueless as to what was going on. He was longing to enjoy a cigar while getting ever better acquainted with the man who'd married his daughter.

I shrugged and got up easy-like. "Excuse me, Mr. and Mrs. McCully." I gladly followed Cassie onto the gallery across the front of the two-story house that featured a commanding view of the vast prairies before it.

She showed me to a swing bench off to one side. "Beautiful evening, Lucas."

I took in how the blue in her dress lit up her crystal blue eyes like twin lights in the darkness. "Can almost see Heaven's Gate from here." I felt just a tad uncomfortable at the closeness afforded by the bench, given that her folks were close enough to be able to see the bench if they so chose. The heady, sweet aroma of Cassie's perfume wafted its way across my nose. It was so very tempting. The extra touch she'd applied before heading out the door was having the desired effect. "Warm, isn't it?"

"I think it's just about right, Lucas Dunn."

I rather liked that she didn't call me Junior like everyone else. I was her husband, my own man for her, not my father's namesake. My eyes shifted from the vista before us and locked in on hers. The magnetic draw of their deep crystalline blueness lit early evening. I was at once uncomfortably nervous yet magnetically drawn to her gaze. Despite five years of marriage, I still felt awkward.

"I want you to know that I support you joining the Texas Rangers." She didn't really, but she knew better than to say otherwise.

My hand seemed to act independently, as it found its way

to her cheek. Her face turned slightly upward toward mine. I was about to gently caress her but instead leaned forward and pulled her to me. Lips touched ever-so-softly and then pressed harder. To hell with her parents' seeing anything.

Cassie felt a warm wave of passion course through her body. She gently pulled away and blushed. My kiss was always like a match to kindling.

I rightly figured that another kiss might throw our evening fully out of control. I held her gaze locked into mine. I so wanted to once again mouth the words declaring my undying love. The future might be uncertain, but Cassie McCully Dunn was real and now. My yearning was written all over my face. "Cassie...I...er...love..." It was dredged up deep from my heart, but never easy to release from its moorings.

She smiled. Why were those words always so difficult for men? Her mother had provided no explanation. It seemed to be one of life's mysteries. "I love you, Lucas..." She paused as though carefully weighing her next words. "I...I have a secret."

I felt my face warm, as a curious expression found its way across my face. "Secret?"

"I missed my bleeding."

"You mean?" I was at once overjoyed and concerned. My decision to join the Texas Rangers suddenly seemed terribly ill-timed.

"I haven't even told ma." She looked up into my eyes. "Are you happy?"

"Er...yes...yes, I'm happy, sweetheart." I couldn't help but look disconcerted.

"Don't look so out of sorts. Everything will be just fine. We'll get some help with the ranch as we need it." Cassie tried to be reassuring. In the deep inner recesses of her mind lurked the worry of me being out hunting down lawbreakers.

I took a deep breath. I knew that my folks had handled the challenges of my dad being a lawman, running a ranch, and raising a family. I knew enough to give Cassie comfort and encouragement. Looking deeply into her eyes, I took her in my arms and gave her an even longer, deeper kiss. I held her for a bit before pulling away. "I love you, Cassie Dunn. You're going to be a great mother." My finger gently wiped a tear of joy from her eyes. "We're blessed, sweetheart."

The future seemed so uncertain, yet my words brought comfort. She surely knew that my love was true and strong. We'd deal with this new dimension to our lives.

"We'd better be heading back to the ranch soon. I've got to get up early." I knew that those words had likely dashed a bucket of cold water on the evening, but I wasn't prepared for where our feelings were heading, especially here at the McCully's place. I so wanted her right then and there, but it wasn't to be.

She understood. She didn't want to leave either. She yearned for all that would normally follow that passionate kiss. Wild sensual urges were still lingering within her.

TWO
TEXAS RANGER FRESH MINTED

I HITCHED Tornado outside the old schoolhouse. Pausing and taking a deep breath, I climbed the steps, swung open the door, and was greeted by the nervous glances of other recruits shifting their weight from foot to foot.

"You must be Mr. Dunn. Just fall in over there." Captain John Hughes pointed to a spot beside one of the recruits.

"Yes sir," I mumbled. I stood where Hughes told me and stole a glance at the other recruits. They were a tad shopworn. Ragtag might be a good description. I was at least a head taller and packed substantially more muscle. While they were well armed, my twin 38-caliber double-action Colt revolvers were brand spanking new.

"Ah-hem," Captain Hughes coughed to get the recruits' attention. "Gentlemen, raise your right hands." Hughes smiled broadly, as he administered the oath. By his reckoning, more justice would soon be served in Texas.

The three recruits—myself included—dutifully repeated the words.

Moments later, Hughes was pinning a Texas Ranger badge on my shirt. He offered up an aside, "I hope you're half the

Ranger your father was, Lucas. If so, you oughta do right well."

I had resigned myself to such comparisons. They would likely dog me throughout my lawman career, however long that lasted. "Thank you, sir. I'll do my best." Lurking in the inner recesses of my thinking were the threefold pangs of Cassie's reluctant acceptance of my decision, living up to my father's legacy, and the new responsibility thrust upon me by Cassie's pregnancy.

Hughes wasn't finished. His eyes bored into me as he addressed the three of us. "I'm sure it's been drummed into you growing up, but never forget that bringing individual lawbreakers to justice will eventually ensure a just society." He wrote the word "justice" in large letters on the chalkboard behind him. It stood out boldly against the cartoonish drawings left by the school children that normally occupied the building. The Nuecestown schoolhouse was considered the biggest one around these parts, and it had naturally been a convenient place for a few Texas Ranger recruits to gather for a swearing-in ceremony.

"Yes, sir." I understood the well-intended advice, but also was all too well acquainted with the vagaries of what constituted justice. It was an ill-defined word from all I'd come to figure, especially having watched my father in action. Whose justice was it after all? Justice by the law, first and foremost, I figured. But even right and wrong could get all too nuanced. I'd be called to make judgments that wouldn't be easy. There was justice per the law, per moral principles, and as delivered through punishment. I knew that some folks saw justice as a social issue concerned with equitableness, but I saw that as more difficult to define as that sort of justice depended on the sway of the citizenry.

Hughes turned to face us newly minted Rangers and the half dozen Texas Rangers attending the ceremony. I had been so nervous that I'd been unaware of the Rangers attending the swearing-in ceremony. Hughes addressed us all. "You men will leave tomorrow morning for Brownsville. I'll meet you there in a few days after I take care of some business with Sheriff Tyler in Corpus. Texas Ranger Dunn here will be joining me." Captain John Hughes was all business and every inch the very same man who'd avenged the ambush killing of Texas Ranger Captain Frank Jones by the Olguin family in Mexico a couple of years back. The Texas Rangers, under Hughes's leadership, had disposed of eighteen Olguin family members by gun or noose. Nobody messed with John Hughes. It was as though he was a throwback to a bygone era.

As the other men strode from the schoolhouse, I made a move to follow them.

"Hold on there, Dunn. Did you hear me? You're joining me on this visit to Sheriff Tyler." He smiled as I froze in my tracks.

I was perhaps an inch or two taller than Hughes. Together, the two of us would make an imposing force in any sort of saloon brawl or back-alley encounter. The old adage applied to the Texas Rangers of "one riot, one Ranger" went double for us.

"Seems there's a killer or killers running around bush-whacking lawbreakers. Sheriff Tyler has finally asked for Texas Ranger assist..."

"Yes, sir. I spoke with the sheriff just yesterday, when he was bringing in a body."

"Dunn! Dang! Don't ever interrupt me!" Hughes's face flushed a hot shade of red. He might be cool under fire, but could exhibit a quick temper when he figured he was being even a little bit disrespected.

"Sorry, Captain."

"As I was saying...there have been three such incidents around Nueces County recently. Each victim has been killed with a single shot, most likely from a .406 Winchester or .50 caliber Sharps. The sheriff is experienced, but his sleuthing abilities are being strained. My thinking is to loan you to him.

You know the territory and the folks living here. They respect you, just as they respect your father." Hughes let that sink in. "Now, since you spoke with the sheriff, do you have any thoughts?"

I appreciated both the slap down and the show of respect for my familiarity with the region. It was clear who was boss. "Couple questions come to mind, Captain. Sheriff Tyler told me the killings occurred at night. He thinks it's the work of one killer, and the apparent use of the same weapon in each killing points to that...but we can't be certain. Also, the killer seems to think he's meting out some sort of justice. Can't say as the victims haven't deserved killing." I stroked my chin absentmindedly.

Hughes smiled, as he recalled seeing my father stroke his mustache in similar fashion.

I continued. "Folks in Corpus are calling these vigilante killings. That begs the question of where the vigilante is getting his information about his victims. Reckon whoever this killer is, he's no dummy. The sheriff says he's found no evidence at the scene except for the devastating bullet wounds in the victims." I paused and nodded to indicate I was about finished with my assessment.

Hughes wasn't quite ready to admit how impressed he was with my early assessment. "How are you at tracking varmints, Junior?"

"My dad taught me pretty much all he knows, Captain. We've never gone hungry." I chanced a little grin at that. I was confident that I could draw upon the real-world education my father had sought to instill in his children. I knew the where-abouts of secret watering holes, what plants were edible, how to make medicinal poultices, the nature of just about any wild or domestic animal that could be encountered, the tricks of being hunter versus hunted, and more. "If he can be identified, I can find him."

"Well, just in case you could use a second set of eyes and

ears, I'm going to introduce you to an old friend of the Rangers, name of Buffalo Watts. He's an ornery old codger, but he's likely bagged one of just about every big game beast in America if the mounted trophies in his cabin are any indication. One way or the other, you'll learn a thing or two from him."

I nodded. I hadn't the heart to steal Hughes's thunder and tell him that I was already acquainted with Buffalo Watts.

"Let's mount up and go see the sheriff, Junior."

The Longhorn Saloon was as dusty and musty as ever. A near half-century of wear and tear with all manner of blood, sweat, booze, smoke, and piss coupled with the sweet perfumes of aging whores will tend to give a place a unique signature. That it still attracted anyone was testament to the fact that lawmen mostly let it be- a sort of tacit understanding. As a consequence, the Longhorn attracted those varmints who were unwelcome in the more upscale drinking establishments in Corpus Christi.

Jim "Eagle Eye" Smith, the half-breed Kiowa renegade, was one of those varmints who had been pulled into the Longhorn sort of like iron filings to a magnet. His Kiowa heritage kept him out of other saloons around the region, so he more than made up for that prejudice by regularly drinking himself under the table. Besides, he felt obliged to uphold the image of ne'er-do-well drunken savage that he seemed to cultivate. On the other hand, when he was sober, he could be the meanest of the mean. His heart and soul were filled with rage at what had become of his people. No matter that he'd been born of a White mother and Kiowa chief father not unlike the famed Kwahadi Comanche chief Quanah Parker but without Parker's smarts and resourcefulness. Smith understood that similar to Parker's mother, she was a captive from a wagon train, but he discounted the Anglo side of his heritage as illegitimate. His father wasn't much of a chief, as he fell in a Comanche ambush in West Texas when Smith was a mere teen. The Comanche left the youth for dead, even partially scalping him. It left behind a scary-looking, jagged scar along one side of his head. Could be said that he was just plain angry at the world.

The breed was eventually found by a party of trappers, who took kindly to the boy. Once his wounds healed, the youngster proved his worth as a hunter. It seemed that he could spot game at considerable distances. Importantly, he was adept at spotting hidden hostiles in even the densest natural camouflage. It was thus that he earned the sobriquet Eagle Eye.

The frontier, like the mountain men and Indians, began to play out. Eagle Eye found himself cold and alone even in the company of the men who'd become his family. One day, he awoke to find the last two of his companions deathly ill. The half-breed had no idea what cholera was, even when it had taken the lives of some of his fellow tribesmen several years back. The next morning, he was indeed very much alone. So began a lifelong odyssey that brought him to the Longhorn at least a couple of days a week. Folks seemed to pity him, likely influenced by the rather gruesome scar. With drinking and years in the prairie sun, he looked far older than his forty or so years.

Oddly, no one...at least, no one around the Longhorn... seemed to question how Eagle Eye made ends meet. He always paid for his own booze and the occasional whore.

The half-breed lounged against the bar, one foot on the bar rail. His clothes were mostly raggy-looking with muddied boots, rusted spurs, unkempt pin-striped black trousers, and a gray shirt topped off with a red bandana and brown broad-brimmed hat with two eagle feathers stuck in the hatband. He wore the last vestige of his heyday on the frontier: a well-worn fringed buckskin coat. Armed? He wore a black leather holster with an old 44-caliber 1875 Remington revolver. He was thusly outfitted when the door was filled with two large dark shadows.

John Hughes had decided that he and I should whet our whistles before trudging over to the jail to meet with Sheriff Tyler.

I fell in behind as we sidled up to the bar.

Smith kept a suspicious eye on the two lawmen. What the hell could they be up to at the Longhorn? The question appeared to linger in Eagle Eye's thoughts. He ordered another drink, though he was already feeling that his sobriety had deserted him. He offered up a guttural greeting punctuated by a belch. "What brings two such fine representatives of the law to the Longhorn this evening?" That he'd even delivered a full sentence was a feat unto itself, given his condition. He had of a sudden become scarily close to acting sociable.

Hughes leaned on the bar and motioned to the barkeeper for two drinks. The whiskeys were promptly delivered. The Texas Ranger Captain slowly and deliberately turned his head toward Eagle Eye. "Just passing through."

I nudged Hughes and whispered, "That's Eagle Eye Smith, the local drunk. Half-breed Kiowa by background."

Hughes nodded toward Eagle Eye. "Nice evening. That dun cayuse hitched outside belong to you?"

"You fixin' to buy it?" Smith was all ears.

"Nope. Just curious about that 1895 Winchester setting in the scabbard. That's a fine piece for most anyone these days."

My eyes grew wide. Even I hadn't noticed the rifle as we entered the Longhorn.

"You…sure…you don't want to buy the horse?" Smith belched again, slid down the front of the bar, and wound up sitting on the floor with legs akimbo.

The barkeep gave a nod to two men sitting at a nearby table who had been observing the half-breed. They shook their heads resignedly, went over, carried Eagle Eye out the front door, and deposited him in the dirt alongside his horse.

Hughes could do naught but shake his head in dismay.

"Didn't know old Eagle Eye owned a Winchester," I said.

"Doesn't look like he could afford it."

The barkeep smiled. "He's what they call an enigma, Mr. Texas Ranger. No one knows where Eagle Eye gets his money, but he always pays for his drinks, food, and the ladies. Don't surprise me none that he's found hisself a new rifle, leastways a different one from the Sharps he used to sport. We don't ask too many questions around here."

Hughes offered an understanding smile and motioned to me. "Let's mosey on down to the sheriff's office." Hughes downed his drink, smiled at the still nearly full glass in front of me, and led the way out the front door and past Eagle Eyes's still somnolent form lying spread-eagled beside his horse. The Texas Ranger paused long enough to lift the half-breed's Winchester from its scabbard. "See this insignia, Junior? This is a service-issue rifle. Wonder where he got it?" Hughes slipped it back in the scabbard, and we renewed our walk toward the jail.

"You think he could be the killer?"

"Not likely. The barkeep wasn't tellin' us anything new. From what I've heard from folks around these parts about old Eagle Eye, his killin' days are long behind him. Still, the rifle does match the caliber the sheriff claims." Hughes looked down at Smith with a touch of pity in his eyes. "Nuts. Sheriff Tyler likely figures the man isn't even worth locking up overnight to sleep off his drunk."

"How many of those 1895 Winchesters do you figure might be around?" I asked.

John Hughes smiled mischievously. "Guess you're going to find out."

★★

Bode McCully had watched the two Rangers come and then go from the Longhorn. "Have to keep an eye on that young Dunn buck," he muttered to himself. He stared into the half-full glass, sitting in a puddle of spilled booze on the table. It troubled him that his granddaughter's husband had joined the Texas Rangers. It wouldn't do to have the young man hurt. He picked up the tumbler and gently swirled the liquid around. He seemed mesmerized by the golden-brown liquid, but his stare belied how very open his ears were. Bode had become quite adept at picking out conversations that mattered to him. He couldn't care less about what might have happened to Mrs. Wilson's cow, but he was all ears at the comings and goings of folks that might be up to no good. A little conversation from the table to his left caught his attention mostly because of a familiar name that was dropped. It brought back memories of his Texas Ranger days. Old habits of listening to local rumor mills were hard to break. It was at times entertaining, as when someone revealed an embarrassing event.

"You heard about Trey Bolton?" The speaker, a local ne'er-do-well cowpoke, leaned in toward the man he was talking to. The woman that sat fetchingly on his knee tried not to appear bored. She placed one hand on the man's upper leg in an effort to keep his attention drawn to her special wiles.

"What about him?" the other man responded distractedly, as his eyes were riveted on the woman's ample breasts, seeming to ooze from her bodice.

The prostitute continued to struggle to keep the cowpoke's attention, as the cowpoke pondered further. "He dodged the law in Victoria the other day. Seems they haven't been able to lay a hand on old Trey." He lowered his voice to a near whisper that was hard to pick out above the ambient noise. "You didn't hear it here, but word has it he's fixin' to put another gang together for a little financial work." The man wasn't especially good at keeping any secrets. Bolton was known to favor heisting banks.

Bode listened in as best he could.

"They're gathering out toward Nuecestown, but the opposite side of the river."

With all the surrounding chatter, all Bode could pick up was Nuecestown. It was a clue. He expected Sheriff Tyler would find such information invaluable. A looming question would be whether the sheriff would, in fact, pursue Bolton? Danged lawbreakers seemed to be acting with impunity lately.

I followed Captain Hughes up the step to the jail, nearly bumping into the Ranger when he stopped to knock.

"Not so close, Junior." He chuckled at my momentary bumble.

About the time the words were out, the door opened and Sheriff Tyler was welcoming them in. "Good to see you, Captain Hughes. Whatcha got with you there?"

Hughes strode past the sheriff as though he owned the place. I followed close behind, paying no never mind to the not-so-subtle rebuff of the sheriff. Hughes didn't waste time with niceties. "I expect you're already acquainted with Junior here. He's Texas Ranger Lucas Dunn, Junior, now." Hughes took a seat and motioned me to grab the chair beside his.

Tyler flashed one of those uh-oh expressions with raised eyebrows and a slightly gaping jaw. After our brief conversation the day before, he expected I'd be following in my father's footsteps, so half expected this development. He caught himself, as he moved to his desk. He was no rube, but figured Hughes was about to offer me on loan to help with the vigilante case. He tried his best to look respectful, even cordial toward me. "Congratulations, Junior. I'm sure your dad is proud of you." Sometimes familiarity could breed some level of contempt. He likely still thought of me as some wet-behind-the-ears ten-year-old kid.

I remained silent, acknowledging Tyler with a slight respectful nod.

Hughes ignored the personal dynamic in the sheriff's tight little office. "Hear tell you've got a problem you're looking for help with, Sheriff. What can you tell me about it?"

"Care for a smoke, Captain?" Tyler offered up a box of cigars.

"Thanks. I'll pass." Hughes noted that the sheriff hadn't offered a smoke to me.

"Suit yourself." Tyler made a show of carefully selecting a cigar, clipping one end, lighting up, and taking a few long drags. He coughed involuntarily. Embarrassed, he took a swig of whatever was in the coffee cup on his desk. "Well, to answer your question, we've found three dead bodies in the past couple of months around Nueces County. All victims were killed with a single bullet. Appears to be a .405, likely from one of those new 1895 Winchesters. Pretty much ruled out other rifles. All the killings have been at night."

"What about the victims?"

"Lawbreakers one and all. One was a bounty hunter, but wasn't especially careful about confirming the identities of the folks he'd shot and killed."

"Any suspects?"

"Nope. Can't even be certain the three victims are the only ones this killer has bushwhacked. Could be more victims out there somewhere."

"You think he's acting alone?"

"Far as I can tell, but you never can be sure."

I figured it was high time I earned my keep in this conversation. "Any clue as to how the killer is selecting his victims?"

Tyler answered while looking at Hughes rather than me. "That would be helpful, wouldn't it?"

Hughes didn't much care for the obvious slight. "I believe Ranger Dunn here asked the question, Sheriff." Hughes nodded toward me.

Tyler took a puff on the cigar and another sip from the cup. "Sorry. You gents care for some coffee?"

I replied respectfully, "No thanks, Sheriff." I smiled politely and leaned in just a tad. "Now, do you have any thoughts on how this vigilante is choosing his victims?" I strove to be as lawman-like as possible.

Tyler resigned himself to the inevitable. I was going to be on loan from the Texas Rangers. "He sure isn't getting information from this office. Other than wanted posters at the post office, newspaper reports, and talk at the local saloons, there are plenty of free sources to draw from." It was an obvious answer to an essentially rhetorical question, but it opened the communication between Tyler and me.

I seemed to be on the beginning of a roll. "Assuming he identifies a victim, he still has to figure out where that person is going to be and at what time. Don't figure he's going to lie around night after night waiting for his bushwhack target to show up. He's got to study his victim's habits. That likely means he's doing some stalking."

Hughes noted from the sheriff's body language that he was growing ever-so-slightly more receptive to my thoughts about the crimes.

Tyler actually smiled. "We figure that out, Junior, and we'll be a lot closer to figuring this case out. Hear tell you track game like your daddy, so maybe you can figure out how this vigilante does it." A peal of thunder rolled in from the distance, signaling what might be a storm. They'd been few and far between of late. Any rain was welcome. "Guess he won't be doing any stalking today."

Our laughter broke any remaining tension.

We spent another half hour jawing about general goings-on around Corpus Christi. Finally, Hughes had enough. The sheriff's cigar smoke was ever more nauseating, and the Ranger captain had a few odds and ends to gather before heading out in the morning for Brownsville. "I'll count on you and Junior here staying in communication, Sheriff. I appreciate that your jurisdiction is limited. Ranger Dunn here has got my full authorization to do whatever is necessary. If y'all need more manpower, the telegraph will likely catch up with me."

As we stood, Hughes turned to me. "Oh, one more thing, come on up the street with me. I'll introduce you to Buffalo Watts."

Tyler had just begun to rise from behind his desk to see the Rangers out. "You're going to what?"

"Problem with that, Sheriff?"

"Just had the impression that old Buffalo was getting close to meeting his maker."

"There's still a lot of knowledge in those old bones, Sheriff. I expect Junior here will yet learn a thing or two. We'll be moseying along." He led the way out the door. "Oh, you might like to know that old Eagle Eye Smith is littering the street up at the Longhorn."

Tyler shook his head. "Passed out likely. Thanks, Captain."

"And thanks for your time, Sheriff Tyler."

As we prepared to mount up, I caught the captain's attention. "Captain, you should know that my dad and I hunted with Buffalo Watts a few years back. He helped me stalk and bag a mountain lion. I figure I can yet learn a few things, but he's taught me pretty much anything my dad didn't."

"Well, shoot. If you're already acquainted, I'll let you connect with Buffalo on your own. I could use the time to pull my poke together for traveling."

As we sat in our saddles, I extended my hand to Hughes. "I appreciate this opportunity, Captain. I'll not disappoint you."

"Shoot, Junior. You wouldn't be here representing the Texas Rangers, if I figured you'd disappoint anyone." He smiled broadly, turned his mount, and began to head away. He drew up. "One more thing."

"Yes, Captain?"

"I hear you've got yourself a right sweet little wife. Don't let that distract you." He winked and continued to ride off.

Eagle Eye awakened enough from his stupor to see a shadowy form ride by. His urge was to follow, but his head said otherwise. At least, he was finally sober enough to be able to stand and lean against the hitching post. He made a mental note as best he could under the circumstances to follow the trail in the morning. A second rider passed by moments later. Smith was a bit taken aback by the sudden increased traffic on the little section of Corpus Christi byway he was standing on. He attempted to leave the support of the hitching post, tried twice to get his foot in the saddle stirrup, and finally decided to simply stagger home with horse in tow.

Bode McCully paid little more than glancing recognition to the tottering half-breed as he headed out toward Nuecestown. He was of a mind to see whether he might learn more about what Trey Bolton was up to. His blood still ran with the instincts of a Texas Ranger.

"Hey, Mr. McCully. Wait up!" I had found myself riding just a few yards behind my sweet wife's grandfather.

Bode cringed. Having company didn't suit his present intentions or state of mind. He was focused on his evening's mission. He resigned himself to the inevitable. "Oh, Junior. Fancy meeting you out here. Where you headed?"

"Home. Mind if I ride with you?"

"Sure. The road's plenty wide for two abreast." Bode seemed even older by contrast to me as a newly minted Texas Ranger. He rode silently for a couple of minutes. "Nice that you spend time with your folks, Junior. Family is important, especially these days." Bode continued, "You are close with yours, aren't you? Cassie talks glowingly about them."

"She's prejudiced." I couldn't help but smile.

"By the way, congratulations on signing up with the Texas Rangers. From what I've heard from Cassie's father, you'll likely make the Rangers proud to have you onboard. Your father was near legendary."

"Thanks, Mr. McCully."

"I expect since I was a Ranger and you are one, you can call me Bode. Sounds more comfortable, doesn't it?"

"Sure, Mr....er...Bode."

"You know, Rangering is more than about a badge and a gun. Your father knew how to use the gun, but he always tried to avoid shooting. He had a mind for getting inside lawbreakers' heads. I think they call that psychology. It's about outthinking your prey. Sometimes it leads to justice, sometimes to redemption of sorts." He wanted to add how painfully slow the law seemed to move.

I interrupted that thought. "That's pretty much what my dad taught me, Bode. You always try to outthink your prey."

We rode on silently for a while over terrain bathed in a patina of deep oranges and magentas as the sun began its inevitable sinking below the western horizon. We were both familiar with the road and appreciative of a certain beauty it held that many folks might not appreciate. All manner of critters were out among the grasses, shrubs, and occasional mottes of live oak, stands of cypress, and the ubiquitous pecan trees. Coyotes were getting restless, prairie dogs nestling in their borrows, and an owl occasionally made its presence known.

"Where you headed, Mr. McCully?"

"Nuecestown," he answered.

"Business?"

"Junior...I'm no Ranger anymore. Figured I'd visit a few folks."

"So, it's social."

"Seems like." Bode weighed a question he had on his mind but decided to ask anyway. "How come you didn't head to Brownsville with Captain Hughes?"

"The captain wanted me to help Sheriff Tyler with a case in Corpus." I wasn't ready to expand on that, even to my wife's grandfather and a trusted former Ranger.

"Any case in particular?"

I rubbed my chin thoughtfully. "You know I'm not supposed to discuss ongoing cases, Bode."

Bode nodded. "True. Good for you to stick to your knitting. But I have to figure the sheriff is looking for Texas Ranger help to deal with those recent killings folks been talking about. Captain Hughes must think highly of you."

"I expect so."

Blessedly, the entrance to Heaven's Gate loomed ahead. That would bring the questioning to an end. I shifted in my saddle just a bit awkwardly. "Here's where we part. Enjoy your visit in Nuecestown, Bode."

"You be sure to give my best to your folks, Junior. I'll put in a good word with Cassie about you next time I see her." He laid a hand aside his hat to bid me goodbye and rode on.

I took a trail to the right off the entrance to Heaven's Gate. It was a shortcut to mine and Cassie's spread. I was anxious to share the news that I'd be starting off my Texas Ranger career close to home rather than riding off to Brownsville and places unknown.

I rode on up to the barn and led Tornado to his stall. The old stallion had served me well and still had a few good years left in him. As I stored the tack and curried and fed my beloved steed, my mind drifted to Cassie's grandfather. Strange that he'd chosen to make a seemingly random trip to Nuecestown after dark. I'd noted the butt of a new rifle jutting from the elder McCully's saddle scabbard. I couldn't quite tell what make it was. Wonder was about all I could do. The man was retired, after all, and was free to live his life when, how, and where he saw fit.

I was about to turn, when a voice froze me in place. I hesitated and then smiled knowingly, as I completed my turn. "Buffalo Watts! What the…what are you doing here?"

"Shucks, yuh wet-behind-the-ears tadpole, yuh didn't even know I tracked yuh all the way from Corpus. Wagh! Yuh and that goldarned Bode McCully hadn't a clue." Watts chuckled. "Hell, I coulda been that vigilante killer that's rumored about." Watts was bust-a-button proud that he still had his tracking skills.

"But you're not, and McCully and I are not the vigilante's type of targets."

"So, yuh say." Watts grinned broadly and shook his head ever-so-slightly.

"You don't agree?" I asked.

"Best to ne'er make assumptions, son, Wagh! Yuh ne'er know when hunted prey might do the unexpected. Sometimes prey'll turn on yuh soon as they look at yuh. Besides, I'll bet yuh ain't hardly begun to git nuf evidence to have a clue. Could be anybody bushwhacking them desperadoes," said Watts taking a deep breath. He wasn't used to uttering long sentences much less stringing thoughts together as such.

"You're right there." I grinned sheepishly and nodded toward the house. "Care for a bit of late refreshment?"

"Nope. Heard from Sheriff Tyler that yuh might be lookin' fer me. I'll be moseying on my way. Yuh know where to find me. Wagh!" He began to turn, then paused. "Expect yuh know you've got a big advantage goin' fer yuh, son. Not many folks can point to havin' livin' legends fer a father."

"Except I've got to agree with you there."

Buffalo offered up a seriously thoughtful expression before letting loose a slight grin and a wink. "A man without heroes is a lost soul, Junior. It's in yer blood, son. The fruit never falls far from the tree, an' I see in yuh that belief in the strength, courage, and noble purpose that is yer father. You're gonna be a great Texas Ranger, Junior, just as sure as the sun rises and sets."

I swallowed uncomfortably at the wholly unexpected praise. "When I finish with this business, maybe we can do a little hunting."

"I'd like that, son. You've got a tough nut to crack meantime."

I couldn't deny that. "Can't argue with you there. Stay safe, my friend. *Via con Dios.*" Indeed, I had a very hard nut to crack.

"Shucks, I gotta go back and git my old friend Eagle Eye. Seems they stuck him in the hoosegow after all." As if beckoned by some call from the shadows, Buffalo Watts disappeared from my view about as quickly as he'd appeared.

I grabbed my rifle and walked up to the house and Cassie's waiting arms. I hadn't had much time to think on becoming a father. Holding her would bring the reality of it home. The coming months would herald a few new beginnings for me. As my hand reached for the door, I could already smell the aroma of fresh-baked apple pie. Suddenly, it swung open, and I was greeted by a hug that nearly bowled me over.

Cassie pulled me inside. "Let me see it! Let me..." She pulled back my vest to reveal the shiny new Texas Ranger badge. "I'm so proud of you, Lucas!"

I pulled her close. Mixed feelings tossed round and round as though in some sort of whirlwind through my head. Sure, I was proud to be a Texas Ranger but...Cassie was now pregnant. My priorities and responsibilities had necessarily shifted. Life called me to reach beyond me and Cassie. Lord knows, I needed to stay alive for all of their sakes. I wondered how my dad had ever managed it...wondered what my mother had thought when her husband was seriously wounded by some lawbreaker and lay dangerously close to death's doorstep? Could I put Cassie through that? Could she handle it?

"Come back to me, Lucas." She saw that faraway gaze that told of my immersion in some sort of heavy thinking. "What's troubling you?"

Dang, but she read me like the proverbial book. I looked deeply into her eyes. "Just thinking of us and you being with child." I kissed her, lightly at first and then with greater passion. I pulled back and was silent for a moment. "It's something I'd never really thought on before, love. It's wonderful... but..."

"I know." She grinned. "Not to worry, Lucas. Not to worry."

At that, I felt something nuzzling my boot. "Where the... what the?"

"I had him hidden away, but now you know."

"Dang, he's handsome even as a pup. Reminds me of..."

"The Blue Lacy your folks had...El Gato...the one your dad found on the trail that bested the lynx." She smiled at the memory of my love for El Gato. The Lacy was a blue-colored mix of English shepherd purportedly mixed with greyhound and wolf. The handsome breed had been conjured up by some fellow named Lacy, thus, the name. "I needed company while you're gallivanting over the countryside, bringing lawbreakers to justice."

I squatted down and cradled the pup's head. Its tongue slobbered across my cheek. "You name him?"

Cassie beamed impishly. "Not yet. What do you think?"

"Hmmm. Not rightly sure. He's a right-friendly puppy. But if he's like El Gato, he's likely going to keep guard over you and our child. He'll be sort of like having a Texas Ranger at home."

Cassie smiled broadly. "I think I see where your thinking is heading, Lucas Dunn." She kneeled down and stroked the puppy, then placed her hand over mine. "Ranger."

I pushed forward over the pup and kissed her. "Ranger it

is." I gave Ranger another rough scratching around his ears and stood. "Now, I believe I smell apple pie."

"And steak, potatoes, and cornbread, Mr. Texas Ranger." She grinned impishly. "I think I just about captured your mother's cornbread recipe." She didn't let on that she'd figured out that it had something to do with the smoke from the Dunn's stash of mesquite logs, so she'd helped herself to an armful.

I rode out early, a freshly minted Texas Ranger heading to Corpus Christi to meet with Sheriff Tyler. The vigilante case was now an official assignment. The night had been bitter-sweet and pretty much sleepless, as Cassie's passions seemed more unbounded than ever. Likely as not, it was from the inevitability of my leaving in the morning coupled with her pregnancy. I struggled to focus on the tasks ahead. I thought back to having briefly ridden the previous evening with Cassie's grandfather and wondered what he'd found in Nuecestown if anything. Perhaps...just perhaps, the retired Texas Ranger might have some thoughts helpful to me.

Riding along, I couldn't help but think on the challenges I was inflicting on my beloved Cassie. The ranch was a burden. The weather had been dry. We'd lost several precious cattle to drought and heat. Money was tight despite having sold a few head, though now we had the prospect of Texas Ranger pay meager as it was. The drought had been the worst on record. That wasn't saying much, given that record-keeping had only begun a couple of years back. I recalled my folks enduring the "Big Die-Up" back in 1887, in which millions of head of live-stock perished from Montana to Texas. Dust storms plagued the land, and many folks had to give up on their dreams of making a life on America's western frontier. Worse yet, it had caused free range to be relegated to the annals of history, as barbed-wire fences proliferated. Even winter had brought no relief. Blizzards struck and starving livestock froze to death in their tracks. Thousands of dead cattle were found stacked against drift fences and still more along those barbed-wire barriers. If cold didn't kill, then it was starvation. Ranchers lost up to three-fourths of their beeves. Come spring thaw, dead cattle clogged streams and spoiled drinking water. I could do naught but pray that 1895 wouldn't be so bad as that. It was in God's hands.

THREE
THE FUTURE BEGINS

BODE DISMOUNTED. He'd caught the day's last crossing of the ferry just before the sun was sinking to the horizon and casting a pinkish-golden glow in its aftermath. As luck would have it, he'd boarded for the night with a farmer and his wagon, so he felt as though he was able to cross the Nueces River without particular suspicion. So far as anyone might think, he was simply a traveler on his way to San Antonio or beyond. Once he reached the opposite bank of the river, he led his cayuse a hundred yards or so into the scrub lining the north riverbank and hitched him to a nearby pecan tree. It wouldn't do to risk the steed ambling off into Trey Bolton's camp. The camp? Well, it was hard to miss. Bolton was making no effort to hide his assembly drawn from the dredges of society.

Sneaking up on the encampment wasn't so difficult. It would be easy enough to get a handle on how many men had joined the outlaw's gang. Tougher, however, would be identifying Bolton in the dim firelight and trying to hear what he was up to. He dared not lose sight of the fact that the outlaw was also a killer of some repute, and there was no telling how many of his newly forming crew might have a notch or two on their guns. There was plenty of cover in the brush and tall grasses among the cypress trees surrounding the camp, so getting close was no special challenge. So far as Bode could make out, there were no sentries posted. Big fire? No sentries? To add further, a full moon had begun to rise like a balloon on the horizon? Had Bolton become so cocky as to become careless?

The retired lawman wasn't getting any younger, so creeping close through the dense and thorny brush took a tad longer than it might have a few years back. Bode dared not stir anything that would draw attention to himself, so extra caution was in order. He darkened his face with dirt to camouflage himself. An unusual noise here or there could give him away. He amazed even himself that he was able to draw within roughly twenty feet. He could even make out Bolton himself in the dim light and feel the warmth cast off by the fire. There were perhaps seven gang members hanging with the gang leader, so far as he could tell. Bode lay patiently listening to random conversation for what seemed like an hour, perhaps more.

One of the men got up and paced anxiously. "Let's git to it, Bolton. We din't come here to make nice talk."

Bode's wasn't the only patience wearing thin.

There was a general grumbling murmur of support for the outlaw who'd ventured to call Bolton on his game.

"You have a problem, Cal? I'll truck no whining here. There's a big payday ahead, and y'all must be all in." Bolton's squinty eyes eyeballed the men, and his hand rested all too comfortably on the revolver at his hip.

Bolton's calling out the attempted assertiveness of one of his gang members had grabbed Bode's totally undivided attention. The outlaw gang leader offered a smile that would have done a rattlesnake proud. A forked tongue flicking out would have made for a perfect image. "They've got that new bank in Alice, boys. This time of year, the ranchers are stuffing their profits into the bank. I've checked it out, and it's bursting at the seams with money. Yep, it's ripe for plunder."

A uniform murmur arose from the gang. "Alice?" Each looked to the other.

Cal spoke out. "What 'bout a big haul like Corpus?" He was the boldest and had taken the role of spokesman for the others. He was likely the top gun of the outfit, save for Bolton himself. Cal wore twin revolvers, one in a holster and the second stuffed in his waistband. The gun in the holster had the trigger guard filed away for more rapid firing. But he was likely pushing his luck a bit, stretching the bounds set by Trey Bolton.

"You're welcome to leave, Cal?" Bolton glared at the man and struck a pose that begged for the complainer to test him. "Absolute loyalty to me and this job is a must."

Cal sighed and shrugged. He had just enough sense to back off. "Naw, boss...I'm with ya."

Bolton relaxed. "We're going to come in from the east in the morning with the sun behind us. We've hung close to Nueces-town plenty long enough. We don't want to raise suspicions, so we're going to break up and rendezvous about a mile east of the town. We'll hit the bank on Friday." He smiled deviously. "They'll expect us to escape to the west, but we'll go east toward Nueces Bay and take the old shell road across the bay that the Indians used. Then, we'll head north to Victoria and divvy up the loot." He looked from man to man to be certain all were on board. "Gonna fool them, men. No one will expect us to be heading east."

"How ya pullin' it off, boss?"

Bolton went into a more detailed description of the role of each gang member and the layout of the bank itself, falling just short of describing the nails holding the boards of the bank's wooden sidewalk.

About this time, Bode was visited by a need for a sneeze. Inconvenient, to say the least. He'd be a dead man if he didn't contain the danged thing. It was all he could do to suppress it, as he pulled back while holding his nose and covering his mouth. He took a few painful scratches from thorn bushes as he hurriedly and as quietly as possible, slunk away. As he drew near his horse, the sneeze finally exploded from his nose and mouth. He fumbled with the tie of his horse's reins and managed to climb into the saddle just as he heard alarmed voices and scrambling of boots of gang members as they initiated pursuit. Thankfully, they were on foot, so he was able to quickly put some healthy distance between himself and the pursuers. It was far too close for comfort. Worse, they had been alerted. They might now change their plans, given the risk of having been overheard.

Bode far out-distanced the men, though he was still just close enough to hear the fading shouts of his frustrated pursuers.

A well-winded Bolton finally stopped giving chase. The rest of the gang, realizing they hadn't a prayer of catching any interloper on foot, had apparently given up the pursuit and fallen well behind him.

"Think it was a deer, boss?"

Bolton frowned. "Damn deer don't sneeze like a man," he grumbled.

Cal couldn't help but suggest the obvious. "Mebbe someone snooping, boss?"

Bolton didn't respond. He waved Cal off as he rubbed his forehead, trying to think through this new development. Robbing banks was a risky enough business as it was. The sneeze had come from a way off. It could have just been some traveler passing by. Finally, he turned to his gang. "We aren't changing our plans." He hadn't shared that this was more than about the bank robbery. He had a secret, an inside advantage. A brief dalliance in Alice with a bank teller had secured plenty of inside information about how the bank was operated, its internal layout, and especially the location of the vault. Corrie was her name, and he'd promised to take her with them on their escape from the robbery. He'd painted a picture of adventure for her that he never intended to share. He shook his head so as to dismiss his little daydream. "Anyone have a problem?"

Cal and the others shrugged their acquiescence and ambled off to their bedrolls.

Bolton figured morale was good. The prospect of money tended to do that, especially to mostly desperate men. The bank heist was only two days off. His biggest challenge would be to not let boredom gain a foothold.

Bode meanwhile took a few deep breaths. Narrowly escaping discovery wasn't part of his plan. He'd dang well have to take greater care, if he was to enjoy a long retirement. Late as it was, he'd be spending the night north of the river.

★★

"Dang! Who the hell's out here ridin' in the brush at this time of night? Gotta be crazy," Buffalo Watts grumbled to himself in a near whisper. He peered out into the night, trying to make out who had just ridden past his campsite.

For his part, Bode sensed that he wasn't alone but figured it was plenty dark enough to not be recognized.

Watts nestled back under his blanket. The frontiersman and Indian tracker in him were in high gear. He found his mind roiling over the sound of the horse and rider. There was something familiar about the sound from the rider, but he couldn't place it for the moment. His need for sleep overcame his curiosity, and he decided that daylight might reveal clues and answer his question. He'd sprung his friend Eagle Eye from the jail and lost half a night's sleep in the process. Just getting Smith settled in back in Corpus had been a challenge, given the man's still inebriated condition. He'd felt the need to head back up to Nuecestown, even swimming his horse across the river. He'd seen Bolton's campfire off in the distance but wasn't up to making the man's acquaintance in the middle of the night. Generally, it wasn't a good practice anyway.

He thought back to earlier in the evening when he was having a little fun tracking me and my grandfather-in-law. He'd noticed a slight squeak from Bode McCully's saddle. Could that have been the distinctive sound he heard passing by? If the rider was McCully, what on earth was the man doing out in rough country at night on the north side of the river? He stored away the tidbit of information.

"Sheriff Tyler. Good morning," I announced as I dismounted.

Tyler was sitting on a bench in front of the jail taking a long sip from a cup of hot coffee. He nodded to me with the customary salute of a couple of fingers to the brim of his weather-worn hat. He brought his lanky legs up under him and stood to welcome me. "Guess you're reporting for duty," he drawled.

"Only here to help, Sheriff."

"Look, Junior. I fully appreciate Captain Hughes assigning you to help with this vigilante business. Truth be told, I was sort of forced into it by the mayor and a couple of commissioners. So, to be honest, I'm none too happy about it."

I was quick to realize that the sheriff saw the assistance of a wet-behind-the-ears lawman as impugning his abilities. I mustered up a dose of confidence. "I have a couple of thoughts on how we can make this work, Sheriff."

Tyler sighed uncomfortably. He'd lost sleep, dreading my arrival. "Well...come on in and grab a cup of coffee," he finally groused.

I picked up what appeared to be the cleanest of tin mugs on the side hutch and poured myself a cup of the thickest-looking rotgut black coffee I'd seen in a long while. Cassie had certainly spoiled me as to coffee. I walked over to the window, looked out thoughtfully, and ventured an idea. "I was thinking, Sheriff, how you've got a whole county to worry about here, especially Corpus Christi itself. My being a Texas Ranger gives me a pretty broad jurisdiction around these parts." I turned to Tyler. "How about if I do my snooping around for this vigilante mostly beyond the Nueces County limits? I can check in with you now and again so you stay informed. Last thing you need is surprises."

Tyler looked up from his seat behind the gnarly old oaken desk. It occurred to him that maybe this kid wouldn't be so bad after all. He caught my gaze and nodded with feigned gravity. Tyler was a stubborn man and hated to admit that my proposal made sense and that he should have thought of it himself.

I took a swig of coffee and set it down. I swallowed hard. "Damn, Sheriff. How do you drink this stuff?"

Tyler smiled and drew a whiskey bottle from the bottom drawer of his desk. "Secret ingredient, Junior...secret ingredient. Want a bit?"

I chuckled and shook my head. "I'll pass, Sheriff, but thanks for the offer. Too early to be drinking." I fully faced the sheriff. "Do you like my approach?"

Tyler nodded. "We'll give it a try. Can't hurt." The words felt dry and stuck in his mouth a little. "You dig anything up since the other day?"

"It occurs to me that the large caliber rifle that the vigilante used doesn't narrow things down much in these parts. I've spotted four of those new 1895 Winchesters just riding in here this morning. Eagle Eye Smith owns one...even my wife's grandfather owns one. And it could've been an old Sharps rifle. We've...I've got a lot of digging yet to do."

"Well, you're welcome to read my reports, Junior. Maybe checking out where the bodies were found may lead you to something. The scenes will be cold, but something may have been overlooked." Tyler laid three sheets of paper on the desk. "I'm heading down to the livery to check on my horse. Be back in an hour. Help yourself." He stood and began to move toward the door but stopped. He extended his hand. "I do appreciate your help, Junior." It wasn't the easiest admission, but there was no point for things to be setting off on the wrong foot. We shook hands, and I was left to ponder the sheriff's reports. First, I grabbed the coffee pot and dumped the swill behind the jail. I drew water from the pump, found some coffee grounds, and began a fresh brew.

Bode had pretty much figured to spend the night under the stars north of the Nueces River, since the ferry didn't run at night. The river was running a tad shallow, given the past several months of drought, but snags and even quicksand along the shoreline dictated caution. The retired Texas Ranger didn't figure on being so achy after slithering through the brush to find out what Bolton's plans were and then having to escape while stifling a sneeze. He cursed under his breath at the travails of aging.

The silvery rays of the rising sun did cheer him a bit, as he struggled to massage muscles and joints made sore by sleeping on the hard ground. He didn't have far to go to the ferry landing, but he'd have to wait a half hour for it to pole across. He'd had an uncomfortable night sleeping, or trying to. Wrestling with the information he'd learned kept him awake more than asleep. The lawman in him nagged at his craw. He knew he must tell Sheriff Tyler.

If Tyler failed to take action on the tip...well...that would be another matter. In any case, the sooner he rode down to Corpus Christi and shared the news, the more likely Tyler would be able to thwart Bolton's plan.

The ferry finally pulled to the landing.

"Yo, Bode! What you doin' up these parts so early in the mornin'?"

Bode cringed and turned slowly to face the sound. He strove to put on his best face. "Buffalo Watts! I'll be hornswoggled. Didn't expect you up here at the crack of dawn either."

"Heard yuh ridin' last night. Yuh huntin' for somethin'?"

Bode resented the inquiry. Besides, how the hell did Watts figure it was him out riding at night? "Just restless to get out in the night air. Sort of miss the old days of tracking lawbreakers."

Watts chewed on that for a minute before accepting the response. "Yep. Guess we're not gettin' any younger. Miss the good old days. Wagh!"

"Dang, I figure you've got a bunch of those so-called good old days ahead of you." Bode tried right hard to make conversation. It wasn't something he enjoyed, and he had to take care to not reveal the true purpose of his nocturnal wanderings.

The two continued small talk about their past exploits as the ferry labored across the river, though it seemed to take forever. Once on the south landing, they parted company.

Watts watched as Bode took the road toward Corpus Christi. Something wasn't sitting right, but he couldn't put his finger on it. The old Ranger was keeping some sort of secret. Watts's years of tracking wild and human game—often one and the same—had sensitized him to a sort of intuitive thinking. He decided it might be worth following Bode, though he'd have to be extra careful so as not to be discovered.

About mid-morning, Bode rode slowly up to the Corpus Christi jail. He brought his horse to a halt and sat his saddle another moment to gather his thoughts. He heard footsteps from inside coming to the door, so finally dismounted.

"Bode McCully. Good morning." Tyler smiled friendly-like.

"I saw you ride up and was waiting for your knock. What brings you here this fine morning?"

The old Ranger was silent, as he absorbed the sheriff's greeting. It was a little too much of friendly for this hour of the day. "Well, good morning to you, Sheriff." Bode coughed, reached down for his canteen, and took a swig of whatever was inside. "Dang dry weather." Actually, the absence of humidity was unusual, so there was a touch of humor in Bode's observation. "Have a bit of information for you."

Tyler cocked his head curiously. "Information? Sounds serious."

"Could be. I've done a bit of investigating and come to find out that a fella named Trey Bolton is fixing to rob the Alice Bank of Texas, day after tomorrow."

"Where'd you hear this, Bode?"

"Direct from the horse's mouth, so to speak." Bode couldn't hold back a smile. "He's got a gang with him. Seven hired guns."

Tyler sighed. There was a lot of ground to cover in Nueces County. It'd likely take him a couple of days to rustle up a handful of extra men for any sort of posse. He only had three deputies, and he'd need to leave at least two in Corpus to watch over the city. "Appreciate you coming to me, Bode." He noted a hopeful look on the old Ranger's face. "Er...you are retired." He knew it was a euphemism for feeling that Bode was too old to be asked to join any posse. "I'm figuring to ask the Dunn's and Whelan's to join me."

I had headed out at the crack of dawn and unknowingly barely missed crossing paths with Bode. I did manage to interrupt Buffalo Watt's little tracking venture.

"Buffalo, what are you up to this fine morning?"

Watts had been fully focused on trying to figure what Bode

had been up to so responded a tad disconcertedly. "Just moseying along, Junior. Nice day to mosey, wouldn't yuh say?"

I sighed. I could read Watts like a book. "Who or what are you tailing after this morning, my friend?"

Watts wasn't quite ready to reveal what he was up to, but I was the son of a good friend and a lawman. He reckoned I rightly should know. "Yer lovely wife's grandfather was out prowling around north of the river last night. Claimed he was restless." The old mountain man paused thoughtfully. "Figured to foller him to see what he might be up to."

By now, my attention was aroused. What might Bode McCully have been up to? "Thanks, Buffalo. How about you go ahead and tail Mr. McCully? I'll cross the river and see what I might find."

Watts nodded and turned his mount eastward toward Corpus Christi.

I watched after him for a couple of minutes before heading Tornado toward the Nuecestown ferry.

As I approached the ferry landing, my eye caught a thin column of smoke wafting a few yards back from the north bank of the river. It was perhaps a quarter mile downstream. I thought it might be wise to check it out, as not so many folks camped in the area these days. I checked the loads in both revolvers and my rifle more out of habit than from any outright sense of imminent danger. The grasses and scrub along the shoreline would effectively screen my water crossing. The ferry was convenient and sure beat riding a mile or so upstream to cross at the shallows.

As I dismounted and led Tornado onto the deck of the ferry, I kept an eye on that telltale smoke. Just as the ferry was about to pull away, I saw a puff of steam as though someone were extinguishing the blaze. My natural lawman suspicions kicked in, and I decided I didn't want to be stuck midstream when whomever it was might reveal themselves. That was a tad too vulnerable. Upon seeing that, I nodded to the ferryman and backed the Appaloosa off onto the landing. "I think I'm going to take a ride upstream, Bert. Have a fine day."

I rode about a half mile upstream. Taking advantage of the lowered water level, thanks to the extended drought and plenty of overhanging cover, I easily found a place to wade across.

By the time I'd doubled back toward the ferry, the smoke had disappeared. I had a general idea as to where the campsite was. Upon reflection, I deduced that the best course would be to approach the campsite easy and friendly-like, as though it was a chance encounter. Any noise I made was purposefully as normal as possible so as not to cause any alarm. So it was that squeaking leather and jingling spurs that alerted the campers.

Cal turned to Bolton, as the outlaw finished cinching his saddle. "You hear someone coming, boss?"

"Ease up Cal. Nice day...there'll be a few travelers about."

"This traveler sounds like he's headin' our way."

Bolton sighed. "Damn, Cal. Just act real easy-like." The last thing he needed was them to appear as though they were up to no good. No sooner had the words left his mouth than I rode into the campsite.

Cal's hand reflexively stroked the butt of his revolver at the sight of a big man on a decidedly big horse.

Apparently, several of the gang had ventured out the night before and planned to stay away until the planned rendezvous near Alice, so only Bolton, Cal, and two others remained.

Bolton put his hand out toward them palm down as

though to set them at ease. He looked up at me. "Welcome stranger. You passing through these parts?"

I nodded and tapped my fingers along the brim of my hat. "Yep. Pretty much passing through. Saw your smoke and was curious." I glanced about. "Coulda used a cup of coffee, but I see you're breaking camp. Guess I'll just mosey on down the road." I kept my badge hidden beneath my vest. There was no point in arousing unwanted attention.

"Well, you travel safe now, ya heah." Bolton let the words slither snakelike off his tongue as he smiled as friendly-like as possible.

By now, I had taken in about all I needed to see. These men were heavily armed, not just cowboys traveling through. This wasn't the time to stir things up, but my gut instinct told him they were likely up to no good. I returned Bolton's smile, turned Tornado, and rode on away.

Once I was out of earshot, Bolton turned to Cal and the others. "You men have to be careful. We can't afford anything suspicious...or stupid. If he was a lawman, we might have had a fight on our hands."

"Maybe he was a smart lawman, boss."

"Did you see a badge?" Bolton cast a hard eye on Cal.

"He sure was outfitted like one of them Texas Rangers." Cal shrugged and hung his head as though his instincts weighed heavily on his all-too-feeble brain. "Had that Colt in his holster, a Bowie knife, and one of them fancy Henry repeating rifles alongside his saddle. Coulda been a lawman checkin' us out, boss."

"So, you want to call off the bank robbery, Cal?" Bolton wasted no time challenging him. It definitely wouldn't do to have a doubter in their midst. "You can leave now, if that's your druthers. I won't hold it against you." Bolton laid a squinty eyed, challenging gaze on the man.

"'Spect I'll stick it out, boss." Cal sighed just a tad too audibly.

"Just don't be doing anything stupid, Cal." He turned to tighten the cinch and climbed into the saddle. "I'm thinking this spot is too busy. I'm gonna set up camp downriver a bit. Meet you at the rendezvous east of Alice before dawn. The bank should be right vulnerable."

Cal looked up at the outlaw leader. "You have been inside the bank?" It was as much a serious question as a challenge.

Bolton shook his head. "I can tell you how many floorboards from the front door to the teller window and to the vault." He began to turn his mount. "And I've got dynamite to blow it to smithereens." With nary another word, he put spurs to horse flanks and rode away.

FOUR
BANK HEIST THAT WASN'T

IN THE DIM PRE-DAWN LIGHT, Bolton sat astride his cayuse, awaiting the arrival of Cal and the rest of the gang. He was ever alert for the slightest sound of a possible threat. Other than the sounds of a gentle breeze and the occasional singing of frogs and crickets, there was nothing unusual to raise concern. He let his cayuse's head drop to chew on some choice grasses. It seemed as though time was on hold.

The metallic click of the bolt action on the Winchester was lost among nature's sound. The blast from the muzzle was not.

The outlaw was lifted from his saddle by the force of the 40-caliber slug and landed hard on his back in a cluster of cacti. The fall alone was enough to knock the wind from him, but the hole in the center of his chest fully took the last breath from him. Bolton was dead within moments of hitting the ground.

The bushwhacker heard the loud retreat of several riders that had been approaching and couldn't suppress a satisfied smile. There'd be no bank robbing in Alice on this morning, and one more troublemaker's lawless career was ended. It sure beat the long process of forming up a posse, capturing the outlaw, and waiting for a long trial simply for dame justice to be served.

I was headed to Alice this particular morning to meet up with a special visitor. A quite secretive rendezvous had been arranged. As it was, my path would inevitably take me past Bolton's rendezvous spot east of the town. My rookie Texas Ranger mind was focused on the meeting ahead and curiosity as to whom I was going to be meeting.

Within roughly a mile of Alice, Tornado's head began bobbing and his nostrils flared. A few more yards, and a riderless horse came into my field of view. A quick glance upward at circling buzzards offered a stark hint of what I was about to find. I nudged the Appaloosa forward while being ever on high alert to my surroundings. There was plenty of tall grass and cacti. The odor of death wafted my way. Wasn't long before the source became readily apparent. As I drew closer, a pair of coyotes slunk grudgingly away from the body of a man who was quite obviously no longer of this world.

Trey Bolton lay with open eyes, staring off into nothingness. I cussed under my breath to the extent that the bandanna now covering my nose permitted breathing. I'd had my suspicion that Bolton might be up to no good, but this was a surprise. It was an all-too-obvious bushwhacking. Could the vigilante have struck again? Sighing resignedly, I dismounted and secured the dead man's horse. I appreciated that the cayuse had hung around. Thus began the distasteful task of wrapping Bolton's body in his own bedroll and tying him over the saddle of his horse. Once finished with that inglorious task, I began nosing around the area for any clues left behind by the shooter.

I'd walked perhaps a hundred yards up the road toward Alice, when I noted a set of fresh horse tracks and a spot on a knoll where the grass had been tamped down by someone lying in a prone position. Try as I might, I found no notable sign. A shell casing or fragment of cloth might have been right nice, but such evidence wasn't to be. Whoever had gunned down Trey Bolton was meticulously careful. Then, I followed the tracks a bit, but there was nothing special as to horseshoe configuration or where the tracks headed. I decided that I would do a more thorough tracking on my way back from the meeting in Alice. Besides, I now had the added burden of dropping Bolton's body off with the sheriff's deputy. If there was a reward, I could lay claim to it. That would be right handy given Cassie's pregnancy.

The Taberna Bandana was a saloon named after the moniker given the railroad hamlet of Alice upon its founding a few years back. The establishment was a welcome watering hole to cowboys, laborers, travelers who didn't know better, drifters, hard cases, and the like. Sawdust covered the oak floor, already permanently stained with booze, cow manure, piss, chaws, and most anything else itinerant visitors might leave behind as a signature to their passing through or frequenting. Bode McCully sat back easy-like in the chair and nursed what he'd dubbed as a well-deserved beer. His crossed legs extended straight out, being careful not to let the rowels of his spurs damage the boot leather. Bode's eyes kept scanning the room at the comings and goings. He didn't get to Alice often, and he wasn't quite sure why he headed this way. Maybe it was to listen to more local chatter. His old Texas Rangering days would occasionally kick in, as he'd perk up his ears and listen for news of local lawbreaking. It was tough to relax when conversations turned worthy of eavesdropping.

Bode simply sat quietly observing. The place was slowly but surely filling up. It was the hard-scrabble riff-raff of the region. They'd bite your nose off as soon as they look at you. They weren't the best-dressed of society, more often wearing their duds out from the inside. There were plenty of guns and knives to be seen, but none were for show. It wasn't hard to imagine Bode's surprise when I strode in to whet my whistle before heading to my appointment.

I had taken but a step inside, when I caught the elder McCully in my peripheral vision. I instantly shifted direction from the bar and strode over to Bode's table.

"Howdy, young 'un. What brings you to Alice, Mr. Texas Ranger?" Bode was nothing if not enormously pleased that his granddaughter's husband had joined up.

"Could say the same for you, Mr. McCully."

"Pull up a chair and set a spell."

"Afraid I've only got a few minutes, but I'm happy to join you for a quick beer."

"Whatcha in an all-fired hurry for?" The old Ranger's naturally inquisitive thought process kicked in. Old interrogation questions never died. He drew his legs in and leaned toward me.

"Have a meeting with the governor of all things." I sat while motioning to the barkeep to send over two beers. "I got delayed a bit."

"Delayed?"

I lowered my voice and glanced around for possible eavesdroppers. "Found a body along the road from Nuecestown. It was that Trey Bolton fella. The coyotes had chewed him a tad, but I recovered the body and dropped it at the sheriff's office."

"Was it an accident?"

"Not unless putting a big hole in the middle of your chest is accidental. I'm of a mind to think it was the work of that bushwhacking vigilante we've been hearing about."

Bode gave an ever-so-slight grin. "At least whoever is doing this bushwhacking ended the ways of another lawbreaker." The old gentleman leaned in secretive-like again. "Do you think it's the work of one man?"

I wasn't certain as to how much I should reveal. "Not sure yet. Evidence points to it, but so far, it's mostly coincidental. Nothing stands out as especially distinguishing other than the targets being men wanted by the law for hanging offenses."

"Doesn't sound like just any old bushwhacking. Whoever's concocting these ambushes is saving Texas taxpayers a bundle of money."

"I can't complain about that, Mr. McCully, other than it's not lawful. Justice should take its course."

"You're right, of course, Junior." Bode smiled to himself and took a deep swallow of beer.

I finished off my beer. "Got to be going, Bode." I slid my chair back. Arising, I couldn't help but notice the retired Ranger's boots. Smiling, I asked, "Mighty clean boots for a man riding the trail. You always keep them so shined up?"

"Dang heel was coming loose. Bootblack fixed the heel and felt obliged to wax them up a bit."

I chuckled. "Shucks, even your spurs were polished." I implied that the immaculate footwear didn't fit with the rest of Bode's trail-dust-impregnated clothes. "You're getting quite duded up."

Bode suppressed a smile. He was impressed that I noticed the slight anachronism of his polished boots. "Give my best to your lovely wife. Hear tell y'all are expecting your first. I'm looking forward to being a great grandpa."

I stood, tipped my hat, and strode from the Taberna Bandana. Thoughts of the elder McCully's boots stuck in my mind. I didn't know why. In fact, it was likely of no significance. Still, there it hung, just a tad perplexing. I picked up my pace, as I realized I was close to being late for his meeting.

★ ★

Charles Culberson...Governor Charles Culberson...was not a patient man. A spit-and-polish military man with steely blue eyes and graduate of the Virginia Military Institute and University of Virginia Law School, he was uncomfortable with anything not by the book. Even his civilian attire featured a fit and finish that harkened back to his days at VMI. Tough as nails, he served as Texas attorney general, successfully defending the Railroad Commission. That led to his election as governor in 1892. Now, here he was, impatiently waiting for some wet-behind-the-ears Texas Ranger to show up. Worse still, his chair squeaked. He'd tried two others, but every danged chair in the room squeaked. He sat alone. This was to be a private meeting.

He'd made a name for himself over concern with railroads, and that was what he had traveled a couple of hundred miles to talk with this lawman about. Alice had become the busiest shipping point in South Texas thanks to the railroad. Now, Uriah Lott and Benjamin Yoakum were fixing to build the first phase of what would become the Gulf Coast Lines, the St. Louis, Brownsville and Mexico Railway.

Culberson's thoughts had just begun to drift off to political concerns, when he heard the tread of cowboy boots and jangle of spurs. There was a brief knock.

"Governor?"

The chair released another squeak as Culberson arose. "Come in."

The apparition that walked through the door nearly caused the governor to drop back into his chair. The tall, broad-shoul-dered, heavily armed man with the Texas Ranger shield was more than he'd expected. "Are you Texas Ranger Dunn?"

"Yes, sir, Governor. Lucas Dunn at your service." I paused at the expression on Culberson's face. "Is there a problem?"

"No. They told me you were a big man, but...well, I hadn't quite..." His words trailed off. "You're Luke Dunn's son, aren't you?"

"Yes, yes I am."

"Damn fine Ranger as I heard it. I hope the fruit hasn't fallen far from the tree." Culberson motioned for me to sit as he returned to his seat. He winced at the chorus of squeaking wood as he sat. "Do you know why you're here?"

I shook my head.

Culberson explained the concerns surrounding planned construction of the St. Louis, Brownsville and Mexico Railway.

I strove to listen attentively, patiently waiting for the governor to get to his purpose. Now and then, the chairs would give voice to their need for lubrication and a touch of glue, but they were ever less of a distraction.

"Dunn, there are some problems that need your special attention. There's the general concern about lawlessness. However, folks seem to be especially worried about some vigilante out there, a man taking the law into his own hands."

I nodded. Had the governor come all this way just to press me about the vigilante? Had he not heard that Captain Hughes had assigned me to root out the bushwhacker?

My body language wasn't lost on Culberson.

"I know that you're hunting that goldanged vigilante. I'm sure it isn't an easy assignment, Dunn." Culberson arose with an accompanying chair squeak, strode toward the door, and pivoted. "Guess you figured the vigilante and railroads aren't the only reasons for my coming all the way from Austin." The governor laid a penetrating gaze on me. "You recall Cheno Cortina?"

I figured that was a rhetorical question. Who in South Texas hadn't heard of Cortina, the Mexican rancher, politician, military leader, outlaw, and folk hero who had been the bane of Texas Rangers for decades until his death just three years ago? I nodded perfunctorily, partly out of respect for the governor and partly a reflex.

"Well, old Cheno had quite a few loyal followers. One of the most dangerous is a bad hombre named Carlos Diaz. We have reason to believe that he's gathered a few of Cortina's old gang and intends to cause a bit of havoc around Corpus Christi."

I now leaned forward. Culberson had grabbed my attention.

"Your Captain Hughes is patrolling the Rio Grande, and we've alerted him. However, we have reliable sources telling us that Diaz has already slipped past the Rangers and is headed north. I've been told that he hopes to make a name for himself by mimicking the Good Friday Raid back in 1875 but with a different outcome."

I was barely five years old when the raid had happened. I'd heard stories about it from my Texas Ranger cousins John and Matt Dunn. In fact, Red John Dunn had added so many embellishments to the family tale that I couldn't be certain as to what was true. I was sure of the outcome: the thieving, murdering Mexican bandits were driven off by a posse and some hostages were freed. "I've heard of the raid, Governor. To be clear, you're saying that this Diaz fellow plans to succeed at what Jesus Seguira failed to do?"

"I understand the Texas Ranger one riot, one Ranger mantra, but I don't expect you to stop a gang of bandits by yourself. I'm asking you to delay them until Captain Hughes arrives. A message has also been sent to Captain Brooks, but he's heading to El Paso and likely won't cover the distance in time to help."

I arose and faced the governor. I must admit that I remained a tad perplexed that the governor had come all the way from Austin, when he could have sent a courier. "I expect there'll be no railroads built or folks settling around these parts with the likes of Carlos Diaz roaming the Nueces Strip, Governor." I had, of course, nailed the underlying purposes behind the governor's visit. Bandits and vigilantes roaming the region were decidedly undesirable in terms of both public safety and economics.

Culberson smiled. "That's about it, Ranger Dunn."

"I'll see what I can do, Governor. Maybe I can do just a tad more than delay Señor Diaz."

"If you're half as resourceful as your father, I expect that I can count on it." Culberson extended his hand.

I put on a serious, can-do facial expression as I firmly gripped the governor's hand. "We'll know soon enough how successful I am."

"I'm counting on you, Ranger Dunn. Now, don't let me delay you any further."

I had taken the governor's handshake, an experience not unlike grasping a wriggling fish, swiftly extricated my hand and headed for the door. I paused before walking out. "And, Governor...I do appreciate your respect for my father." With that, I exited and headed for my horse. Time was wasting, and I needed to come up with some actions for delaying this bandit threat until Captain Hughes arrived. He'd have time to think on the road back to Nuecestown. Mounting up, I whispered in Tornado's ear, "Got a tough job ahead, big fella. Let's go home."

As I passed Taberna Bandana, I saw Bode standing beside his horse. I wanted no distractions, so avoided inviting Bode to ride with me. I said nary a word but gave the traditional fingers aside the brim of my hat by way of recognition.

For his part, Bode quickly figured that I was avoiding him but decided not to press the issue.

I nudged Tornado into a loping stride to put distance between myself and the retired Texas Ranger. I was so focused on the prodigious task ahead that I didn't even entertain the thought that Bode might have some ideas to share toward delaying Carlos Diaz.

★★

Governor Culberson's charge to delay Diaz was huge. Tactics for accomplishing the task were jumping around in my head like a bucking bronc. Naturally, it was critically important that I not get myself killed. I was barely a half mile out of Alice when I pulled up. The task had fully captured me. I shook my head, as though shaking out the jumble of thoughts in my brain. I recalled the hunting advice of Buffalo Watts about keeping calm when stalking prey. I took a deep breath and looked about, realizing that I was near the site of the ambush and recollecting that I was going to reconnoiter for clues. I figured that focusing on the bushwhacker ought to settle my thinking a bit.

I dismounted and searched for the spot I'd found where the vigilante had lain in ambush. Fortunately, the ground was undisturbed from earlier in the day. I found the place quickly enough. From that location, I sighted up the road to where I'd found Bolton's body. I swept the area slowly with ever-more-practiced eyes, as I searched for whatever telltale signs might be revealed. Nothing much to be seen other than prairie grasses, cacti, and some scrubby mesquite interspersed with an occasional live oak.

There was nothing unusual about the hoofprints of the bushwhacker's horse. I was about to give up surveying the scene, when a couple of imprints caught my eye. They were beside where the shooter's horse had been hitched to a tree. It was an impression made by the heel of a boot, and it was slightly askew. I locked the visual image away in my head. While it was the first defining clue of any significance, I realized that it would be easy enough for the killer to have the heel repaired. I sighed, shrugged, and mounted Tornado.

I'd report my discovery of the vigilante's attack to Sheriff Tyler along with the news of the special order I'd personally received from the governor. The sooner I could focus my energies on delaying Carlos Diaz, the better. It both excited me and frightened the living daylights from me.

FIVE
FAMILY MATTERS

I RODE EVER-SO-SLOWLY INTO NUECESTOWN. Anyone passing through couldn't help but notice how the town was showing the beginnings of going to seed. News that the railroad would pass the town by was already having its effect. The corral around the livery was in disrepair, a couple of planks were missing from the ferry landing, the jail needed a new roof, grasses grew untended around graves at the cemetery, ruts seemed deeper in the streets, and only the schoolhouse seemed to have dodged time and weather. Alice, a few miles to the west, was thriving by comparison. Governor Culberson's words about the railroads being links to prosperity seemed quite poignant.

I gave serious thought to stopping, but concerns over Carlos Diaz had given way to a burning need to get onto my ranch and Cassie's waiting arms. I dreaded sharing my new assignment with her, given its very real danger. I wasn't about to make her a young widow if I could help it, but she'd surely fear for me.

As I left the outskirts of Nuecestown, the sound of a horse approaching from my rear caused me to pull up. My hand went to the butt of my Colt revolver, as I half-turned the Appaloosa to face the sound.

"Junior. Wait up!" Bode McCully wasn't but fifty yards behind. He'd been keeping pace with me since leaving Alice and only now had decided to catch up.

"Mr. McCully...er...Bode. You been following all this time?" I recalled seeing the retired Ranger preparing to mount up back at the Taberna Bandana in Alice. Bode must have closed the gap considerably when I stopped at the ambush site. I had a fleeting thought that McCully might have watched me surveying the scene. If so, it surprised me that the former lawman hadn't joined me sooner with some sage advice from his years as a Ranger. Then again, I scolded myself for being so caught up in the Diaz matter, that I hadn't checked my own backtrail. Most any friend or foe could have snuck up on me.

McCully quickly closed the gap between us. "Figured I'd eventually catch up with you. You stopping at Heaven's Gate?"

"Yes sir, Bode."

"Guess you miss Cassie, when you're on the trail. Rangering can be a tough life."

I nodded.

"Looks like you've got the weight of the world on you, son. You okay?"

I was near bursting to unload the burden of the critically important assignment I'd been given directly from the governor. "Er...yes. Yes, Bode. I'm okay." I nudged Tornado forward. "Just got a new assignment on top of finding the bushwhacker that's out there somewhere."

"You need help?"

I glanced over at McCully, who had spurred his mount enough to keep pace alongside and just a little behind. "Afraid I've got to handle this on my own, Mr. McCully, sir. Can't be getting non-lawman folks involved. It's not the days of posses anymore." I turned away. With relief, I saw the gateway to Heaven's Gate just ahead. "I'll catch up with you, when I've finished."

Bode reined in and watched as I rode up the trail to my folks' home on the Heaven's Gate Ranch and then over to my own humble spread. Cassie's open arms would be waiting, and it likely gave the retired Texas Ranger a bit of peace at the thought.

I was relieved to be able to focus on my beloved Cassie. My visit would be all too short. More difficult than the brevity of my return would be explaining to Cassie what I could of this assignment.

Bode found his way to one of his favorite haunts, the Longhorn Saloon in Corpus Christi. The place seemed even more gone to seed, since his visit a few days back. The floor-boards had nearly maxed out their capacity to hold the mix of booze, blood, sweat, and urine shed and spilled on them over the years. Sawdust had its limits so far as compensating. Nasty aromas impregnated the place from wall to wall. No matter to Bode McCully. The Longhorn was a veritable font of information, rumored and reliable.

It was late morning when he set himself at his usual table near the rear. It gave him a view of everything and everyone with the bonus of picking up most conversations. His brief conversation with me weighed on his mind. He was curious as to what assignment I had been given. After watching me ride out of Alice, he'd observed Governor Culberson emerge from the place I had just left. To draw the governor down from Austin signaled that something big was surely afoot. He was dying to learn about it. He figured it just might be worthwhile to keep an eye on me, at a distance, of course. Perhaps there'd be a rumor or two floating through the thick air of the saloon.

Guests who'd imbibed tended to speak a tad louder than sober folk. Thus, it was that his attention was drawn to a couple of cowboys engaged in quite animated conversation just two tables away. Bode was all ears, as he sipped his beer and concentrated on the two.

"Honest, Cal. I heard it from one of them Mexicans about a day's ride south."

"Bandits?" The second cowboy was incredulous. "This is '95, Jack. We're civilized now. Cortina is long gone. The Texas Rangers patrol the Rio Grande."

"Just sayin'." The cowboy named Jack leaned in toward his companion. "They say it's a fella named Diaz. He's supposed to be crazy mean. Rode with Cortina." Jack looked around furtively. "The Mexican said Diaz was up to no good. Gonna make trouble. Diaz is planning to deliver what Jesus Seguira failed at, back in '75."

"If it's true, what are we supposed to do about it?" Cal looked around and caught Bode's eyes watching them over the rim of his beer glass. "You prying, mister?"

Bode put down the beer and eased back in his chair. "Sorry. I couldn't help but overhear."

"Ain't polite to listen in." Cal was just a little riled consequent to the eavesdropping and the rumor he'd just learned of.

"Sorry, it's a bad habit from my Texas Ranger days."

Bode's response got Jack's attention. "You think the Rangers know?"

McCully couldn't be certain, but he'd now put my distracted state together with the rumor he'd just heard. The math was almost too easy and gave all the more reason to follow me. Culberson must have met with the young Texas Ranger about the Diaz matter. "I have it on good authority that the Rangers will handle it."

Jack rolled his eyes. "Last I heard, the nearest company was down in Brownsville."

"I know there's at least one Ranger nearby."

The cowboys rolled their eyes in unison. Jack was especially incredulous. "One Ranger against better than two dozen bandits armed to the teeth!"

Bode couldn't contain himself, as he fell back on the old adage made famous years before, "You know what they say, gents, one riot, one Ranger." He grinned at having had a chance to use the shopworn phrase.

Cal shook his head ruefully. "Sounds like a dead Texas Ranger to me."

Bode figured this was enough talk. He needed to figure how he'd be best able to trail after me. He surely wondered what I might have in mind?

Cassie's embrace seemed to last forever, yet it wasn't long enough for me. I could feel the press of her growing belly against me, and that alone filled me with dread at what I'd been ordered to do. Suicide mission? Not if I could help it.

"I've missed you so, Lucas." Cassie shed tears of joy, as she pressed against her man. She pushed away and led me into the house. "There's so much to…"

I put a finger to my mouth to gently shush her. "I can't stay long, sweetheart."

Bewilderment swept across Cassie's face. Her eyes grew wide. She'd anticipated at least a few days of marital bliss with her husband. "Er…can't stay long?"

"The meeting in Alice with Governor Culberson…well…he gave me a special assignment while Captain Hughes high-tails it here from the Rio Grande."

"Special assignment?" The question was delivered tentatively. A shiver made its way through her. Intuitively, she sensed danger.

"There's trouble headed north from Mexico. I'm to delay it as best I can."

"Trouble?" Her worst fears were being realized.

I took a deep breath. "Just some rogue bandit." The signs of fear that swept across her face couldn't be missed. "I'll be careful." That was hardly reassuring. I didn't dare tell her that Carlos Diaz had a gang of nearly three dozen heavily armed men. I desperately needed to change the subject. "Is that cornbread I smell?"

Cassie pressed herself against me. She must shake thoughts of my special assignment and its dangers from her head. But for now, she needed the security of my strong embrace.

I sensed her need. "I will be careful, sweetheart." I tried very hard to be reassuring.

Finally, she pushed away. "It's right hot today. The creek's up." Released from my arms and with a hint of seductiveness in her steps, she slipped over to the hot pan of cornbread. "Pour yourself some coffee, Lucas."

My mouth gaped just a bit. She'd lost me at the mention of the old swimming hole down at the creek. An image of naked bodies embracing in cool swirling waters took over my mind. I watched Cassie cut two pieces of cornbread. There was a seductiveness in the sway of her hips beneath the filmy cotton dress. Thoughts of my special assignment were all-to-easily replaced, as I admired how incredibly alluring my pregnant wife was. "The creek...yes." I swept her back into my arms. My kiss caused the plates of cornbread to drop to the floor as she yielded to my passion.

"Lucas...oh, Lucas. I've missed you." Her mouth absorbed mine. "Oh...Lucas...I love..." She wrapped one leg around mine and drew me ever tighter to her. My lips found her neck, sending her into a near-convulsive passion that raged through her body.

We dropped to the floor and satisfied our lust in paroxysms of sexual rapture. The swimming hole would wait—but not too long.

★★

Morning had arrived all too soon for Cassie. She still had no idea as to the full nature of her man's special assignment and wasn't sure that she wanted to know. The fact that I was taking three rifles and much more ammunition than usual aroused her suspicions, but she'd decided not to press me. She figured she'd fortified me as best she could with a breakfast fit for three men not to mention having fully satisfied the needs of both of us last night in the bedroom.

Cassie strove to be supportive, to not show her concern for the known but especially unknown risks. "Lucas? You could ask…" Her voice trailed off. She'd suggested I seek her grandfather's advice before. Why I was so reluctant was beyond her.

It was as though I read her mind. "He's old school, sweetheart." I instantly regretted interrupting. I couldn't miss the hurt that swept across her face at my ill-timed discounting of Bode McCully. She adored her grandfather, pretty much thinking he was a legend as a lawman. Growing up, it had been all-too-easy for her to overlook Bode's foibles, his stretching of the law, and his legal miscues. Bode McCully had been tried and acquitted of murder at least once. While that wasn't fully uncommon among lawmen of the era, it spoke of the nature of delivering justice on the frontier, where there was often a fine line between the legal and the illegal.

"Just a thought, Lucas." She smiled. She was so very convinced that Bode could help her man.

I tried to be reassuring, as I prepared to mount Tornado. I stood for a moment with hat in hand and my forehead planted against my saddle. It was tough to leave. My bedroll and saddlebags were packed. I'd rejected the idea of a packhorse, as I knew that a high degree of mobility would be essential. "I'll be back in a few days, sweetheart." I hoped it'd be only a few. I looked searchingly into her eyes. There was so much

love in them...and fear. Words were inadequate, but I
ventured anyway, "I love you, Cassie."

Cassie knew better than to offer a lingering embrace that
would delay the inevitable parting. This Texas Ranger business
was trying enough. She closed her eyes and said a little prayer
to herself for my safe return.

As I swung up into the saddle, my peripheral vision caught
her bowed head and closed eyes. I softly murmured, "Amen,
sweetheart." I'd surely be trusting in divine providence. As her
eyes opened, I stretched down for a parting kiss before turning
Tornado away to the task at hand. The taste of her sweet lips
lingered on mine.

I couldn't bring myself to look back as I headed up the trail.
I knew she was watching me. Her eyes wouldn't be leaving me
until I was out of sight.

Bode McCully rightly reckoned that I would not appreciate his
company. There was the fact that by virtue of being retired, he
was a private citizen and no longer a lawman. There was also
the consideration that he might mess up whatever plans his
grandson-in-law might have in mind. The story about Carlos
Diaz that he'd picked up at the Longhorn Saloon, coupled with
his own experience as a Texas Ranger gave him a pretty fair
idea as to how the Mexican bandit operated. While Diaz's
gang might seem an ominous threat to most folks, they'd be
facing challenges in their travel from the Rio Grande. Feeding
and supplying thirty or so rough characters with gear and
horses was no easy task, even with the occasional support of
Mexican sympathizers along the trail.

Bode decided to hang well back from my path and look for
an opportunity to help where needed. It hadn't taken any
particular mental prowess to put the pieces of my mission

together. The governor had undoubtedly tasked me with delaying Diaz until Captain Hughes arrived with the full company of Texas Rangers. The big question that remained was what did Lucas Dunn have in mind that wouldn't involve getting killed.

SIX
BANDIT DRAMA

WITH A RESPECTABLY LARGE gang of bandits, Carlos
Diaz was feeling properly confident in his mission to wreak
havoc on Corpus Christi and environs. Most of the bandits
were veritable arsenals on horseback, armed to the teeth with
enough firepower to put most Texas Rangers to shame. He
remained ever-driven by memories of the Good Friday Raid of
1875 and his plan to atone for the cowardly retreat of Jesus
Seguira's bandit gang in the face of a small posse of Texans.

The sweltering heat had already caused two of his men to
drop with heat exhaustion, and some of the horses were struggling. Consequently, Diaz was forced to travel at night in unfamiliar territory or risk losing more of his gang. The moon and
stars barely revealed the nature of the vast prairie with its
grasses, rolling terrain, arroyos, and occasional stands of
mesquite and live oak that conspired to make travel slow,
especially given the long distances between watering holes.
The land was sparsely populated, as his band happened on
small clusters of civilization spaced many miles apart that
might ultimately become towns. The bandit leader hadn't
quite figured on logistics being a problem once he'd left
Brownsville.

Diaz reflected on having crossed from Matamoros at night and escaped northward from Brownsville while the Texas Rangers were on a wild goose chase up toward McAllen. He'd been successful in sending a half dozen of his men up river toward McAllen to raise enough of a ruckus to lure Captain Hughes away. The men had shot up the town a bit before heading to rendezvous with Diaz just north of Brownsville near what would become Harlingen. The bandit hadn't counted on word getting north to Austin via telegraph, though he calculated that the Texans would be unable to muster any meaningful defense in time to stop his push north to Corpus Christi. He ultimately employed an old Apache trick of cutting the telegraph line and splicing in strips of rawhide that made it hard to detect the ruined connection.

As the gang slowly plodded northward under the stars and had made it roughly halfway between Corpus and Brownsville, they rode to the crest of a rise in the prairie and were greeted by lights ahead of them in the distance. As they drew closer, Diaz realized that a ranch lay before them. The light from the windows was being cast by kerosene lamps. There were multiple buildings, giving the bandit reason to figure there were several folks populating the place. That translated to his thinking there'd be plenty of food, water, fresh horses, and even more armament to be had. He sent two bandits ahead to scout the place. With a starry night and near full moon, the odds of a successful attack under cover of darkness were decidedly in his favor.

I recognized that Diaz's gang of cutthroats had a significant head start in their drive north from Brownsville. The country the Mexicans traversed offered little shelter from the blazing heat of the summer sun. It was like traveling through an open-air sauna. Neither was there much civilization to speak of so far as towns. I was about as familiar with the landscape as most anyone, thanks to years of hunting with my dad and Buffalo Watts.

I reckoned that the bandit leader would surely avoid large ranches along his route like the Kleberg's King Ranch and Lasater's La Mota de Falfurrias with their well-armed vaqueros. While Diaz might be averse to crossing those vast ranches, they'd be hard to fully avoid. With the bandit chief slowed by the dimly lit landscape and the need to feed his men and water his horses, I reckoned I might be lucky and reach Los Olmos Creek before the bandits. I calculated that they'd have to pass that creek where the terrain most favored me. Despite no mountains or the shelter of thick woods, there'd be plenty of places from where I could harass the Mexican rebel pretender. It had been fortuitous that word of Diaz's march north had reached Governor Culberson in time to take action in defense of Corpus Christi. And it was just as fortuitous that Diaz's cutting of the telegraph wasn't done soon enough. That I just happened to be available had been another stroke of luck, though, considering the risks, I doubted the luck would be his.

I headed Tornado south at a slow walk. I was ever mindful of my surroundings, though I had no idea that Bode McCully was following at a considerable distance. I figured to ride through the night. The only sounds other than a light breeze rustling through the prairie grasses were the creaking of saddle leather, an occasional coyote howl, and a few owl hoots. I was startled once by the screech of a lion, but it was too far off to pay it any mind.

Morning found me within but a few miles of Los Olmos Creek.

Despite his passion for delivering frontier justice, Bode had the presence of mind to stay well behind me. Much to his chagrin,

I had not sought his advice. Part of him resented the snub, but part simply couldn't resist the possibility of knocking off a bandit or two. The justice of it was embedded in his soul.

The heat was unbearable. Bode wondered as to my drive to push on in the face of the withering rays of the late spring sun. The parched landscape got him thinking as to the possibility of a drought that would be especially devastating to this part of Texas. He had the foresight to bring a pack mule loaded with plenty of water among the supplies. He'd surely need it, as he wasn't getting any younger. He brought his mount to a halt as he approached a growth of live oak, took out his bandana, and wiped his brow. He wrung it out and wiped again before tying it around his neck to permit the evaporation of sweat to have a cooling effect. It wouldn't really help much. He murmured to himself, "better give the horse a rest." It was he who actually needed the break from the heat.

"Hay ocho vaqueros, jefe."

Diaz smiled at the report of his scouts. Only eight cowboys around the ranch house meant outnumbering his foe nearly four to one. That made for decidedly favorable odds.

"Pero."

No leader wants to hear doubt cast into a budding plan. Diaz leveled a frustrated gaze on the scout. *"Pero?"*

"Algunos son Mexicanos."

The bandit leader let out a forced breath. Countrymen that fraternized with the Anglos were no better than the Whites. He shook his head. *"No importa."* An evil smile creased his mouth that said he'd truck no resistance to attacking the ranch whether there were Mexicans there or not.

Diaz waved his men forward in a line stretching to his left and right. They'd practiced this time and again back in Mexico. The line would move forward at a walk, gradually coaxing their mounts to ever greater speed. Rifles were loaded and at the ready. It was a classic cavalry charge, lacking only sabers and lances.

Neither me nor Bode could have known that a third party was following our trail and had designs similar to McCully's. Rumor often travels blazing fast, and Buffalo Watts had over-heard talk going around Corpus Christi. His feelings were actually a tad hurt that I had not invited him to ride along. Going after a gang of bandits certainly sounded like a chal-lenge worthy of his skills despite his advanced years.

The Mexicans' plan was for half a dozen of the bandits to ride at the corral, firing rifles into the air and rousing the horses to draw the men from the ranch house. Once the occupants were exposed, Diaz's men could cut them down almost at leisure. The fusillade leveled at the vaqueros would be devastating.

At a mere hundred or so yards from the ranch house, Diaz saw one of the vaqueros stepping outside to answer nature's call. Upon seeing the bandits galloping toward him, the man turned to warn his fellows inside. A bullet from Diaz's rifle cut him down before he could utter a sound, but the sound of gunfire alerted the occupants. Simultaneously, bandits raised holy hell at the corral. Vaqueros rushed from the house, few bothering to grab a firearm. Chaos reigned supreme. The vaqueros were cut down to a man while never returning fire.

"*¡Bastante! ¡Bastante!*" Diaz called for a ceasefire. The attack was over in mere seconds. The bandit chief rode to the ranch house and dismounted to survey the damage. Two of his lieu-tenants gathered the bandits together. Well-lathered horses and equally sweaty bandits needed calming from the brief but intense heat of the attack. As Diaz stood rifle in hand with his back to the door and scanned the bodies lying in eternal repose along the corral fence, a noise from behind caused him to pivot. It was too late to duck a bullet that grazed his left ear. Despite the sting, he coolly leveled his rifle at the woman standing in the doorway with the now smoking rifle and put a bullet through her chest. In his evil mind he instantly regretted killing her, as she was plenty comely enough to have provided a pleasant diversion for his travel-weary gang. "Qué pena," he muttered, a pity indeed.

"¡Comida! ¡Caballos!" Diaz called to his men to strip the place of anything of value that was portable, especially food and fresh horses.

Diaz turned to his lieutenants. "Descansamos aquí esta noche." The men would enjoy resting in the ranch house that night. They would spend the early morning coolness cleaning up after the attack and resume their travels the next day at dusk. They even butchered two longhorns so as to feast on a late-night steak dinner. Coffee had already been brewed by the now-deceased occupants. Little did Diaz realize the error of his ways. Overconfidence was breeding carelessness, as he was unwittingly giving me time to set my delaying tactics in motion and Captain Hughes more time to bring his Texas Ranger company northward.

I scanned the horizon before me more often now. I had no way of knowing of Diaz's dallying. Danger could be lurking around the next arroyo, beyond the next rise, hidden among the tall grasses. Each day, I felt more burdened by the weight of my responsibility. I had crossed Santa Gertrudis Creek at daybreak and found myself traversing the easy rolling terrain with its soil of clay and sandy loam. The prevalent grasses grew tall, and the landscape featured mixes of live oaks, mesquite, and scrub brush. Los Olmos Creek in the heart of the King Ranch fed into Baffin Bay. Along the creek, I expected to find the vantage points necessary for what I had in mind. Once I'd sighted Diaz's bandit rabble, I could plot their likely route and set my series of ambush sites. Importantly, I had hunted this area, so figured I could safely retreat from each ambush. It was my hope that Diaz would be sufficiently annoyed to pursue but cautious enough to not try to overwhelm by force of numbers. It was likely a fool's errand for me, but I had neither the time or resources for more elaborate schemes.

I was surprised to have not encountered any of Bob Kleberg's cowboys. They might even have mustered enough guns to take on Diaz directly. Kleberg, having married Richard King's daughter, had only just taken over management of the King Ranch with its hundreds of thousands of acres spreading across the region southwest of Corpus Christi. While it occurred to me that the King Ranch cowboys would have given me plenty of firepower, I had not been given the authority to recruit private citizens. Only now, I had begun to realize that Cassie's advice to counsel with her grandfather might have been a wise course of action. It was too late now.

As I waded Tornado across Los Olmos Creek and climbed the southern creek bank, luck was with me. I caught sight of several riders perhaps a mile or more to the south. So far as I could tell, they were headed directly toward me. The sun was finding its way toward the horizon, so I calculated that they'd just decamped and were heading northward and taking advantage of the relative cool of the evening. An easy breeze traveled from the west, so I had no fear of any low-level noises I might make alerting the bandit column. Clouds sweeping in gave promise of a night with little or no moonlight or starlight to illuminate the bandits' path. The environment could be treacherous at night for folks unfamiliar with the vagaries of the topography. I murmured a little prayer of thanks that I'd hunted in these parts.

I turned my big Appaloosa northward and spurred him to a gallop. I'd identified two hearty stands of live oak roughly a half mile apart that would serve as cover. I set a rifle and ammunition at each site before doubling back to the creek to set my initial ambush. I calculated that I had perhaps a half hour before Diaz would come into range. Tornado was plenty lathered and would now have plenty of time to recover before the shooting started. My hope was to throw Diaz's band into confusion in the dim light of the ever-darkening scene. I might pick off a couple of bandits—three if I was lucky—before I'd have to hightail it northward to my next ambush site. After an ambush or two, I hoped that the Mexicans just might decide not to risk further pursuit at night.

Bode McCully froze at the faint sound of saddle leather squeaking behind him.

"Damn, McCully. What in tarnation yuh doin' out here?" Buffalo Watts leveled his aged Sharps rifle at the old Ranger.

Bode relaxed and let out an audible burst of air. "Damn yourself, Watts! I could ask you the same." He shook his head. "Put up that ancient piece. You ain't shooting me no how."

Watts smiled. "Guess we're up to the same business, watchin' over Junior." He eased his horse up alongside Bode's mount. "What yuh thinkin'?"

Bode scratched his head thoughtfully. "Well, by my thinking, a crossfire might work right well. Junior's set up a couple of fallback ambush sites."

"Sounds good." Watts spat out his tobacco chaw. "Yuh want east or west?"

"Guess it doesn't matter. I'll take the west side." He hesitated before turning his horse. "Figure to stay mounted. Won't be but a couple of minutes afore young Junior will have to pull

up and hightail it to his next tree stand." Bode pulled the
Winchester from its scabbard and nudged his mount forward.

Watts nodded. "Pretty much. Figure we can drop a bandit
or two and give Junior cover. Maybe one of us will get lucky
and drop Diaz." He turned his mount eastward and rode out
about a hundred yards.

Both were distant enough that I was as yet unaware of their
presence.

Diaz spurred his horse to the front of his band. Travel was
necessarily slow. Despite the psychological rush from the raid
on the ranch, the bandit chieftain realized that he'd have to be
ever more alert as they approached Corpus Christi. The
rapidly approaching darkness with its hidden terrain dangers
added to his frustrations.

Dismounting was not an option, as the grasses, cacti, and
scrub brush would tear at clothing and flesh. And there were
rattlesnakes. This was definitely horse country.

Diaz waved the two bandits behind him to go forward.
"*Anímate y abre un camino.*" They were to carve a trail for the
rest of the band. They'd follow single file behind the lead
bandits. It wasn't exactly to Diaz's liking, as it made them
vulnerable. Then again, what idiot would try to attack them in
the enveloping blackness?

Captain Hughes was pushing his company as hard as he
dared. He faced the same terrain challenges as Diaz, though he
was a bit more familiar with it.

There wasn't the slightest hint of grumbling, as men and
horses pushed on with infrequent stops. Rest was necessary
for the horses but begrudged by the men. They knew what lay

ahead. Many had kinfolk in Corpus Christi that could be in danger, plus they craved the very idea of battle.

Hughes was gradually closing the gap between his company and the bandit gang. By his reckoning, less than half a day now separated him from Diaz. He hoped that I was effective enough in slowing the Mexicans' advance.

Lurking in the Texas Rangers' minds was the ranch victimized by Diaz's band. The massacre had been bad, but the mutilation of the corpses was beyond the pale. They wouldn't soon forget the sight and relished exacting punishment on the lawless invaders.

★★

The lead bandits were roughly twenty-five yards in front of the column. They were cautioning each other as they wended their way through the scrub brush toward the creek.

I patiently waited until they'd reached the south bank of Los Olmos Creek. I'd decided to remain mounted so as to speed my eventual getaway. I was camouflaged from view by blending in with both darkness and the live oak standing behind me. I could barely make out the silhouettes of the two Mexicans, as they stopped at creek's edge.

I drew a bead on the second rider. Tornado held steady. I chambered a round, aimed, breathed easy, and squeezed the trigger. The explosion was deafening in the still darkness. The bandit was lifted from his saddle by the impact of the slug into his chest. I worked the lever, chambering a second round.

The lead bandit took a bullet square between his eyes.

My eyes opened in amazement. I hadn't squeezed my trigger. Where had the shot come from?

Diaz's instinctive reaction was to cast caution aside and charge forward at a full gallop to the scene. His men naturally followed. At least three bandits were thrown, when their horses stumbled.

Diaz dismounted and tried to focus on the scene in the darkness. His band was in total disarray. He turned to the bandit standing beside him only to watch in horror as the man's head was blown apart. Splattered with blood, Diaz called out, "¡Hombres! ¡Retirarse!" He sprang into his saddle as three more shots rang out and two more bandits fell from their saddles. In a span of less than a minute, five bandit bodies graced the grasses and scrub brush of the Nueces Strip.

I had no idea from where my covering fire had come or from whom. I figured that Diaz would go only a short distance before rallying his men. He'd surely return with a vengeance. As I turned Tornado to face north, I took a moment to try figuring from where all the friendly fireworks had come. In the darkness, I could make out a silhouetted form on either side. "Who goes?" I shouted.

"Ride Ranger!"

I recognized Buffalo Watts's gravelly voice. I couldn't contain a smile as I spurred the big Appaloosa to a gallop toward the next stand of trees. I called out from the saddle. "Who you got with you?!"

Bode shouted. "Just an old Ranger!"

I reached the live oaks and reached down for the rifle and ammunition I deposited there. As the cloud cover began to break, there was enough starlight to make out McCully and Watts setting up the next defensive line.

They didn't have to wait long. They heard shouts and the sounds of horses splashing through Los Olmos Creek.

"¡Andele hombres! ¡Los matamos los todos!" Diaz urged his men to hurry and kill all the bushwhackers. He had no idea what he was facing but had reckoned that he was facing a small force. He still had nearly thirty bandits in the saddle spewing lead as they climbed the north bank of the creek.

With the cloud cover dissipating, moonlight further illuminated the scene. Me and my companions could more readily make out their targets, but Diaz could now confirm the size of the enemy force he was facing.

I held fire until the bandits were within fifty yards, then began chambering rounds and firing as quickly as possible. McCully and Watts joined in the mini-fusillade. One...two... three bandits were blown from their saddles. Horses screamed agonizingly as bullets inadvertently found them. Mortally wounded bandits cried out from the grasses.

Diaz found himself frustrated. Once again, he ordered retreat. "¡Hombres! ¡Retirarse!"

As the bandits retreated, Bode McCully took careful aim with his 1895 Winchester. This fight had been like shooting wild hogs in a trap. But this target was special. He'd laid a bead on Carlos Diaz. A squeeze of his trigger, and a slug ripped through Diaz's shoulder. Bode shook his head ruefully. He'd hoped for a kill shot.

With the bandits in retreat, I seized the moment to ride to my next defensive position. Watts and McCully followed. This time, we converged on the stand of live oak. I grabbed the remaining rifle and the stash of ammunition hanging from a branch then turned to my two uninvited but much appreciated guests. I smiled sheepishly, knowing I should have sought help in the first place. "Dang, but I'm kinda glad y'all are here."

"You can thank us later. Where the hell is Captain Hughes?" Bode figured they couldn't hold off Diaz forever.

"Don't know. Hope he's close." I gazed southward, figuring that Diaz was rallying his men for another attack. "How many men do you think he has left?"

Bode shook his head. "Too many. Couple of dozen for sure. I winged el jefe, but he's more angry than pained."

Buffalo Watts rode up. A bullet had grazed his left ear, and another delivered a flesh wound just below his knee.

"You hurt bad, Buffalo?" I couldn't miss the blood staining my friend's shirt and chaps.

Watts responded with his typical gravelly voice. "I'd say so, if I was." He joined us in scanning the southern horizon.

I reloaded. "This terrain between here and the last attack is treacherous." I smiled deviously. "After this, we'll head toward Cayo Del Grullo." I knew that the sandy, swampy landscape with its tall grasses would slow Diaz to a crawl.

Watts smiled knowingly. "They're angrier than a nest of rattlers and won't rest 'til they've sunk their fangs into us all."

Carlos Diaz was red hot angry. How dare a mere three men deign to think they could defeat his force. He'd lost a third of his gang, and he hadn't a clue as to whether any of the defenders had been killed or even wounded. If not, they surely lived charmed lives that would end soon enough by his figuring. He turned to his remaining lieutenant. "*¿Cuántos hombres temenos?*"

"*Veinte, jefe.*" He paused. "*Y cuatro heridos.*"

Diaz shook his head ruefully. He'd lost a third of his band. Only twenty-four, including the wounded, remained. They'd expended far too much ammunition with little to show for it. "*Atacamos de nuevo.*" They'd attack again. He gazed thoughtfully northward. The rush of massacring the vaqueros a day earlier had been more than offset by this night's challenges. An evil grin found its way across his face. "*Debemos flanquearlos.*" They'd try to flank their opponents. Head-on had been near suicidal. Diaz figured to split his force and attack from each side. He winced a couple of times as he patiently waited for his shoulder to be bandaged before climbing back into the saddle.

An expression of concern spread across Bode's face. "The sonofabitch is taking too long. He's up to something."

I laid a questioning look on Bode and Buffalo. "What do you think he's going to do?"

Buffalo stroked the stubble on his chin. "The smart thing would be to circle around us and continue north. But he's prideful. Pride under stress breeds stupidity. If I was in Diaz's shoes and musterin' another attack, I'd come at us from our flanks. He sure won't come head-on again."

I searched the horizon. "I'm thinking he'll expect us to defend like we did the first two times. Let's head to Cayo Del Grullo and draw him to us. The terrain will be in our favor."

Bode liked my idea, not to mention my strategic decisiveness. "Sounds good to me. I wouldn't mind another crack at Diaz." He smiled and stroked the barrel of his precious 1895 Winchester.

Watts had already begun to head northeastward. "Works for me," he muttered.

Diaz wasn't about to charge at a full gallop again. With stars and moon, he now had a better view of the landscape. He'd divided his force, sending them forward cautiously at a walk.

It took but a few minutes to arrive at where he thought the bushwhackers would be.

"¡Maldito! ¿A dónde fueron?" he snarled through clenched teeth. Where could they have gone? His frustration at being outsmarted wasn't lost on his men, though none dared voice any opinion.

It was too dark to try to track his prey. Diaz angrily slapped his hat against his thigh, causing excruciating pain in his sorely wounded shoulder. "¡Maldito!" he cursed again. Damning was mild compared to his true feelings. He sighed resignedly and dismounted, grimacing as the pain surged through his shoulder and radiated across his chest. *"Acampamos aquí."* Without knowing where or when they might be ambushed in the dimly lit and unfamiliar terrain and despite still holding a numerical advantage, he'd decided to spend the night where they stood just north of Los Olmos Creek. With water nearby, they could at least relax, recover, and think further on how best to take on their decidedly pesky enemy. Corpus Christi beckoned, and Diaz was determined not to be deterred by whomever was distracting him from his mission.

"Seems like Diaz doesn't want to follow us in the dark." I couldn't suppress a grin as I expressed the obvious. "Maybe we could stir him up just a bit more."

"What do yuh have in mind?" Buffalo Watts had built considerable respect for my instinctive abilities.

"Wind has turned north to south." I let out an evil chuckle. "Anyone got a match?"

Bode McCully nodded with admiration. This young husband of his granddaughter seemed as resourceful as anyone could expect. It would be foolhardy to attack the Mexicans, but a brush fire would sure add to their woes.

Almost in unison, three pairs of hands filled with matches.

"Let's spread out to spread the fire beyond their flanks. The grasses are dry but hold enough moisture to generate plenty of smoke." I waved McCully and Buffalo to spread to the left and right. They trailed their horses, as they'd need a quick getaway back to the relative safety of Cayo Del Grullo.

The grass lit more easily than expected. With a bit of fanning of the flames, it took but a few minutes for a broad swath of prairie grasses and scrub brush to become aflame with plenty of billowing smoke. Not wishing for their horses to be spooked by the conflagration, we quickly mounted up and rode to safety. We'd trust in the wind to do its work.

McCully purposely fell farther behind me and Buffalo. He'd been mulling something over in his mind. If Captain Hughes's Texas Rangers were to capture Carlos Diaz alive, there was likely to be all sorts of expensive, time-consuming legal, and diplomatic wrangling over the bandit's fate.

Yep, the solution was pretty much obvious to Bode. Cut the head off the rattlesnake, and its tail doesn't rattle anymore. Worst case, without Diaz the bandits would give up right quickly and be sent off back to Mexico.

Bode stroked the barrel of his Winchester, as he pulled back on his horse's reins. His two compatriots weren't looking back. Buffalo and I were hell-bent on riding on to Cayo Del Grullo. The old Ranger smiled with the satisfaction of purpose. He'd be disposing of a menace to society. It was a mercy killing of sorts.

"¿Qué es esse olor?" It was a rhetorical question. There was no mistaking the pungent aroma of burning prairie grass. Diaz instinctively knew that the fire had been purposely set. The uttered curse was mild compared to the words filling his head in the fury of the moment. His shoulder screamed with pain, as he mounted. He'd had the presence of mind to leave his cayuse ready to ride, or flames would have licked at his heels as he tried to saddle up. "¡Rápidamente! ¡De vuelta al arroyo!" He ordered his men back to Los Olmos Creek.

Flames chased at the heels of the last stragglers to splash through the waters. The fire reached the creek and began to fizzle out in a cacophony of hisses and spits in the swirling current. Blessedly for Diaz, glowing embers didn't carry across the waterway.

The skin of Diaz's face had turned from light bronze to a

shade of brownish scarlet that betrayed the intensity of his outrage. In his impetuosity to attack, he was being made the fool. That a mere three men were holding him at bay, made him even more livid.

His men dared not approach him. Clearly, they'd now be spending the night south of the creek without food, drink, and bedrolls. They rightly figured that their supplies had succumbed to the flames.

Between the now excruciating pain in his shoulder and his growing frustration, sleep was not an option for the beleaguered bandit chief. He set a perimeter of pickets while he sat on the creek bank among the tall grasses and pondered what daylight might bring. By now, Captain Hughes and his company of Texas Rangers were surely chasing him, and he had no idea how close they might be. As he settled down, he heard a scream behind him. One of his bandits had placed his saddle over a rattlesnake and suffered the error of his ways. Diaz could do naught but sigh, as another man was lost.

What to do? What more could possibly go awry? After the spirit-lifting attack on the ranch but two days earlier, his purposes were being thwarted by all manner of ill fortune. "¡Los matamos a todos yanquis mañana!" he hissed through clenched jaw. He assured himself as well as the nearby picket that they'd kill all of the ambushers the next day. He sat and reflected on having lost nine men in a single evening to pretty much unseen forces. What might he face in Corpus Christi? What might be his fate if the Texas Rangers, the hated *rinches*, arrived? He must reach Corpus as quickly as possible and take hostages, or he was a dead man walking. His hopes of bettering Jesus Sequira's Good Friday Raid of two decades ago seemed ever dimmer.

Carlos Diaz stood and stretched his legs. The gurgling sounds from the creek did naught to calm him. Sleep wasn't a possibility, as his mind roiled and shoulder pained. He leaned forward, straining his eyes in the dimly lit night and strove to see what might lurk beyond the charred prairie. He heard the metallic clicking sound of a round being chambered into a rifle. A quizzical expression swept across his face. A bullet exploded from the muzzle of Bode McCully's 1895 Winchester. The explosive warning in the stillness of the night was far too late for Diaz, as the bullet was well on its fated path. It would be the final sound he would ever hear. In the ensuing split second of silence, he grunted reflexively and looked down at the hole in the center of his chest. His head raised skyward in a final supplicating gesture as though pleading with his Maker. His eyes rolled back, and he fell forward flat on his face in the mud along the creek bank.

The nearby picket near jumped from his skin at the report of the rifle but quickly dove for cover. He collected himself before peeking out to see what might have befallen his leader.

Carlos Diaz desperately tried to lift his face from the mud, spasmed once, and finally breathed his last. There would be no attack in the morning. The bandits could only hope to escape back to Matamoros and safety. Only Captain Hughes's Rangers now stood in their way.

At Cayo Del Grullo, Watts and I had just begun to wonder what had become of Bode when we heard the explosive percussion of a rifle in the distance. Instinctively, I guessed what the retired Texas Ranger must be up to.

Moments later, a smiling Bode McCully appeared. *"No hay problema mis amigos."* No problem, indeed. His sarcasm cut through the night air. *"Carlos Diaz está en el infierno."*

Buffalo Watts shook his head. "Gone to hell, yuh say?"

Bode nodded affirmatively. "No doubt about it. Got the sonofabitch this time." He glanced at Buffalo and matter-of-factly blurted, "I'm pleased to have saved Texas the expense and diplomatic hassle of trying and hanging the sonofabitch."

I was momentarily dumbfounded but held myself together. "Expect they'll be running into Captain Hughes tomorrow. I don't reckon it'll go too well for them." The understatement wasn't lost on Bode and Buffalo, as we enjoyed a nervous laugh couched in relief.

"Can't thank you gents enough. We sure put a licking on Diaz's band." I paused. "So far."

"What's next, Junior?" Bode smiled. "Are we going to nudge the rest of the bandits along?"

I had little choice but to take the retired Ranger's comment into serious consideration. Would I be pushing their luck? How close was Captain Hughes? Would I be unnecessarily placing these companions in danger?

Buffalo and Bode looked on patiently with anticipation.

I broke the silence. "I reckon to follow them at a distance. Might pick off a straggler." I grinned, as I delivered my next thought. "If y'all want to ride along, it's your choice. I didn't ask y'all to ride with me in the first place, and I can't ask y'all now." Call me doggedly stubborn, but I was determined to be clear that I wasn't recruiting civilians to Texas Ranger business. "Make no mistake, I'm grateful."

Buffalo nodded his understanding of my predicament. "Fair enough. Guess I'll tag along a good way behind, just in case."

Bode nodded as well. "Sounds good to me. That rattler won't be sticking its venom into the fine citizens of Corpus Christi." He grinned just a bit.

I gave McCully a curious look. Was the retired Ranger revealing some underlying sinister purpose? This was the grandfather that Cassie loved and respected. I shook off the thought.

SEVEN

RETURN TO THE HUNT

AS THE SUN crested the eastern horizon, I quaffed the last drops of coffee from my battered tin cup, promptly saddled up, and began the ride southward. I surveilled the area but saw no sign of Bode or Watts. They seemed to be good to their word of staying apart and appearing to have come upon the skirmish with Diaz by sheer happenstance. By the time they drew into sight, I had reached the remains of Diaz's campsite. It was clear that the remaining bandits had left in a hurry, even leaving food, ammunition, and booze in their wake. There was nothing worth retrieving save for the remains of Carlos Diaz. I remained in the saddle as Bode and Watts joined me on the south side of the stream. Of course, they followed at a respectable distance.

Bode stopped and dismounted. He looked down at the remains of Carlos Diaz. The bandit chief's cutthroats hadn't even buried their leader. The old Ranger grabbed a blanket from his pack mule, wrapped Diaz's body in it, and hoisted it over the back of the poor beast, as it brayed with the added load.

I paused and nudged Tornado along. Not a word was

spoken. I took a brief look back, shook my head, and urged the big Appaloosa to a trot.

The mule wouldn't budge.

I glanced back once again and could barely suppress a grin.

Bode shrugged and slid the heavy body from the mule. He tied a bandanna around his mouth to shield him from the smell as he severed the bandit's head, wrapped it in the blanket, and tied it to the pack on the mule. It was practical. It was proof. And the mule offered no further protest.

I shuddered at the sight before once again pressing my heels into Tornado's sides. It was an insanely practical but barbarically macabre act akin to the Comanche or Apache scalping their victims. Was this the man Cassie venerated? I sighed and turned Tornado southward.

It didn't take but a couple of hours for the temperature to climb high enough for us to feel as though we were riding through an oven. Fortunately, we didn't have to ride long, as distant sounds gave hint that the remainder of Diaz's gang had engaged with the Texas Rangers.

I heard the gunfire first and prodded Tornado forward at an easy trot. I didn't have to ride far, as I crested a hill to find that Captain Hughes's company was already putting the finishing touches on mopping up what remained of Carlos Diaz's ill-fated band.

Prisoners with arms raised high quickly opened up about the huge army that had attacked them back at Los Olmos Creek.

Hughes was concentrating on organizing the handling of the prisoners as I rode into the midst of the Texas Rangers and manacled bandits. "Howdy, Captain. Can I help?"

"'Bout time you got here, Dunn. What you been up..." Hughes suddenly realized what I had very much been up to. "Did you?"

"Afraid so, Captain."

Bode rode up behind me. McCully slid from the saddle and

released Carlos Diaz's head from the pack mule's load. Bandits and Rangers leaned away in momentary surprise and then aghast with horror as the head rolled to the captain's feet. "This scum won't be bothering the fine citizens of Texas any time soon, Captain."

"Who the hell?"

I stepped forward calmly. "Mr. Bode McCully here is a retired Texas Ranger. He and my old friend Buffalo Watts came upon me by chance and were of great aid in delaying these bandits." I nodded toward the dozen or so remaining Mexicans who gestured excitedly in agreement. I repeated for emphasis, "I was unaware of their following me, but they sure were a huge help in stopping Diaz."

Hughes stroked his chin thoughtfully and turned to me. "I'd say you've earned yourself a break, Ranger Dunn. How about you take a day or so with your wife, then get back to that mission I assigned. We'll escort this rabble back to Mexico." He smiled as he looked over at McCully and Watts. "Texas appreciates your help, gentlemen. However, we'd much prefer you leaving the meting out of justice to our lawmen. Do have safe travels." He suppressed the urge to call out McCully who should have known better than to interfere. He paused and grinned. "Oh, and y'all bury that damned stinking head." That brought a laugh to all but the prisoners. He gave Bode a hard look. "There's a bounty. I'll see y'all get it, Mr. McCully." He purposely didn't refer to Bode as a Texas Ranger.

Bode wasn't laughing. It took the law far too long to deliver justice. He'd saved the government time and money, and it wasn't fully appreciated.

The retired Texas Ranger's expression wasn't lost on me. I did find myself resenting McCully's presumptiveness in killing Diaz. It had not been part of my assigned plan to delay the bandits.

I mounted up, tipped my hat to Captain Hughes, and turned Tornado to the north. I glanced at Bode and Buffalo.

"You gents take your time. I'd prefer to head back alone." It was nothing personal, but then again, it was personal. I needed to digest all that had happened. I nudged my spurs gently into the big Appaloosa's flanks and trotted away.

My brain felt as though it would burst, as I thought on the past couple of days. There'd be no rest until I found some answers. Bode had of a sudden become a source of angst, even foreboding. Killing the Mexican was the very essence of what I understood as vigilantism. The fact that the vigilante operates outside the law certainly wasn't lost on me. McCully's shooting of the bandit chief essentially from ambush could only be described as murder regardless of the evil intentions of Diaz. Taking the law into one's own hands, even suppressing and punishing crime due to the perceived inadequate processes of the law, was inherently immoral, as I saw it. Of course, I was on solid ground per man's law and God's law. I'd learned that when a man's thinking is controlled by his evil self, there is often death of soul and flesh. It took the personal moral control of a man's spirit to ensure life and peace. It worried me that Bode appeared to lack that moral control.

I slowed Tornado to an easy walk more conducive to mulling things over in my mind. Given Bode McCully's actions, I couldn't help but think on the task Hughes had assigned to me to bring a vigilante to justice. Could Bode be the man? He had a Winchester rifle. I shook the very thought of it from my mind. This was the grandfather Cassie so admired. Bode had been a Texas Ranger. He knew the law. That McCully had once been tried and acquitted for murder didn't enter into my thinking. Many Texas Rangers endured accusations consequent to over-exuberantly delivering justice, and some found themselves brought before the courts. But killing, often in self-defense, was often part of their job. Danger and death were consequences of their frontier duties. Bode McCully couldn't be a vigilante...the vigilante.

★ ★

I pulled Tornado to a halt and looked up at the gateway arch to Heaven's Gate Ranch. I thought back to when I was knee high to a grasshopper, and my dad had erected the structure. It stood as a welcome but also as a warning, as more than one desperado with evil intent had met their end passing through. My mind still swirled with unanswered questions. I'd look to Cassie to bring much-needed relief. I sighed, looked up at the noonday sun, and looked up the trail at warped images dancing in the waves of heat rising from the landscape. The big Appaloosa lurched on through the archway.

As I approached the newly constructed stable, I was surprised to see the door hanging wide open. I quietly slipped from my saddle and dropped my reins. Tornado froze, sensing something was afoot and uttering nary a snort. Out of caution, I placed my hand on the butt of my revolver and slowly stepped toward the door. As fate would have it, my spur struck a stone.

The next thing I knew, I was looking down the barrel of a rifle.

Before I could react, the weapon dropped to the ground and Cassie's arms were wrapped around my neck. "Oh, Lucas, Lucas. I was hoping that was you." She pulled back. "Praise the Lord, you're home."

I pulled her back in and held her tightly. After a few minutes, I felt a wet nose nudge my backside. The danged horse had a sense of humor. As if to add to the welcome, Ranger came out with ears flopping and tail wagging.

"I was doing a little housekeeping, sweetheart. Hoping you'd be home soon."

My gaze now fully took her in. She was very much pregnant and gave off a glow that seemed to make her more beautiful than ever. Cassie had let her hair grow longer, and it beckoned to be caressed.

"See to Tornado, Mr. Ranger." She nodded toward the house and winked provocatively as her words flowed seductively. She didn't want a man's thoughts of his horse interrupting anticipated pleasure.

My eyes followed her move toward the house. I grabbed the Appaloosa's reins and led him into his stall, where I made short work of unsaddling the big stallion. The cayuse seemed to have a sense that my mind wasn't into the task at hand, as he endured a quicker and rougher than usual currying. Soon enough, this rancher-turned-Ranger was shuffling off to the ranch house, unfastening my gun belt along the way.

I stopped next to the water trough and liberally splashed water over myself as best I could. It served to turn trail dust to mud.

Cassie's head popped from the doorway. "Lucas…come on. You're plenty clean enough!" She called out impatiently.

"Enjoyed the adventure, Buffalo, old friend." Bode McCully decided to head back to Alice rather than join the old buffalo hunter in Corpus Christi. He reckoned there just might be some interesting goings on connected with the railroad. No telling what he might find out with his ear to the metaphorical rail.

Watts offered up an imperturbable look that left Bode wondering what was cooking in the old fellow's mind. It was the sort of gaze that a hunter might likely wear when stalking prey. He finally caught McCully's eyes in his own. "Twas some fine shootin' the other day, Bode. You ain't lost yer touch." He smiled ever-so-slightly. "Shame yuh only winged him the first time." It was a not-so-veiled dig.

Bode grinned sheepishly. "The sonofabitch was moving right quick." It was a lame excuse, and he knew it. He broke the pregnant pause with a shrug. "Didn't see you shooting at him."

"Figured that was Junior's job. Expect yuh just might have stirred up a rattler's nest of what them fellers in Austin call diplomatic relations. I sure-as-shootin' don't envy what Captain Hughes will deal with at the border."

Bode had enough. He struggled to be respectful. "Ride safe to Corpus, old friend." In a few hours, Watts would likely have over-celebrated and be passed out drunk at the Longhorn Saloon like his friend Eagle Eye.

"So, my grandfather helped?"

I nodded reluctantly as I was winding up my story of taking on the Diaz gang. "He wasn't supposed to be involved, Cassie. He wasn't a deputized lawman." I hesitated. "He acted more like a vigilante."

Cassie huffed just a bit. "You're not comparing my grandfather with the murderer that's ambushing folks around her lately, are you?"

I wanted to say that it was a possibility but didn't dare. "Er, of course not, sweetheart." I tried ever-so-vainly to not be patronizing. Everyone that could fire a weapon was a suspect, including beloved grandfathers. Yes, I'd narrowed down any list of suspects to folks who owned 1895 Winchesters, might be reasonably accurate marksmen, and were familiar with the terrain of the region. "Captain Hughes ordered me to take a couple of days to spend with you before getting back to hunting for the vigilante." I gave her a look that said the topic was off-limits for the next few days.

Cassie shook her head playfully and rubbed her ever-growing belly. "We still have some catching up to do, Mr. Texas Ranger." Her infectious laugh forced him to grin, then blush.

I hoped and prayed that her grandfather wasn't the vigilante. Yes, he had an 1895 Winchester rifle, yes, he'd been near the scene of a recent vigilante ambush, yes, he was a damned good shot, and yes, he seemed to have an outsized sense of frustration with the slow pace of the justice bureaucracy and its cost. I shook the thoughts from my head like a nest of spider webs they were and turned to Cassie. "Let's do some of that catching up."

Bode eased back in his chair, surveilling the guests at Taberna Bandana. Thanks in part to the railroad, Alice was growing by leaps and bounds. Importantly, the telegraph and railroads meant news traveled faster and was arguably more accurate. Reliance on rumors passed along by itinerant cowboys was less an issue, though those sources were often colorful and certainly opinionated. Accuracy did tend to suffer.

A couple of beers later, he strolled from the saloon, took the reins of his horse, and began walking up the street toward the post office. He soon found himself waiting with other bystanders at the railroad crossing. "Long one this morning," he said to no one in particular.

The man beside him nodded. "Seem longer every day." His bearded face stared out from under an especially broad-brimmed Stetson, sported a red flannel shirt despite the heat, wore wool chaps over his jeans, and had an impressive roan stallion in tow. He glanced over at McCully. "You from these parts, old timer?"

McCully's curiosity was piqued, though he didn't exactly take kindly to being referred to as an old timer. The man gave off an aura of hardness that rivaled the steel rails carrying the long train still chugging past car by car. "Pretty much, mister. Name's McCully, Bode McCully."

"They call me Big George. Worked the JA Ranch up north.

Danged barbed wire been messing with my work, so figured to try my hand down these parts."

Bode was familiar with the JA Ranch. It was a large spread way up near Palo Duro Canyon in the Texas Panhandle. The JA was a great outfit that likely paid well. It left him to wonder whether Big George might be fleeing from something. "Yep. Barbed wire sure changed everything. Got it around these parts, too. Instead of trail drives, beeves are shipped by train." Just then, a string of cattle cars rolled by as if to emphasize Bode's point.

The caboose soon squealed by, and folks began getting on with their business.

"Good luck, George." Bode tipped his hat to the cowboy and went on his way. Soon he was performing his ritual of checking the wanted posters displayed at the post office. Some old lawman habits didn't retire. He paused, as one in partic- ular caught his eye. The sketch showed a clean-shaven man hailing from north Texas and wanted for rustling cattle. Bode reckoned the image resembled the cowboy he'd just met. He studied the poster more closely. The wanted man's name was William Riordan and went by the nickname Big Bill. Bode smiled with growing satisfaction. Big George could just as easily be Big Bill. Stealing cattle was still a hanging offense. If Big George was the man, Bode reckoned his luck was about to run out.

Bode still needed to confirm that this Big George fellow was Riordan. From the description, he'd best be right careful. The man was reputed to have a violent temper. The retired Ranger figured he must have caught the man in a good mood that morning at the railroad crossing. Seemed time to visit Sheriff Tyler.

The jail was nestled between the general store and livery just a short walk from the post office. As Bode strode up the street, he observed the man who called himself Big George enter the Taberna Bandana. It was getting to be another scorcher of a day so could hardly blame the man for imbibing a cold drink. It still went against Bode's grain that the man wore those heavy chaps in town. He almost tripped as he stole a closer look at how those chaps covered the business ends of a pair of holstered Colt revolvers. The man was becoming ever more suspicious to Bode, as he built a case in his mind.

"Morning, Brad." Bode looked ahead to barely avoid running into the sheriff. He stepped aside and placed his fingers aside his hat brim.

"I apologize for the rush, Mr. McCully. You lookin' for me?"

"Matter of fact, I am. You have just a tick of a minute?"

Sheriff Tyler paused. "I'm supposed to be at the court-house. Walk with me."

"A fella just showed up in town. I met him at the railroad crossing. Claims to be from the JA up north. Said he was looking for new work. Called himself Big George. He was friendly enough but a bit over-dressed and right heavily armed." Bode struggled to keep pace with the sheriff.

"You haven't told me anything especially unusual, Mr. McCully."

"Well, I happened by the post office."

The sheriff rolled his eyes. He was familiar with the old Ranger's habit of checking wanted posters.

Bode ignored the sheriff's reaction. "There's a poster on a man named William Riordan. Goes by the nickname Big Bill. He's wanted for rustling cattle up in north Texas. Dang it, Brad, but this Big George fella fits the physical description and just left that part of Texas."

"What do you want me to do, Mr. McCully?" He was growing a tad impatient as they approached the courthouse.

"The man's enjoying some libation at Taberna Bandana as we speak. You just might find out whether he's Riordan. If so, you can..."

"Arrest him," interrupted Tyler. "The judge isn't a patient

man, Mr. McCully. I'm already a couple of minutes late. How about you keeping an eye on Big George. When I'm done with the court, I'll come over to the saloon. If your man is still around, I'll have a chat with him."

Bode released a sigh hinting at frustration. The pace of the law could be so frustrating at times. "I'll keep an eye on him, Sheriff."

Eagle Eye Smith half staggered up the steps and through the swinging doors of Taberna Bandana. Likely as not, he needed another drink about as much as another hole in his head.

McCully shook his head dismayingly as he strode up the street. Perhaps, sitting with the half-breed Kiowa would offer a reasonable excuse to keep an eye on Big George. He followed Eagle Eye to a table just inside the entrance. It seemed especially warm inside the saloon, as he swept the room with practiced eyes before taking a seat. Big George sat in a dark corner toward the rear exit. "Mind if I join you, Eagle Eye?"

Smith belched and nodded toward the rickety old chair beside the table.

Bode positioned the chair so as to face Riordan. He raised his hand to the barkeep with two fingers extended. The two were soon enjoying cold beer.

"What's that damned savage doin' in here?" A growl emanated from the back of the saloon. Big George was leaning forward with an ugly expression spread across his face.

"Big George...is that you?" Bode hoped the cowboy would remember him from the railroad crossing.

Three empty mugs already littered the table in front of Big George's ever-more-threatening body language. He belched.

Bode couldn't help but notice that Big George or William Riordan or whomever he was, wasn't sweating. The man was dry as a horny toad's back. "This is my friend Eagle Eye Smith," he ventured friendly-like. "He's no savage, Big George."

"Git yer friend's Injun ass outta here," snarled Big George. He belched again.

Eagle Eye slowly turned to look at the cowboy and laughed.

That the half-breed had the temerity to laugh only served to stoke the cowboy's anger. He stood with his right hand hovering over the grip of one of his revolvers.

Eagle Eye glanced at Bode then back at the cowboy. "Me scalp today?" He burped loudly and laughed again.

Bode was desperate to defuse the situation. "My friend here has had too much to drink, Big George. How about if I ease him on out of here, and you can enjoy your refreshment in peace." He wanted to add that the cowboy could keep his scalp, but more levity was not an option.

As Bode helped Eagle Eye out through the saloon door, he saw Sheriff Tyler approaching. "Yer in the nick of time, Brad. That cowboy fella is drunk and was ready to shoot Eagle Eye here just for being a breed."

Tyler nodded. "Guess I better enter a tad careful-like." He walked past Bode and strode through the door, his right hand already filled with his shooting iron. His eyes quickly adjusted to the dim light. "Is there some sort of problem here?" he announced.

"The problem just got drug out," snickered the cowboy.

"I'm Sheriff Brad Tyler, and I try to keep things peaceful around here." Tyler had studied the wanted poster at the post office before heading to the Taberna Bandana. "Are you the man they call Big Bill?"

The explosion from Riordan's six-shooter was not unexpected. A bullet sent splinters from the doorjamb beside the sheriff's head. Tyler returned fire but realized once the gunsmoke settled a bit that he was shooting at thin air. Riordan had escaped through the back door and had apparently mounted up and departed in a cloud of prairie dust.

The sheriff emerged from the saloon. "Looks as though you were right, Mr. McCully."

"You gonna chase him?" Bode asked, raising his voice over an especially loud belch from Eagle Eye.

"I'll see if I can muster a posse." Tyler wasn't sounding so confident. "Riordan is heavily armed, and I don't want to be riding into any ambush."

With the combination of booze and gunplay, Eagle Eye's head was pounding. He'd had enough and staggered past Bode and out of the saloon. He took a couple of steps, fell forward on his face, got up, and stumbled into the alley. Given the immediate aftermath from the gunfire and Riordan's escape, the half-breed's exit went virtually unnoticed by Bode and the sheriff. It was typical of Eagle Eye's behavior.

Bode was chagrinned. Another frustrating situation loomed. Raising a posse these days was a tall order. Not so many folks cared to place themselves at risk. It was also a time-consuming task, and every minute that passed put distance between a fugitive and the law. "Good luck, Sheriff." Given his retired status, Bode had already resigned himself to not being selected for a posse. The perception that he was older, slower, and likely not so good a marksman dogged him. He watched in frustration as the sheriff headed toward the jail.

As he pivoted to leave the saloon, a groaning sound from the alley caught Bode's attention. He grabbed his horse's reins and led him into the alley beside Taberna Bandana. "Oh my god," he blurted as he dropped the reins and rushed to Eagle Eye's side. Smith's throat had been slit from ear to ear.

The gurgling final breaths of his friend were too much even for a hardened lawman. There was no question in Bode's mind as to whom had murdered Eagle Eye. Maybe Riordan didn't have so great a head start after all.

As yet clueless as to the violence in the alley, Sheriff Tyler had stopped at the post office and sent a telegram to Captain Hughes requesting assistance in the pursuit of Riordan. He rightly reckoned that this would be within the jurisdiction of the Texas Rangers, since Riordan was a fugitive of the state.

The sheriff took a long, almost wistful look at the poster for Big Bill Riordan. He felt fortunate to be living at a time when the Texas Rangers had become a serious force in law enforcement. He thought back to moments ago, when the fugitive's bullet had narrowly missed his head. Like many sheriffs and marshals of the western frontier and even back east, there was a premium on self-preservation. Sheriff Tyler firmly believed in living. If the risk of pursuing a desperado could be shifted to the Texas Rangers, so much the better toward a life of simply enforcing local ordinances. Far safer to serve an eviction notice then take on a William Riordan in a gun battle...or worse, be bushwhacked.

He was about to leave, when the postmaster hailed him. "Say, Sheriff!" He waved a telegram at Tyler.

Incredulous at the unusually quick response, the sheriff nearly tripped over his own feet in retrieving the message. "Thanks, Bert." He began to read.

Sheriff Tyler:
Busy in Corpus. Will send Ranger Dunn at earliest opportunity.
John Hughes, Captain, Texas Rangers.

Tyler hung his head just a tad despairingly. One Ranger? And a wet-behind-the-ears new one at that. No matter Dunn's lineage. He found himself wishing the vigilante would show up and solve the problem. He shook it off. He shouldn't be thinking that way. The job of a sheriff often seemed akin to a spider sitting on its web awaiting its next prey—not knowing what manner of victim it might ensnare. There was surely no end to the treachery, deceit, and violence folks tended to inflict upon one another.

He looked up to see Bode walking straight toward him at a decidedly brisk pace. "Sheriff!"

"No need to shout, Mr. McCully."

"The sonofabitch killed Eagle Eye!" Bode motioned the sheriff to follow him back to the saloon. "Slit his throat!"

Sheriff Tyler paused as they turned into the alley. "Damn!"

Eagle Eye lay lifeless in a pool of his own blood. No one would be insulting his half-Kiowa heritage any longer. The craggy lines around his aged eyes and mouth were already smoothed out with the facial relaxation accompanying death. Eagle Eye had finally found peace in the violence of his death. Bode glanced at the sheriff. "Had to be that Riordan fella. Seems he didn't high tail it like we thought."

By now, a half dozen onlookers had gathered. Eagle Eye was often a public annoyance, but nobody wished him dead for his harmless drunken revels.

The sheriff stood over the breed with hands on hips. He made a cursory scan of the surroundings. "Well, from the hoof-prints, he's long gone now," Tyler sighed exasperatedly. "I'll have Bixby bring a box from behind the livery. Our old friend deserves a decent burial." He motioned for one of the local boys to fetch Bixby and a pine coffin.

Bode grew a little impatient but tried to contain it as best he could. "You raising a posse, Sheriff?"

"Captain Hughes is sending a Ranger."

Bode had been resigned to such an outcome. He never did see Sheriff Tyler having the spine to risk his hide chasing an armed and dangerous fugitive. Plus, he had a pretty fair idea whom the Texas Ranger Captain would send.

The retired Ranger's disappointment wasn't lost on Sheriff Tyler, but that wasn't enough for him to ride off into a bushwhacking. "I have a big county to take care of, Mr. McCully." Indeed, Nueces County likely needed to be divided into more manageable jurisdictions. "I haven't been back in Corpus for nearly a week, and work demanding my attention is surely stacked up." It was a lame excuse at best.

EIGHT
BIG BILL'S ITCH

BIG BILL RIORDAN had headed off to the east at a hard gallop. With any luck, he'd find his way to Corpus Christi and thence south to Mexico. His mind was still filled with the lust of the kill. The drunken half-breed hadn't been sober enough to put up a fight. He wondered whether it even counted as a murder. Many folks around Texas still didn't consider killing an Indian as murder, but this one was half White. Was it a half-murder? He managed a smile at his own philosophizing, as he slowed his cayuse to a walk. No sense burning the beast out.

He kept an eye out for a homestead where he'd be able to shed his rather distinctive red flannel shirt and wool chaps. His horse was a problem, too. Folks often identified a horse before recognizing the human in its saddle.

About five miles east of Alice, a likely target came into view. A one-room cabin with a sod roof and smoke wafting from a makeshift chimney presented itself as likely prey. From a distance, he made out a woman and small child doing some sort of chores in the clearing in front of the cabin. A couple of horses pranced around in a small corral behind the structure. No adult male was to be seen.

Riordan rode toward the cabin easy-like.

Upon the first sound of Riordan's horse brushing a mesquite branch, the woman was alerted. She hustled the child into the cabin, picked up a shotgun, and turned to face whatever threat was approaching. "Who goes?" she called out.

"Easy, ma'am. Just a traveler looking fer a drink of water and maybe barter a bit."

"Stop where you are. Come another step, and so help me, I'll pull this trigger."

Riordan raised his hands to just above shoulder level. "I come in peace, ma'am. Is your man around?"

"My husband be comin' in shortly fer lunch." By now, she'd made out that the interloper was heavily armed. "Very shortly."

The fugitive would have to act swiftly. "Ma'am, I'd like to make this painless. I wish no ill will to you or your child. I need a fresh shirt and look to trade this fine stallion for one of yer horses over yonder."

"Keep away. Ride on!"

Riordan nudged his horse a couple of steps toward the woman.

Both barrels fired. Buckshot whizzed past Riordan's head. The blast would surely alert whatever man she'd been expecting. The woman fumbled to reload.

Big Bill was out of his saddle and beside her in an instant, cracking her skull with the butt of one of his pistols. As she crumpled to the dust, he dismounted and knocked the child over in his dash into the cabin. It took but a second to find a suitable shirt, grab a couple of biscuits from the table, and head for the corral. His cowboy skills came into play as he speedily unsaddled his horse. Luckily, the horse he chose had been broken, so he was able to saddle up right quickly. He spurred the buckskin to a near gallop through the corral gate and disappeared down the trail along the Nueces River. It was none too soon, as the woman's husband arrived, and from what Riordan could hear, was angrier than a stirred-up nest of rattlesnakes. His wife had apparently awakened long enough to point him in the direction Big Bill was riding.

Riordan had a choice. He could turn and ambush his pursuer or keep on riding. The horse under him seemed strong enough. He fought off his natural inclination to rid himself of the pesky husband. He had a long lead. There were plenty of places to hide if necessary.

As he rightly reckoned, the pursuit didn't last long. The angered husband likely figured he'd made a decent show of defending against his wife's attacker, and there was no point in taking undue risk.

Too often, telegrams failed to bring good news. Captain Hughes's name on this one didn't exactly bode well to my mind, as I luxuriated in the second day of my vacation with Cassie. She'd sure shown me how she could make up for lost time in the bedroom. I even had to admit to myself that I was getting plum-tuckered out.

I stood in the ranch house doorway and began to open the envelope just as Cassie emerged from the bedroom wearing just enough to be semi-modestly clothed. The sound of the courier had awakened us both, though I was quick to throw on a shirt, jump into trousers, and pull on my boots so as to be sufficiently dressed to receive the telegram. Cassie placed her hand on my shoulder and rubbed her leg provocatively against mine. "Cassie, give me a chance to open this thing."

"We don't want to know," she pouted.

I read the message. "Dang. Been a murder in Alice. My old friend Eagle Eye Smith was murdered by a fellow named William Riordan. The captain wants me to bring Riordan in."

Cassie sighed. Another dangerous mission loomed. Would they ever have a peaceful life ranching and growing a family?

I gazed into her eyes. "This Riordan fellow is on the run.

Might be headed toward Corpus Christi." My voice trailed off as her eyes melted my resolve. "No point in rushing the hunt. I'll head out day after tomorrow," I finally offered up, as my gaze followed each of her steps toward the bedroom.

Cassie turned, puckered her lips, struck a fetching pose, and beckoned me with a come-hither look that might have melted forged iron.

Bode McCully rapped on the post in front of my house. He waited. And waited. He finally dismounted and took a seat on the gallery.

"Dang, Grandpa, what are you doing here this early?" Cassie, barefoot and still dressed in her nightgown, offered him a cup of coffee. "Lucas will be out shortly." That was code for me still pulling myself together after an especially amorous night.

Bode pointed to the sun already risen high above the horizon. "Ain't exactly break of dawn, Cassie darlin'."

She blushed and ducked back into the kitchen.

Aromas of eggs and biscuits and the sizzling sounds of bacon quickly dispelled any lingering annoyance on Bode's part at having had to wait for the Dunn household to awaken.

"Come on in, Bode." I urged the retired Ranger to join them.

We were soon seated around a rather ample oak table, more suitable to seating the sort of large family that we hoped to raise. It had been a hand-me-down from my folks. The notches and squirrelly gigs carved into it held mostly wonderful memories stored within its bulk.

"What brings you out this way today, Grandpa?" Cassie broke the ice.

"You heard from Captain Hughes, Junior?" It was more a rhetorical question.

"Grandpa, I'm over here." Cassie felt just a tad put off that Bode had directed his answer to me rather than her.

"Sorry, darlin', I had lawman's business on my mind."

Cassie found it difficult to knit her brows at her beloved grandfather, but did offer a rejoinder. "If it's about Junior chasing any fugitives, do understand that it affects me, too. If something bad were to happen...well...you understand."

I took a long sip of coffee as if to avoid the little tiff between Cassie and her grandfather.

Bode was nevertheless persistent and asked, "So, are you going after him, Junior?"

I took another long sip of coffee.

"Er, breakfast is right delicious, Cassie." Bode tried desperately to make amends with Cassie over the perceived slight.

I poured another cup of coffee and topped off Cassie's and Bode's. Finally, I eased back, swallowed a final forkful of eggs, and turned to Cassie. "What did I say about this assignment last night, sweetheart?"

She kept her eyes on me, as she directed her words to Bode, "Grandpa, Junior heard from Captain Hughes and plans to begin tracking Mr. Riordan tomorrow morning."

Bode strove to suppress the redness welling up from his neck. It wouldn't do to be overly frustrated with his ever-loving granddaughter or her—to his thinking—mostly capable husband. Swirling through his mind was his ongoing frustration with the slow pace of law enforcement and feeling that the young lawmen of these days weren't so committed to justice as they were back in the day...his day.

It was hard for me to miss the sense of frustration that exuded from Bode as the retired Ranger squirmed in his seat. "He's not going to be hard to track, Bode."

"You know he's headed to Mexico."

I didn't especially appreciate the patronizing comment and tried not to show it. I stood and wiped my mouth with one of the new napkins Cassie had purchased during a recent trip to

Corpus Christi. "He's not going to get that far, Mr. McCully." I refolded the napkin, stood behind Cassie, and gave her a gentle hug. "And don't you be following me."

Bode's facial expression lingered between frustration and annoyance. "I'm sure you're up to it, Ranger Dunn." He arose and turned to Cassie. "Thanks kindly for the delicious breakfast, darlin' granddaughter." He grabbed his hat. "Good to see y'all. Guess I'll be headin' to Corpus. Sheriff Tyler mentioned he had business to tend to there."

I walked Bode to his horse. "Good to see you, Bode. By the way, I didn't tell Cassie about you and Buffalo helping with the Diaz business. Didn't figure to worry her overmuch. Reckon we ought to keep it that way."

Bode smiled. I apparently seemed just a tad wiser than he'd given me credit for. "I'm sure you'll catch Riordan, Junior." He swung into the saddle with a grunt. He rubbed his belly. "Careful that wife of yours doesn't turn you into a chub. She sure can cook up a meal." Off he rode.

Riordan stuck to the trail along the south side of the Nueces River and thence along the shores of Nueces Bay. There was no point in raising any more attention than he already had squabbling with the homesteaders. At least, he hadn't added another killing to his credit. As it was, he was walking a fine line between life at the prison in Huntsville or the hangman's noose. He reckoned to yet stock up with enough supplies to last for the ride to the comparative safety of Matamoros.

He'd used the old trick of doubling back a few times, and it was clear that no one was pursuing him just yet. That made him a bit uneasy. He figured that there'd be a pretty fair price on his head by now, so he'd best be cautious. Obtaining supplies was the first order of business, and he figured that there should be some sort of general store on the outskirts of

Corpus that would be ripe for robbing. He might even find some money to add to his stash from selling rustled cattle.

As he rounded a bend in the trail, he found himself face-to-face with a pair of travelers sporting an arsenal that didn't exactly inspire confidence in peaceful intentions. He pulled his horse aside to allow them to pass.

Rather than skirt around him, the two riders split so as to pass on either side.

Riordan had plenty of experience in recognizing potential trouble. "Howdy," he offered and touched his fingers friendly like to the brim of his hat. He wasn't what the dime-store novels would have called a fast-draw gunman, but Riordan was no slouch. At the sound of gun metal scraping leather, one of Big Bill's Colts found its way into his hand and fired a slug through the midsection of the man to his left. The second man's horse reared at the explosion and sent its rider tumbling off backward into the dust.

"Meant no harm. Please! Don't shoot!" The second traveler breathlessly pleaded with Riordan.

The fugitive sat in his saddle with the smoking Colt pointed at the fallen man's chest. He glanced at the man he'd shot as the poor soul writhed in agonizing pain. A gut shot was often as painful as it was deadly. He waved the barrel of his revolver at the second man. "Drop your gun belt."

The traveler readily and cautiously complied.

Riordan realized the man posed no further threat. Without his gun, he was about as cowardly as they come. "Tend to your friend." He motioned with a wave of his gun. "I'm headed up the trail. If y'all try to follow me, I'll kill you both and leave you to the buzzards." With that, the fugitive nudged his mount to as easy a loping stride as it could muster and headed up the trail. The encounter had been a bit too close for comfort. Worse yet, he'd begun to realize that the buckskin was no colt and might not be fully up to the long ride to Matamoros.

★★

It was almost a relief—physically, at least—for me to saddle up Tornado and be heading out to pick up Riordan's trail. Cassie had plumb worn me out as she insisted on making up for lost marital time of the carnal variety. Of course, there had also been myriad chores to tend to around the ranch, from exercising horses to mending fences. I felt blessed to have a couple of capable vaqueros to tend the several hundred head grazing the range. Housed in modest cabins with their wives on some property I had carved from the ranch, they also offered a modicum of security when I was away.

As I pondered where William Riordan might be heading, I hearkened back to my days tracking game with my dad, Buffalo Watts, and occasionally Eagle Eye Smith. I'd miss the ever-colorful Eagle Eye. These men had taught me hunting skills I'd not soon forget. Likely, the best advice had come from a Comanche chief called One Arrow who had been friends with my dad and intent on trying to learn the ways of the White man. One Arrow told the story of how the hunter must never become the prey, as his own chief Three Toes had been tracking my father and found himself captured by my wily and now legendary Texas Ranger father. The confrontation had turned into a mutual respect and then an enduring friendship. One Arrow's advice was to embed yourself into the mind of your prey. What might be driving the animal—or human—to run? How desperate might the prey be? Most importantly, One Arrow advised that the prey would eventually and invariably make a fatal mistake. I thought on this. What might Riordan's fatal mistake be?

I decided to track along the southern shores of the Nueces River. It seemed the most logical route for a man on the run who was unfamiliar with the territory. I reckoned that the Riordan would need supplies before heading to Mexico, and there'd be homesteads between Nuecestown and Corpus that would be vulnerable to the outlaw's predations. Once adequately supplied, Riordan would surely make a beeline for the Rio Grande.

I hadn't been riding but a couple of hours when I happened upon the homestead Riordan had attacked. As I approached the cabin, I heard the clicking of a shotgun hammer being pulled back.

"Who goes?" a deep voice called out.

"Texas Ranger Lucas Dunn." I spoke firmly with the sort of confidence a badge bestows. "Drop your weapons. I'm coming in." I heard the cocked hammer being released and found myself breathing a sigh of relief. The humble homestead reminded me of tales my folks shared about eking out a living on the frontier. While Nueces County was hardly frontier these days, there were still homesteads to be had and lands to be cleared and cultivated for farming and ranching. The pecan trees framing the cabin lent an air of quaintness to the scene before me, yet I quickly sensed that there had been trouble.

"Come on in, Mr. Ranger."

I rode slowly into the clearing in front of the cabin with hands raised to shoulder level. "What happened to get you folks so riled up?"

A woman with a bloodied bandage around her head stepped from the house.

The man set the shotgun by the door. "Name's McCormick. This here's my wife. Big fella pistol-whipped her yesterday. He took one of my shirts, swapped horses, and lit out toward Corpus."

I shook my head. "Sorry for the trouble. Is your wife okay?"

"Nasty knot and cut on the back of her head, but she don't want no doc." McCormick more than likely couldn't afford any doctoring, and his wife was forced to tough it out.

"What color shirt did he take?" I wasn't going to argue with the man about caring for his wife.

"Took a blue shirt. Left us his red flannel abomination." McCormick paused in thought. "Oh, and the horse he took is a buckskin." He nearly smiled. "Actually, I think we got the better of that trade. That buckskin ain't gettin' any younger."

"The man that attacked y'all is William Riordan. He's wanted for rustling and murder, so y'all were lucky to get away with your lives. I've been assigned to bring him to justice." I didn't want to appear too anxious to move along, but I was excited by having confirmed picking up Riordan's trail and change of horse and clothing. "You folks going to be all right?"

"We'll feel better when you bring this Riordan fella to justice, Ranger Dunn." The man paused. "Say...are you kin to..."

I sighed. "I'm his son." I tucked my chin to my chest to hide an ever-so-slight blush and turned Tornado. "I'd better get along." Tipping my hat, I headed eastward. Riordan was obviously heading toward Corpus. It was reassuring to know that my prey was behaving as expected.

"Any horseflesh for sale or trade?" Riordan had stopped at the livery on the outskirts of Corpus Christi. The stable and corral were ramshackle affairs at best and had seen better days. Big Bill reckoned this wouldn't be the only livery in town, but he wasn't anxious to get hung up in Corpus proper, and this was convenient.

The stableboy took a brief gander at the buckskin and shook his head apologetically. "Can't say as yer cayuse is worth swapping, mister."

Riordan made his own scan of the corral and had to admit to himself that none of the stock looked to be an improvement over his current mount. There seemed no point in pressing the issue. "Can you recommend anyplace 'tween here and Brownsville?"

The stableboy thought a moment. "There be a couple of ranches 'long where yer headed. Might try yer luck with one of 'em."

The outlaw sighed. "Thanks kindly." He turned the buckskin to the city proper. It occurred to him that a pause for a drink seemed a decent idea about now. It would be a long, lonely ride along the coast.

Bode was miffed, to say the least, by the all-too-casual attitude of law enforcement toward Riordan. Even his grandson-in-law seemed to be letting him down. As he finished purchasing supplies for a couple of days camping on the trail, he decided to stop by the Corpus Christi post office. There for all the world to see and mounted dead center on the wall was a brand spanking new poster announcing a $2,000 reward for William "Big Bill" Riordan—dead or alive. *That'd be nice money,* he thought.

His long experience hunting fugitives told him that Riordan was likely to skirt Corpus itself. The city would be a bit too hot for the fugitive's liking. Consequently, he decided to grab a quick drink at the Longhorn Saloon before attempting to pick up the outlaw's trail. Finding the trail itself was going to be a huge challenge, given the vast, unbroken terrain of the Nueces Strip between Corpus Christi and Brownsville. The sandy loam soil made tracking next to impossible, even assuming that there would be anything distinguishable from Riordan's horse. Maybe a bit of whiskey at the Longhorn would bring him luck.

Bode stepped through the café doors at the saloon entrance with a certain flair typical of one long experienced with drinking establishments like the Longhorn. He wasn't the least surprised that it had gradually gone to seed as cattle drives waned and saloons became better known for drinking, gambling, and entertainment of a less civilized crowd. In the case of the Longhorn, the rooms upstairs still served certain clientele seeking to drown their gambling losses in a bit of debauchery with aging but enthusiastic soiled doves. Bode nodded to the barkeep. "Nice to see you, Clyde."

"You heading out, Mr. McCully?" The Longhorn barkeep always held the now-retired Texas Ranger in admiring respect. When in Corpus Christi, Bode tended to stop in for a libation before heading out on his travels. As if be habit or reflex, Clyde checked to be sure the double-barreled shotgun was handy. Any time a Texas Ranger entered a saloon, whether active or retired, there was the possibility of actions that just might get out of hand. Clyde poured a shot of whiskey and set it on the bar.

Bode quaffed the whiskey and set the glass down. He waved off a refill. "Have some hunting to do, Clyde." He made a cursory scan of the area around the bar but saw nothing amiss.

"Deer? Lion?" The barkeep was naturally curious.

Bode shrugged. "Maybe." He didn't figure to give even a hint of his true intentions. He was intent on being far more efficient and effective than the sheriff or Texas Rangers or bounty hunters could ever dream of being.

"Well, good luck, Mr. McCully."

Bode initially failed to see the figure lurking in the shadows at the rear of the room. With the change in wardrobe and clean-shaven face, it was little wonder he'd find it difficult to recognize his prey. Bode finally paused and made a more complete scan of the saloon guests. Again, nothing suspicious caught his eye. There was no red flannel shirt to be seen in any case. He wordlessly dropped a coin on the bar, pivoted, and headed out the door. Once outside, he suddenly realized that he had actually seen Riordan. The outlaw had been concealed from view in the dark shadows at the rear of the saloon. He thought to head back inside but decided not to press his luck. He'd not be likely to win any sort of shootout.

Bode mounted up. He gently patted the butt of the 1895 Winchester nestled in its scabbard hanging from his saddle horn. He failed to notice the horseman that emerged from behind the Longhorn and headed southward. The hunt was on, and the prey was getting a head start. But not for long.

William Riordan smiled. He had recognized Bode from back in Alice. It was sort of ironic to have run into the half-breed's friend. He chuckled to himself, as he figured the old man to be harmless, and likely lacking the courage to respond to the outlaw's murder of his Injun' companion. It was time to get himself to Matamoros. It would be a long ride, but he felt little concern. No one seemed to be tracking him, even after murdering the half-breed, robbing the homesteaders, and killing the traveler on the Nueces River trail. Having stocked up with just enough jerky and coffee to tide him over until Matamoros, he found himself becoming right confident of his seeming ability to avoid confrontation with the law.

Big Bill eased his horse through the back alleys of Corpus. There was no point in arousing unwanted attention. So it was that he didn't duck quite far enough under a clothesline from which various female unmentionables hung. He found himself tangled. It was decidedly embarrassing. With a sweeping motion of his arm that brought half the laundry into the dust of the alley, he finally extricated himself.

"Hey, cowboy! What the hell do you think you're doin'?"

Riordan looked up to see a half-naked young woman—at least, he figured she was young—hanging from the second-story window. She was none too happy.

"Pick up my laundry, you careless sonofabitch!"

Young but foul-mouthed so far as Riordan could figure. He found himself nonplussed, nevertheless. "Er…my apologies, ma'am." His first inclination had been to ignore her and ride on, but he found himself slipping from his saddle and gathering the now dirty laundry into a bundle. He stood helplessly as the offended woman emerged from the back door and swept the bundle from his arms.

"You clumsy oaf! I've got to wash my clothes again because…" She stopped as she finally took in the man standing before her. He was big. It was as though someone had flipped a switch inside her brain. "I'm Dolly, cowboy. What's your name?"

A broad grin traced across Riordan's face. He reckoned he had plenty of time to hit the trail to Matamoros. "Big Bill."

"How big are you, Big Bill?" She cast a fetching come-hither smile and leaned toward him to reveal most of her ample chest.

Riordan's grin turned to a laugh. "Big enough."

Dolly beckoned Riordan to come inside. "Come on in, Big Bill. I'll wash these later." She threw the bundle aside while simultaneously leading him into a room furnished with the requisite bed. The walls were a bit seamy, but the bed was adequately plush.

As Riordan stepped through the threshold and unbuckled his gun belt, Dolly pulled him to her. Her hand caressed the arousing manhood beneath his jeans. She nearly tore the shirt from him, drew his pants to his knees, and put herself on top of him on the bed. Dolly's clothes went helter-skelter among a tangle of arms and legs as she expertly had her way with him.

For Riordan, it seemed to be over before it had begun. It hadn't struck him as to how long it had been since he'd had a woman.

"Well, Mr. Big Bill, I must say you didn't disappoint." Her broad, self-satisfied smile pretty much lit up the room. "Damn, but this one is on the house." Dolly was luxuriating in the afterglow of their wild romp between the sheets. "You stayin' long in Corpus?"

Riordan stood and pulled up his pants. "Headin' south beginning this very second, Dolly."

She let out a deep sigh. "You sure you wouldn't like to help with my washin'?" It was a back-handed invitation but a stupidly phrased question.

Big Bill laughed it off. "Got to be on the road, darlin'."

Dolly's eyes looked Riordan up and down, coming to rest upon the gun belt he was buckling with the twin holsters. She began to put the pieces of the man together. Riding through the alley, heading south, and heavily armed. He was on a mission...or escaping one. She felt a chill course up her spine. Fear? Of a sudden, she felt lucky to be alive. She watched him mount up and continue his ride up the alley. On the other hand, he'd been a damned good lay. Besides, she hadn't checked with the doc lately and just might have given him something to remember her by.

Riordan sported a self-satisfied smile as he worked his way free of the back alleys of Corpus and nudged his cayuse into an easy lope. He'd soon be free of the city. The sea air wafting from the gulf across Padre Island filled his nostrils and gave him a sense of confidence that he'd be in Mexico right soon.

★☆

"Where the devil did that sonofabitch go?" Bode asked himself. He reckoned that Riordan wouldn't hang around the city very long, but hadn't figured on the outlaw being waylaid by a local soiled dove. He found himself on the southern outskirts of Corpus looking off into the distance at mostly nothingness save grasses and sand dunes. There was no evidence of any riders passing through. It was tough enough trying to find any sort of tracks in the dry sandy soil, and he was not likely the only traveler. Tougher still, it was unlikely that there'd be any distinguishing features from Riordan's bronc.

This was not a good start. The last thing he needed was to be ahead of his quarry, and he had a sinking feeling that Riordan was behind him. Bode reluctantly turned his mount and traced the edge of the city limits. He wasn't about to risk running into the outlaw. After all, it likely wouldn't take much for Riordan to put together their impromptu sighting at the Longhorn with the retired Ranger coincidently being on the trail south from Corpus.

He turned eastward, figuring to ride well off the trail. He spurred to a loping trot to put some distance between himself and the path Riordan was likely to travel. The greater the distance, the better, as a rider could see for miles on the mostly flat terrain. Besides, there'd be places ripe to set an ambush. The poster did say "dead or alive."

I had barely gone another half dozen miles beyond the homesteaders when I came upon a man at trailside putting the finishing touches on a grave. I rode cautiously forward, double-checking to be sure my Texas Ranger badge was fully displayed.

The gravedigger had just plunged a makeshift cross marker at the head of his companion's final resting place when he heard me approach. Unarmed, he stood and raised both hands. "Don't shoot. I ain't armed!"

"I'm Texas Ranger Lucas Dunn. What happened here?"

The man lowered his hands and wiped his brow with a bandanna. "Me and Petey here...er, Pete Skaggs,"—he nodded toward the fresh diggings and continued—"we was traveling west along the bay trail when we met this big fella. We figured to have a little fun with him, but he took quick offense and plugged Petey here. The gunfire spooked my horse and dumped me back yonder. The big man then rode off. Petey took a gut shot an' bled out right quick. I tried to get him to a doc, but we didn't get far. Passed on right slow."

"Sorry about your friend," I replied. I'd heard that a gut shot could mean a slow death. At the same time, I was thinking that these two paid the price for their shenanigans. "The big man...was he heavily armed, riding a buckskin, and wearing a blue shirt?"

"Yep. That was him."

"You should be grateful to be alive. That was Big Bill Riordan. He's wanted for rustling and murder." I had by now begun to wish I'd started tracking the outlaw a day earlier. It was clear that Riordan was headed for Corpus Christi and just as clear that he'd be heading due south once resupplied. I sighed resignedly. "I'd appreciate it if you'd let Sheriff Tyler know about your friend's untimely demise. Did Mr. Skaggs have any family?"

"Just a brother up in Victoria. I'll see to it, Ranger Dunn."

I nodded and turned Tornado toward Corpus. I picked up our pace. Riordan needed to be brought to justice before he could wreak more havoc. To that end, I made a conscious decision to avoid the city altogether. Better to skirt round and pick up the trail south. As I rode on with new urgency, I recalled advice my dad had given about fugitives on the run eventually growing careless. I already surmised from the outlaw's increasingly reckless behavior that Riordan was possibly of a mind that he wasn't being followed.

I pulled up at a cousin Matt's homestead on the southwestern-most outskirts of Corpus to water and feed Tornado for the trek ahead. From what I knew already about Riordan's aged mount, horses could well be the key to catching the desperado.

"Where you headed, Junior?"

"Got business south of here, Matt."

Matt Dunn knew what the business was. He recalled the exploits of our cousin Texas Ranger "Red John" Dunn and my legendary father, Luke Dunn. "Happy hunting, cousin." He scratched his chin thoughtfully. "This has been busy territory in the past few hours. Saw you wife's grandfather off in the distance riding south and still further out, a big man on a buckskin also headed south. Now you come by." Matt smiled knowingly. "I smell something in the wind."

I was just short of incredulous. "You say you saw Bode McCully?"

"Oh yes. Sort of surprised he didn't stop by."

"You're certain it was him?"

Matt nodded. "He sorta sticks out with that black cayuse and black hat...even at a distance. It was him for sure."

"Damn."

"Pardon?"

"Matt, do you have something to write on? I'd be much obliged, if you could get a message to Sheriff Tyler."

"I gather Mr. McCully might be doin' something untoward?"

I shook my head resignedly. "He thinks he's still a Texas Ranger. Now, he looks to have turned bounty hunter." In the innermost recesses of my mind, I had begun to think he was more like vigilante than bounty hunter. I wrote a brief message to the sheriff.

With Matt's assurance that he'd deliver the note to Sheriff Tyler, I resumed the hunt. The new dimension of dealing with McCully had put a quite undesirable wrinkle into the pursuit of Riordan. I felt obliged to save the desperado from Bode so he could face a sure death sentence at trial. I now found myself in a race to beat my wife's grandfather to the prey.

An itching between Big Bill's legs had begun to worsen. This wasn't saddle itch. Worse yet, his privates were swelling. He thought back to his impromptu dalliance with Dolly and cursed her under his breath. The soiled dove apparently hadn't complied with the city's tough requirement for damsels of the local brothels to receive regular medical attention. With a long ride ahead to Matamoros and no towns at which to find relief, Riordan was going to have to tough it out. He now found a new incentive to hurry himself to the sanctity of Mexico and—hopefully—a good doctor.

He turned his horse toward the waters of Laguna Madre between Padre Island and the Gulf of Mexico, reckoning that a dip in the soothing waters might bring some relief. Afore long, he crested a sand dune and rode to the water's edge. He dismounted, impatiently stripped down, and waded into the crystalline waters. He was met with a combination of relief and pain, as the salty water did his condition no special favors. He examined himself and wasn't pleased at the progress of the gift the Corpus whore had bestowed upon him. Adding a bit of insult to injury, jellyfish floating by gave the outlaw a reminder of their presence by leaving a couple of itchy red welts across the back of his legs and buttocks.

Between whores and jellyfish, Riordan's escape was fast becoming a nightmare of nagging misery. He escaped the spineless denizens of the gulf and managed to get dressed, mount up with notable discomfort, and renew his ride southward. The itching and now soreness was quickly proving to be a serious distraction. He was becoming increasingly careless, but was as yet, still too overly confident to be aware of it.

NINE
AN OUTLAW'S DEMISE?

BODE FIGURED THAT BY NOW, Riordan should be well on his way southward. It perplexed him that he hadn't sighted the fugitive as yet. To complicate his situation, he had to watch his backside for any sign of me. Perplexing...a tad frustrating indeed.

With his natural tendency to impatience, Bode decided to push his luck and head eastward. The downside was a lack of cover. Sneaking up on any prey was a trying proposition among the coastal sand dunes and grasses. Had he been aware of the physical distractions Riordan was enduring or of me trying to recover from my early delays in pursuit, he might have relaxed just a bit.

On the second night of tracking Big Bill, Bode saw the faint glow of a campfire in the distance. Given that it was mostly comprised of grasses, it gave off more smoke than flame. The moonlight struck the billows of smoke as though blaring an announcement of the outlaw's presence. It occurred to Bode that the smoke just might draw rogue Lipan Apache that occasionally wreaked trouble on the Nueces Strip. With Geronimo safely tucked away at Fort Sill in Oklahoma, there remained a stubborn few that occasionally struck out on their own to vent their frustrations. It also hinted that Riordan was growing ever-more-careless.

He decided that it was time to get ahead of Riordan and find a suitable sand dune from which to set an ambush. He preferred to shoot his prey in the early morning while the sun was barely above the horizon. It created a silhouette of rider against sunrise. There seemed something appropriate in that image. Maybe it had to do with ridding the earth of an evil before the beauty of the day got underway.

I pushed Tornado hard all night, and the big Appaloosa didn't let me down. It was as though he sensed his rider's imperative. Sticking to the coastline along the Laguna Madre made for far fewer obstacles than I'd encounter inland among the shrubs and grasses. I was ever on alert, lest I be a target for Big Bill Riordan or—accidentally—Bode McCully. I hoped my cousin had been good to his word and delivered my message to Sheriff Tyler.

Around mid-morning, I came upon the dying embers of what appeared to be the outlaw's campfire. I dismounted and scouted around the site. Nothing stood out as unusual, except that the fugitive had decided to head due west rather than continuing southward. I reckoned that he was using an evasive tactic. Little did I realize that Riordan was looking for a place where he could get relief from his ailments.

I looked out at the horizon to the west, eventually resorting to sighting through the telescopic scope of my rifle. There was nothing to be seen except grasses waving gently in the gulf breezes. Had Riordan encountered some trouble? At the same time, it distracted me that there was no sign of McCully. Where had my wife's revered grandfather hidden himself?

Doggedly, I decided to follow the tracks heading west from the gulf shore. It was obvious that he had closed the gap between me and my prey. A day had become hours, and now I was but minutes behind and closing. It was a matter of kill or capture while keeping an eye out for McCully who was seeming ever more unpredictable.

As I headed Tornado through a gap between the sand dunes, I heard the report of a rifle from south of my position. A second shot exploded in the sea air. Then silence. Nothing. Was it a hunter?

I sighed heavily and turned southward toward the gunfire.

I used utmost caution, scanning the dunes and listening intently as I rode along. Tornado's ears stood straight up as though sharing the alert. There was an eerie silence save for the rustling of grasses in the breeze. Barely two miles from where I'd heard the shot, I heard cussing from the top of a nearby sand dune. I drew my Colt and nudged Tornado up the dune.

"Damn, Mr. McCully! What have you gone and done?"

Bode was lying on his back, waving his hat and cursing to high heaven. An Apache bullet had gone clean through the crown. An inch lower, and the bullet would have put a bloody part in his thinning hair. He shook his head at the familiar sound of my voice. "Stupid. How in tarnation?" he grimaced.

I dismounted. "Do you know who..."

"Damned Apache...that's who. They're supposed to be up north at Fort Griffin." He looked around. "Sonsofbitches stole my horse, but I think I winged one."

I kneeled beside the old Ranger. "Are you wounded, Bode?"

"No, dammit. Just ruined a good hat. Just my pride that took a licking."

I noted the blood on his hand, but ignored it for the moment. "What were you doing up there in the dunes anyway?"

"Now, you can't be delayed because of me. I know you've got an outlaw to catch. Sorry to mess you up, Junior."

I shook my head resignedly. I'd need to see to the now horseless retired Ranger before continuing the hunt for Riordan. It was frustrating, given that I was certain I nearly had the fugitive in my grasp. "I'm not leaving you three days walk from Corpus and wounded." I helped Bode to his feet. "Can you climb aboard? We'll have to ride double." I figured there'd likely be a homestead not too far off. "Where'd you get hit?"

"I'm not that old, dammit! Of course, I can mount up behind." Bode climbed up behind me and awkwardly held on to his Winchester. His nonplussed, frustrated expression spoke loudly, as he tried to get comfortable straddled behind me on Tornado's rump. "Fools just scratched my backside," he admitted.

I didn't want to insult him by mentioning how unwieldy carrying the rifle made the journey, especially when it occasionally poked me in the back.

The ramshackle cabin seemed to loom ahead larger than life to Big Bill. He was desperate to relieve the agony in his crotch that seemed to worsen with every lurch in the saddle. The slow, plodding nature of the buckskin's gait didn't help any. Perhaps, there was something—anything—among its stores that would bring relief.

The smoke curling from the cabin chimney gave sure evidence of human residents. Three horses stood in an adjoining corral. Strangely, they were all saddled. Riordan figured to play it real cautious like. He pulled one of his revolvers from its holster and rode quietly to within a few yards of the front door. The faint squeak of saddle leather and the buckskin's occasional snort were the only noises save for a ruckus going on inside the cabin. Just as he was about to hail the residents, he was startled to see a long-haired figure backing from the doorway with a recently scalped body in tow.

Riordan immediately recognized that he'd come upon the very end of an Apache attack. He aimed his gun carefully and caught the savage fully unawares with a shot dead center in the back. Not bad for a man with a crotch itching like crazy. The sound of the shot alerted two more hostiles inside, and they quickly appeared in the doorway. They were still caught up in the adrenaline rush of the attack.

The outlaw's eyes riveted in on the first Apache through the door just as the savage began to bring up the muzzle of his rifle. Riordan's prejudicial hatred of the Redman kicked into overdrive. "Damn...you be Apache sonsofbitches." He pulled his second revolver and began blasting away. The Apache's rifle went flying with the White man's first volleys, and he fell in a heap on top of his brother. The third Apache never saw the bullets that shattered his face. In but seconds, all were dead, and the stillness of death hung over the scene. "Damned savages," cursed Riordan. He'd kept pulling the triggers even as the hammers of both guns struck dead rounds. Such was his madness. The scene reeked of blood and death.

He dismounted, having calculated that there were no more living souls close by. He poked his head inside the cabin. Only one other scalped White man lay inside, and he was sucking his final breaths of life. Riordan ignored the man's raspy groans and began searching for any unction or salve that might relieve his condition. He soon came upon a tin of bear grease. He unfastened his gun belt, dropped it on an old oak table, dropped his drawers, and began applying it liberally.

Just as physical relief began to take hold, the neighing of an approaching horse started him. He tried to pull up his pants, as he staggered to the table. With a gun in each hand and his pants hanging around his knees, he made it to the doorway. He found himself facing the business ends of two large bore rifles.

"William Riordan, you are under arrest. Drop those guns and raise your hands."

Big Bill sought to go down fighting. No way he'd be taken in and stand trial. He pulled the triggers on his guns, but nothing happened. He had failed to reload after killing the Apache. He frustratingly threw his guns at me and Bode. We neatly ducked them. "Who the hell are you sonsof—"

"Watch your tongue, Riordan. I'm Texas Ranger Lucas Dunn, and you are under arrest. Get those hands high."

With that, Riordan's trousers dropped to his ankles. His jaw dropped at recognizing Bode. "Sonofa..."

Bode couldn't suppress a chuckle. "Dang if he didn't get himself in a fine fix, Junior."

"I've got him covered, Mr. McCully. Dismount and put these manacles on him, if you'd be so kind."

Bode slid from behind me. He was anxious to please his grandson-in-law. It was like old times as a Texas Ranger. He slipped behind Riordan and secured the manacles around the fugitive's wrists, turning away at the odor wafting from the prisoner's backside.

With Riordan cuffed, I scanned the scene. There were five bodies to be buried before heading back to Corpus. It was already midday, so I rightly figured to spend the night at the cabin. There would at least be horses for the ride home.

Bode examined the Apache bodies. "Same trio that tried to get me back in the dunes, Junior. I think this one in the red shirt is the one I winged." There were enough of Riordan's bullets in the bodies that actually confirming Bode's marksmanship wasn't in the cards. No matter. Bode would have another story to tell future grandchildren about holding off an Apache attack.

With Riordan in cuffs and Bode given grub duty, it was left to me to dig a pair of shallow graves. One grave was for the two homesteaders and the other for the Apache. I was wiping my brow soon enough, as I dug the graves during this hottest time of day. I tried to consider it a blessing that the excavation was easy, given the loose sandy soil. The carcasses were already giving off a nasty odor, so I had plenty of incentive to get them underground as quickly as possible.

With Riordan's manacles securely wrapped around the brace supporting one of the legs of the heavy oak table, I took the first watch. While I was reluctant to have Bode involved, I was glad to have some relief guarding the prisoner. It wasn't long, however, before the day's ride in the hot sun began to catch up with me. I grew ever drowsier, and my head would occasionally drop involuntarily in the early throes of sleep. That would awaken me, and I'd shake it off with renewed determination to stay awake.

Bode was already snoring loud enough to wake the dead but not keep me awake.

Riordan was unable to sleep. The itching drove him just short of full-bore crazed. Sweat seemed to ooze from every pore. Despite having been given plenty of water, his mouth felt as dry as the sand dunes that he could see beyond the windows in the bluish-white moonlight. The horses were peacefully standing in the adjoining corral with their tack hung over the fence rail. Escape was ever-so-tempting, ever-so-close at hand. He watched his captors as he sought the right moment to attempt an escape. Bode remained asleep, and I was close to nodding off. He pulled gently on the wooden support. It squeaked just a tad. A strong tug, and it would surely come loose. For him to pry it loose and escape successfully, we would have to be fully asleep.

Finally, I succumbed to the beckoning call of sleep. My arms still cradled my rifle, but I was in dreamland.

Riordan gritted his teeth as another wave of itching coursed through his crotch and thighs. He saw the tin of bear grease on the shelf beside the door. He wouldn't be forgetting to grab that on his way out. He twisted the manacle chains tightly to gain leverage against the table support and slowly began to pry it loose. After a slight squeak, it finally came loose. He stood unsteadily at first. With the prospect of escaping unscathed readily at hand, he wasn't about to search me for the key to his shackles. Awakening one or both of us presented far too much risk.

The desperado tiptoed from the cabin, being sure to grab the tin of bear grease on his way out. He looked over the horses. He considered Tornado, but decided the steed was much too spirited for his tastes. Even manacled and despite mind-numbing itching, he found it easy enough to saddle a horse. Rather than risk stirring them, he selected the closest cayuse. It happened to be the buckskin. As he opened the gate to ride out, he paused. He realized that he had forgotten his guns. He dismounted cautiously, crept back into the cabin, grabbed his gun belt with twin holsters and revolvers, and snuck back to his horse. He mounted up, reopened the gate, and freed the remaining horses from the corral. Just as I stirred noisily inside the cabin, Riordan gave a whoop, spurred his horse, and escaped as quickly as the old buckskin could carry him.

It took but a moment for me to realize that Big Bill had escaped. I staggered to the doorway only to see the outlaw fading into the distance. A quick scan revealed that Riordan had let the horses loose, though the fugitive hadn't counted on Tornado staying close at hand. "Sonofa..." escaped my lips just as Bode appeared beside him.

"What's the ruckus, Junior?"

My face reddened in anger and embarrassment. "Guess I fell asleep. He tore loose from the table and escaped." I'd already whistled Tornado in and grabbed his tack.

"Where you going in such an all-fired hurry? He ain't getting far." Bode had taken a quick inventory of the remaining horses. "Looks like he took that broken-down buckskin." He turned back inside. "I don't figure to ride into some ambush at night. Might as well catch some more shuteye."

I nodded resignedly. Bode was right. There was no point in getting myself bushwhacked. We managed to gather the horses in the darkness and secure them back in the corral. I looked skyward. "Sky is clouding up. Let's put the tack inside in case it rains."

★★

A misty rain greeted us next morning. While the cabin afforded a temporary respite, we could take some comfort in reckoning that our prey would be decidedly uncomfortable.

Bode finished off the last sips of coffee. "I expect you want me to head back to Corpus."

"I expect no trouble from Riordan, Bode. He's in pretty sad shape, and the weather is on my side. He'll leave an easy trail to follow." I stated the obvious, as I held a not-so-hidden desire for the retired Texas Ranger to leave the pursuit of Riordan to the law. I didn't want to deal with any complications in once again explaining Bode's presence to Captain Hughes.

Bode nodded. "Okay. I'll head back."

I thought Bode's response came far too easily, but accepted it. "Stay put, Mr. McCully." I excused myself to go behind the cabin and answer nature's call.

Bode managed to hustle outside, grab his tack, and saddle up.

I returned to the cabin to see McCully riding off into the distant sand dunes. "Dang you, Bode McCully," tripped from my lips. I sighed and gathered what supplies I could before saddling Tornado and heading southward. I hadn't exactly been reckoning on playing a game of catch and release. This hunt had suddenly become more challenging than I'd expected or much liked.

Riordan already had a half-day start and, knowing he was being pursued, would likely push as relentlessly as the old buckskin would permit. McCully presented a different problem for me, as I felt responsible for the old man's welfare. It might be difficult to explain to Captain Hughes but quite a bit more challenging to deal with Cassie, if something serious were to happen to the old Ranger.

I mounted Tornado and headed southward. The rain had stopped. I'd ridden but a couple of hours when I came upon something metallic in the sand that caught the sun's rays. It turned out to be the now empty tin of bear grease. He smiled. Riordan's misery must be fully intolerable by now. The outlaw would surely be increasingly careless.

"No...no...not now," Riordan mumbled under his breath. The aged buckskin had begun to limp badly. He reckoned that he was perhaps two days from Matamoros, but it would take longer if he had to walk. Added to the fire raging between his legs and the decidedly uncomfortable metal shackles binding his wrists, his prospects for successful escape were seeming ever dimmer.

Unbeknownst to the fugitive, Bode had not only caught up but had managed to pass him by skirting around behind a dune just before dawn. The old Ranger had found a comfortable spot a few hundred yards south atop a sand dune overlooking where Big Bill was sure to pass. It became a matter of waiting to deliver a kill shot. Bode savored the task at hand, not to mention the bounty on the outlaw's head.

Riordan plodded along, moving ever-closer within range of Bode's Winchester. Every rocking motion of his horse sent paroxysms through his loins. It was as though the saddle had been made from thousands of burrs. He'd begun to think of another dip in the gulf, jellyfish and all. He pulled up and seriously entertained the thought of dismounting.

"William Riordan, halt!" The voice boomed from behind the outlaw. I had caught up.

Big Bill froze.

Bode couldn't see or hear me but saw Riordan pull up. He had no idea why the outlaw had stopped, but his patience had run more than thin, it was plumb tuckered out. He aimed at Big Bill's broad chest, partially exhaled, and squeezed the trigger. The blast was near ear-shattering in the still sea air.

Riordan had just raised his hands to his chest. The slug ricocheted from the outlaw's manacles and struck me in my left side. Despite being partially spent, it packed plenty enough wallop to penetrate the flesh, bring Tornado to an abrupt halt, and spin me from the saddle. I landed with a cringeworthy thud that knocked the wind from me.

Riordan's wrist hurt like fire from the concussive force of Bode's bullet against the hardened steel of the manacle. He struggled to get the now fully spent buckskin to turn so as to make an escape. With his cayuse failing at his moment of utmost need, the panicky outlaw dismounted awkwardly. He took a quick scan, saw me struggling on the ground, and began making a beeline toward Tornado. Having applied the very last of the bear grease, Big Bill had neglected to refasten his pants. As the waistline fell to his knees, he found himself staggering clumsily toward my horse. He couldn't know that the big Appaloosa was a one-rider cayuse. While I was still writhing on the ground in serious pain and trying to catch my breath, the outlaw gripped Tornado's reins and attempted to mount. The Appaloosa would have none of that. He reared high, wrenched the reins from Riordan's grip, and struck him a crushing blow on the chest with his hooves. Driven to his knees and now laboring simply to rise to one knee with his pants twisted at his knees, the outlaw pulled one of his revolvers, aimed it at the horse, and heard the click of hammer on empty cartridge. Careless and distracted by his physical miseries, he'd still forgotten to reload.

By now, Bode realized that he hadn't felled his target. Like a hunter that wounded his prey and was obligated to finish it off, he mounted up and headed toward Riordan.

Riordan dropped bullets in the damp sand, as he hopelessly strove to reload.

I managed to clear my head and catch my breath enough to unholster a Colt and open fire at Riordan. One...two...three... four...five blasts filled the air. The outlaw's body jerked convulsively as each bullet found flesh and bone. He was dead before he hit the ground. I struggled to my feet, standing unsteadily as blood began to seep from the wound in my side. The pungent odor of gunsmoke displaced the sea air and had the effect of bringing me to my senses.

Upon hearing the gunfire, Bode spurred his horse to a gallop. He still had no idea as to the mayhem his bullet had caused, but multiple gunshots meant trouble. He arrived at the gory scene, halting his horse in a shower of sand to find me with smoking gun in hand, standing over Riordan.

I looked up at him. "What the hell were you thinking?" was all I could gasp, as I held one hand tightly against my wound and with the other, waved the now empty Colt erratically down at Big Bill.

Surveying the scene and realizing what he'd done, the old Ranger instinctively grabbed his saddlebag and dismounted. What could he say?

I dropped to my knees. Blood now oozed steadily from my wound, its scarlet stain absorbed in the folds of the cotton shirt Cassie had made for me. My side hurt real bad.

Dodging the muzzle of my empty gun, Bode strode over to take a closer look at the wound. "Open your shirt, Junior," he directed. He realized I was still focused on Riordan. "The sonofabitch is dead and ain't getting a halo, Junior. Pay him no never mind." He gently relieved me of the revolver. "Let me look at your side."

I gritted my teeth and obliged.

Bode drew upon his experience dealing with gunshot wounds from his Texas Ranger days. "Looks like the slug went clean through. Tore the flesh a bit, but went through. Didn't hit nothing vital. We need to get a bandage on this." He rifled through his saddlebag and came up with some cloth strips.

I sat patiently but couldn't hold back my anger. "Damn it, McCully. If it weren't for Cassie, I'd arrest you this minute."

Bode ignored the threat and began wrapping the wound to staunch the flow of blood. "You need a doc, son. I think we're closer to Brownsville, so let's head down thataways."

I began to gather my wits after the initial shock and aftermath of being shot. "Load Riordan's carcass on what's left of the buckskin and help me mount up," I growled. With extra effort and a helping hand from Bode, I managed to stand.

As if on cue, Tornado walked over, sniffed at me, snorted gently, took in my hand signal, and lowered himself to permit me to climb more easily into the saddle.

Bode was momentarily impressed at the bond between horse and rider. He opened his mouth in the now sheepish thought of offering an apology. He found no voice. He shrugged instead, figuring it wouldn't matter at this point. He turned resignedly back to the business at hand, removing the saddle from the buckskin to ease the anticipated load of dead weight. It was a struggle, but he managed to push and pull Riordan's big bullet-riddled body over the buckskin's back. He fought off an urge to laugh at the outlaw's raw-skinned, sand-and-grease-laden naked butt facing the sky. He covered the body with a blanket and lashed it in place. He couldn't help but note the clustered pattern of wounds in the middle of Big Bill's back. Even wounded, I was a hell of a marksman. Bode picked up Riordan's revolvers, shook them, and blew away the remaining sand. Closer inspection caused his jaw to drop.

"Junior, lookee here." He held the weapons up to offer a better view. "No live rounds. He never reloaded after shootin' those Apache."

I nodded. "Happens every time, doesn't it? They eventually make some careless mistake." I took a deep breath and winced just a tad. "I would have preferred to deliver him alive back in Corpus." It was difficult to not resent Bode's interference. I sighed. "Sheriff Forto will surely find a place to bury Riordan's sorry butt in the Brownsville cemetery." I grinned slightly at the thought of the sorry condition of the outlaw's posterior.

TEN
UNEXPECTED TWIST

THE WOUND in my side hurt like hell, but I remained silent. It served no point to berate Bode. I took some solace in reckoning that the wound wasn't going to kill me so long as it didn't fester. I'd seen worse and recalled my brother dying a slow death from an infected gunshot wound. Riordan, on the other hand, hadn't had a prayer of survival once I opened fire on him. A cluster of 44-caliber bullets in the middle of a man's back will tend to do that.

"You figure two days to Brownsville, Bode?" It was pretty much a rhetorical question, as I'd hunted these parts with my dad and Buffalo Watts. Still, I couldn't stand Bode's embarrassed silence.

"Reckon." Bode wasn't exactly feeling talkative.

I winced as Tornado half-jumped over a large piece of driftwood.

Bode realized that with the old buckskin in tow, progress toward Brownsville was necessarily slow. "Maybe we could cross over to Point Isabel. It's a tad closer."

"We'll stick with Brownsville," I said stoically. I straightened up, even though it caused considerable discomfort. I was still wrapping my brain around McCully's vigilante-style antics, first at Los Olmos Creek and now along the Laguna Madre. I earnestly wanted to pass it off as coincidence, though this second incident was stretching credulity. Could Bode McCully be the vigilante I sought or not? McCully was quite open with his frustration with how justice was being delivered in Texas. I shook it from my mind. Cassie's grandfather was a straight shooter, a man that stood staunchly on the right side of the law. The circumstances of these shootings were surely just coincidental. Had to be. I sniffed the air. "Dang, Mr. McCully...lengthen the lead on the buckskin. Big Bill is stinkin' the place up." I suppressed a laugh as even the thought of humor caused renewed pain from my wound. "Not funny," I said through gritted teeth.

"Take a gander yonder, Junior," exclaimed Bode. The tracks of the Rio Grande Railroad came into sight.

I looked up. I'd nearly fallen asleep in the saddle. I shook loose the cobwebs of sleep. "Dang, but that's a sight for sore eyes, Bode." I brought Tornado to a halt. "Let's follow the tracks straight into Brownsville. Maybe we'll get lucky and grab a ride." I knew there wasn't much chance of that, as the twenty-two-mile line kept to a rather sporadic schedule, shuttling between Point Isabel and Brownsville. The railroad did feature a few bridges spanning marshes and waterways. I logically reasoned that bridges were preferable to skirting the unknown depths of any wetlands we encountered.

Bode nodded agreement. "We'd better keep our heads low and eyes and ears open from here on out, Junior." He was all too aware of the long-held attraction of Texas Ranger companies to this region, as the law of the gun ruled supreme. The bandit Cheno Cortina's ranch wasn't far, and Ranger companies led by the likes of Leander McNelly and James Callahan had caused their share of diplomatic disasters in meeting out justice against Apache predations and roving gangs of Mexican bandits.

It was near sunset, as we pulled up in front of the Brownsville jail. The last golden rays of sunlight reflected from a placard on the door that announced, "Emilio Forto, Sheriff, Cameron County." I stared at it a moment, then grimaced as I dismounted. I fought off the urge to shake out my stiffened muscles, as it wouldn't do to set my bullet wound to bleeding. Glancing intensely at Bode as though telling him to stay put, I stepped up on the wooden planks that served as a makeshift sidewalk and knocked on the door. There was no response. I knocked again. Same result. I shook my head resignedly, as I wanted to rid myself of Riordan's now quite odoriferous body and then get some medical attention for myself.

A voice sounded from the street. "Y'all won't find the sheriff there, gents. Try up the street at Doc Jones's place." It seemed that Sheriff Forto was still recovering from multiple wounds received in a gunfight with outlaws near La Tasa Ranch out near the meandering flows of the Arroyo Colorado a few weeks back.

"Thanks kindly." I nodded to the man and led Tornado, Bode, and our ever more foul-smelling prize in the direction the passerby pointed.

"Mr. McCully, please guard our gift to Brownsville, while I inquire as to Sheriff Forto's situation and see to this hole in my side." The last couple of words were uttered with a certain resentment that had been building ever since the shootout up on the beach of the Laguna Madre.

Bode nodded affirmatively. He really wasn't in any position to protest or offer any alternatives.

I strode up to the door as swiftly as my now stiffened gait would permit and knocked loudly. The sun had set, and only a dim kerosene lamp shed enough light to avoid tripping on the rickety stairs. "Doc Jones?" I called.

Shuffling steps were followed by the skin-crawling creak of

the weather-beaten door and the gnarled and wrinkled face of Doc Jones himself. "What's the damned racket about?" Jones gave a cursory once-over of my tall presence standing before him. His eyes paused at the Texas Ranger badge and then the dark brown stain of dried blood. He opened the door wider. "Come on in." He'd seen this sort of thing before.

"I'm Texas Ranger Lucas Dunn, Doc. I'm needing some medical attention and also looking for Sheriff Forto."

Jones looked past me at Bode and the body draped over the buckskin. "Why don't you have your friend come in, Ranger Dunn?" He glanced again at my side. "You might be a while."

I thought but a moment. "He can wait for a bit." I wasn't about to reveal that I was punishing the old man. "The body draped over the cayuse is a gift for Sheriff Forto, if he's up to accepting it."

"The sheriff is in the back room on past my examination room, Ranger Dunn. I think he's awake. He took a few slugs in a shootout a few weeks ago and is still recovering."

I took a step in the direction Jones indicated but was stopped by a gentle hand on my arm.

"Let's take a look at that wound before you go talking with the sheriff. Gather it's from a bullet. Lots of that going on around these parts lately." He pointed me to the exam table. "Grab a seat and let's have a look."

I paused and turned back toward Bode. "You can hitch the buckskin, and come on in."

"Who's your friend?" Doc Jones inquired.

"My wife's grandfather. He thinks he's still a Texas Ranger." I smiled at the irony buried in my words.

"Have him pull up a seat while I take a look at your side, Ranger Dunn."

It didn't take long for the doc to tend to my wound. Disinfecting as best possible and stitching the jagged edges together was a painful exercise, but Doc Jones applied a salve to ease the discomfort before re-bandaging my side. "Take it easy for a few days, Ranger Dunn. I take pride in my sewing skills. It wouldn't do to have those stitches tear loose."

"What do I owe you, Doc?"

Doc Jones nodded his head toward the body draped across the back of the buckskin. "This one's on the house. It's the least I can do. We appreciate you Texas Rangers around these parts." The doctor paused. "You can go talk with Sheriff Forto, if you like." He pointed to the next room.

As I buttoned my shirt and turned, I found myself face-to-face with the sheriff.

"I hear about a Texas Ranger?" Forto leaned against the doorjamb.

"Gather you're Sheriff Forto?" I forced a friendly smile, cringing a bit at the slight pull of the stitches in my side. "I'm Texas Ranger Lucas Dunn."

"And I'm Sheriff Emilio Forto at your service. Sorry about my condition." Forto's eyes traced my wounds. "Being a lawman's a tough business. How can I be of assistance?"

"I'm with Captain Hughes's company. I've brought…"

Forto interjected, "Are you Luke Dunn's kin?"

I sighed as respectfully as possible. "He's my dad."

"Damned fine lawman. A legend in these parts." Forto closed his eyes a moment as though trying to remember something but shook it off. "I'm sorry, you were saying?"

"I've got the remains of Willian Riordan draped over yonder saddled." I directed my thumb at the hitching post out front. In the dim light of the kerosene lantern, Big Bill's swollen remains could be seen. "He was wanted up north for rustling, robbery, and murder. Seems there's a reward. I just need you to certify receipt and bury what's left of him."

Forto limped to a front window and peered out. "Looks like a bit of a storm gathering." He turned to me. "Ought to be a box up at yonder livery," he suggested, pointing up the street.

"You gonna certify it's Riordan?"

Forto sighed. He wasn't up to the pain, much less stumbling to the jail to undertake the time-consuming task of sorting through wanted posters simply to verify that the body draped over the saddle was, in fact, William Riordan. The possibility of traipsing through rain and mud made the task even less inviting. A Texas Ranger's word was good enough for him. "I'll take your word for it, Ranger Dunn."

I glanced over at Bode, who nearly imperceptibly nodded to accept the sheriff's offer. "Well, it's Riordan, and the slugs I put in him testify to his being dead." With that, I reached into my pocket, pulled out a pretty much shredded piece of yellowed paper, and unfolded it. "Here's the poster, Sheriff." I handed it to Forto.

The sheriff skimmed the description on the poster and gazed squinty eyed at the body adorning the buckskin. He coughed and pulled his bandanna over his nose. "Er, sure looks to be him."

Doc stepped in. "With a storm brewing, y'all better get that body boxed. I expect the stable will keep y'all warm and dry for the night. Doubt y'all will catch a room at the hotel at this hour."

Sheriff Forto seemed relieved. "Meet me at the jail in the morning. I'll get the papers done up for your reward." He offered a half wave and hobbled to the back room.

"Thanks, Doc." I winced as the stitches in my side pulled a little with the sudden movement. I grimaced a tad and motioned Bode to follow me out.

Doc saw us to the door. "Remember to give that wound a day or two afore you head north, Ranger Dunn."

Heavy humidity from the previous night's rains greeted me and Bode as we roused at the break of dawn. Home was a long way off, and we yet needed to stop at Sheriff Forto's office before heading north.

The simple task of pulling on my boots caused me to wince. I tried to hide it from Bode.

"Hurt a bit?"

"Just stitches pulling a tad." I grabbed my gun belt and began to strap it on.

"Where you going?"

"Got to visit the sheriff, and then we can head north."

"You'd best heed doc's advice, Junior."

Impatient to leave Brownsville, I nevertheless nodded affirmatively. "Maybe we could ride gentle-like over to the south end of Padre Island." It was crystal clear that sitting in one place for any length of time sufficient to permit my wound to heal wasn't part of my thinking.

The idea didn't exactly excite Bode. "Shucks, it's just sand and seagulls out there. Sounds boring."

"Cousin Patrick hasn't found it so boring. His longhorns are thriving up on the north end." My cousin Patrick Dunn and his brother Lawrence had been raising cattle on North Padre Island for the past sixteen years. With Laguna Madre to the east and Gulf of Mexico to the west, there was no need for fences and fresh water was plentiful. The beeves fattened up on sedge grass, sand crabs, and dead fish. When ready for market, the Dunns simply waded the longhorns across to Corpus Christi. Wasn't long until Patrick bought out his brother and named the spread El Rancho de Don Patricio.

"Yep. He's made a go of it."

I chuckled as I recalled my cousin putting the initials D.P.I. after his name. When asked, he laughingly replied, "Duke of Padre Island." Indeed, it was his fiefdom. "Patrick calls himself the Duke of Padre Island. Has a nice ring to it."

"You're not thinking…"

"No, I'm not going to ranch on South Padre Island, Bode. I don't expect Cassie would cotton to the isolation."

Bode sat back and looked off in the direction of South Padre Island. He reckoned it was about a twenty-five-mile ride, at least a full day at the snail's pace my wound would require. "So, you gonna be Duke of Nuecestown?" He chuckled at his own humor.

I glanced at Bode. "I know what you're thinking." I released an emphatic sigh. "And you're right. We'll spend the night here in Brownsville and begin the trek north tomorrow."

"Still too soon, but makes better sense."

"Might visit Judge Wells."

Bode's jaw dropped just a smidgen. "You thinking about politics, Junior?" Jim Wells was the political power broker of Cameron County, even having been Brownsville city attorney and state district judge. He was the protégé of Democratic Party boss Stephen Powers up in Corpus Christi and had become tight with Archie Parr, the party boss in Duval County near Alice and but an easy day's ride from my ranch.

"Doesn't hurt to have influential friends, Bode. You never know when it might come in right handy." I was well aware that my dad stayed outside politics, and how it caused difficulties for the family during post-war reconstruction. It wasn't that Luke was unaware of the political landscape, just that he chose to not play in it. I figured to be just a tad more involved. I didn't reckon on being a Texas Ranger as a career and still held hopes of growing mine and Cassie's ranch. One could never be sure as to when it might be beneficial to have friends in high places, even if they were of debatable morals.

Bode considered politicians anathema. From his perspective, they were the ones concocting the rules that made delivering justice more difficult. "You gonna take a bath afterward?"

"Let's go grab some grub and then visit Sheriff Fortas." I had enough of small talk before breakfast.

We stepped off the sidewalk to cross to a ramshackle but—judging by the number of horses at the hitching rail—a popular local restaurant. We slogged across the muddy detritus of a midnight rain as mucked up by wagon wheels and horse hooves. We finally stepped up on the wooden sidewalk of the restaurant and availed ourselves of sticks provided for the purpose of scraping mud from boots.

Despite the packed room, breakfast was promptly served. Bode scanned the room, looking for a worthy target to observe and perhaps overhear some juice gossip. "Look over yonder, Junior."

None other than Jim Wells his very self was enjoying breakfast on the opposite side of the room.

I glanced over through a sea of red-checkered tablecloths and about as diverse a set of diners as might be conceived. I looked across the table. "Mr. McCully...please. Keep your voice down," I whispered. We ordered breakfast and soon the aromas of bacon, hot buttered biscuits, and a stack of flapjacks were far too alluring than any chance engagement with Jim Wells. I kept my voice at a whisper. "He's still eating. It's not proper to interrupt a man in the middle of his meal." With that, I stuffed a forkful of syrupy flapjack into my mouth. I was quick to grab a napkin and wipe away the syrup drooling from my scruffy beard.

Bode allowed himself a bit of a guffaw before shoving a forkful of breakfast into his own mouth.

I kept a watchful eye on Wells. As the man began to swipe the last remnants of egg yolk with his biscuit, I decided to make my move. I turned to Bode. "This is on you, Mr. McCully." I arose, nodded to the serving girl that McCully was paying, and ambled easy-like over to where Wells was about to get up from his chair. "Pardon, Mr. Wells. Have you a moment?"

Wells proffered one of those *should I know you* expressions common among overly-popular folks before realizing that a stranger was addressing him. He gave me a quick hat to boots once over with a brief pause at the dried bloodstain on the side of my shirt. "Howdy…er, my office hours are posted and my secretary will be pleased to make an appointment." He made a motion to move past me.

"I'm Texas Ranger Lucas Dunn, Junior, Mr. Wells. I'm acquainted with Mr. Parr up north." I knew that was a stretch, as the closest I'd come to even meeting Parr was walking by at a community meeting in Alice.

The mention of Parr's name caused Wells to pause. "I see. How can I help you, Ranger Dunn." It was obvious that Wells was combing the inner workings of his brain at the all-too-familiar Dunn name.

"Just delivered a fugitive to Sheriff Fortas and thought I might make your acquaintance before heading back north. I'm with Captain Hughes's company."

"Fugitive? Guess he'll show up in my court."

"Likely not, Mr. Wells. William Riordan has already met his Maker."

Wells smiled. "Then I reckon it's congratulations for a job well done." Then it hit him. "You related to Luke Dunn?"

"Yes, sir. He's my dad." I waited for the inevitable retort.

"Seems the fruit doesn't fall far from the tree."

I smiled politely. "My dad was a fine Texas Ranger, Mr. Wells. In any case, I won't hold you up any further. I just wanted to make your acquaintance. I'll be sure to tell Mr. Parr of our chance encounter."

Wells nodded, then paused. "You wouldn't happen to know anything about that vigilante up around Corpus, would you?"

"I'm working at tracking him down, Mr. Wells." I couldn't say that it was possible that the vigilante just might be finishing breakfast in the very room in which me and Wells were carrying on our chance meeting.

Wells bowed his head ever-so-slightly in acknowledgment. "Well, I won't hold you up from your duties, Ranger Dunn."

We shook hands, and I turned to find myself face-to-face with Bode.

"Two minutes? That's what you call a meeting?"

"Just getting acquainted, Bode. You never know when some help might be needed on down the road. It's sort of akin to riding at night to keep the herd quiet. You never know when a storm hits or rustlers appear and you need help. Good help can be hard to find."

We exited the restaurant, and I turned in the direction of the livery.

"Where you headed, Junior?"

"We're saddling up and heading home, Bode."

"But the doc said…"

"I'll be fine." I hadn't taken more than a half dozen steps when I stopped suddenly, causing Bode to nearly bump into him. I looked across the street at a general store. "Might be a good idea if I bought myself a new shirt. I don't think Cassie would appreciate me showing up in this one." I smiled at his understatement.

Upon crossing the street and once again scraping mud from my boots, I entered. I began to scan the interior with its neatly arranged goods only to find my gaze halted by a young woman behind a display counter.

"May I help you, sir." Her voice had the heavenly lilt of a lass fresh from the green heathers of Ireland. Waves of chestnut-colored hair cascaded across her shoulders, setting off green eyes, full ruby-red lips, and alabaster skin that seemed translucent.

I was momentarily speechless.

"May I help…"

"Er, yes. I'm in need of a shirt."

She couldn't help but stare at the bloodstains and torn fabric on my shirt and the white bandage peeking through the gaping tear in its side. Then, her eyes ventured up to the silver Texas Ranger badge pinned to my chest.

Noting her distraction, I gave her a wink and repeated. "I'm in need of a shirt, ma'am."

She blinked.

"Perhaps we should start over. I'm Texas Ranger Lucas Dunn, Junior. I've just completed some business a ways north of here, and I'm in need of a new shirt before heading back to Corpus Christi."

The young woman blushed and quickly sized up my muscular frame. "I believe we have a shirt that should fit you, Mr. Dunn." She walked briskly to a shelf, selected a suitable shirt, and returned. "This should do. Oh, and my name is Lilith." She held the shirt up for him.

"I expect I'd best try it on." With that, I naively stripped off my shirt, revealing rippling muscles along with a serious bandage. I hadn't given a second's thought as to the impact on young Lilith.

She blushed a deep scarlet and turned away, though she couldn't resist a peek just as I slid the new shirt over my washboard abdominal muscles.

"Seems to fit just fine."

Lilith gasped slightly but held back the urge to agree wholeheartedly.

I forced myself to tend to the business at hand. I needed a shirt, not a woman. "What do I owe you?"

Her blush had begun to transition to a healthy glow. "Are you staying long in Brownsville?" The lilt in her voice was softer, as she drew out the words as more of an invitation.

I had given her the sort of once-over that only us men seemed capable of when she'd gone to fetch the shirt. Were I not Cassie's man...well, as it was, I was sorely tempted. I found myself grateful to hear Bode enter. The distraction broke the tension like an axe splitting wood.

"Er...two bits, Ranger Dunn." She couldn't hold back

another blush, as she as she took in the manly apparition before her and imagined herself passionately stroking my muscular chest and more...so much more. Her eyelids fluttered involuntarily with both nervousness and near-orgasmic surges that were overcoming her body.

I felt a bit warm myself and it wasn't from the weather. I fished coins from my pocket, placed them on the counter, and nearly fell over myself following Bode out of the store. I paused and looked back for the blood-stained shirt.

Lilith was holding it close as though to absorb its very essence.

I shrugged and hurried out to the sidewalk.

"Dang, Junior. You always have that effect on women?"

Silence.

"Really?"

"Just Cassie, Mr. McCully. She's all that matters."

We headed toward the livery, using wooden sidewalks so far as possible to avoid the muddy street.

I slid a bit as I ill-advisedly leaped from one sidewalk to another. The pull on the stitches caused an involuntary gasp. I stood for a moment to collect myself. "Maybe we'll spend one more night bedded down in the stable," I said with just a touch of sheepishness.

Bode smiled and nodded knowingly.

ELEVEN
TRUTHS ON THE SANDS

THE SUN CAST its golden glow across the eastern horizon as Bode and me saddled up. We'd held on to the old buckskin that Riordan rode, as it was serviceable as a pack horse. I figured we could return the cayuse to its owner up near the Nueces River.

Tornado seemed to sense that we were headed home, as the big Appaloosa's natural energies fought back at my urgings to ride gently. I looked forward to the $2,000 reward that would be awaiting us back in Corpus Christi. We emerged from the livery into the brightness of a South Texas day. The trail up the eastern boundary of the Nueces Strip beckoned. It would be slow going.

I glanced over at the general store. Lilith was standing out front, still clutching my battered shirt. She waved, and I managed to ignore her. I turned to Bode. "Do you think Sheriff Fortas was exaggerating about the dangers of traveling in Cameron County?"

Bode looked off thoughtfully at the distant grasses as if to come up with some profound retort. "Don't think we have much to worry about, Junior. A pair of heavily armed travelers might tend to make a bandit think twice."

"Even a wounded Ranger and a," I paused. "A retired Ranger?"

Bode chuckled. "Tell that to Carlos Diaz."

The reference back to the recent engagements with the ill-fated Mexican bandit stirred my investigative juices. Bode was riding to his right a half horse length behind. I glanced at the 1895 Winchester in its scabbard hanging from the saddle horn.

Bode noticed the nearly imperceptible change in my demeanor. "What do you figure, Junior? Five days ride to Corpus?"

I once again shook off my line of thinking. The ride north could get right uncomfortable were I to resort to sleuthing about finding the vigilante. "Reckon so, Bode." I found myself tempted to pick up our pace, but yielded to good sense. It wouldn't do to bloody a new shirt. I smiled as I couldn't help but wonder why young Lilith was still fondling my old shirt. The very thought sent a revulsive shiver up my spine.

We happened upon an abandoned wagon that furnished wood for a respectable cooking fire and enjoyed beans and jerky topped off with simmering coffee more likely to keep us awake than settle us down.

The night was crystal clear and, but for occasional hoots of an owl and mournful howl of coyotes, it was so quiet that you could hear the stars blink. I poked at the fire with a stick. I was once again pondering the challenge of finding the vigilante that plagued the region. I sort of wished I'd learn of the vigilante striking while me and Bode were in Brownsville so as to take Cassie's grandfather off my list of suspects.

"What's on your mind, Junior? You seem to be carrying a heavy load, sort of like a hog fattened up and ready for butchering."

"What do you think of this vigilante fellow folks around Corpus are worried about?"

Bode knew the question would eventually come. "Seems he's intent on delivering justice to wanted fugitives from the law."

"What if he makes a mistake and kills an innocent man?" I gently rubbed the bandage covering my side.

"Whoever it is, he seems to identify his targets before pulling the trigger."

I flipped a plank with my stick, causing a shower of coals. "Is it murder?"

"No question, it's killing. However, the target is accused of crimes normally punishable by hanging."

"True, Bode. So true." I stuck my stick in the coals and blew out the flame at the tip of the stick I was stirring with. My eyes seemed to penetrate deep into Bode's psyche. "But the accused isn't convicted."

"Is this for you to decide, Junior?"

"It goes to motive, Bode. Just maybe, this vigilante figures he's answering to some noble purpose." I stared at the rekindled flame at the end of my stick. "It's not my place to approve or disapprove. That's God's judgment, not mine."

"Texas Rangers are called upon to deliver justice." Bode found himself donning his old Ranger persona.

"Justice, but not punishment, Bode. I can arrest a lawbreaker to face trial and can kill one in self-defense. Shucks, my dad reckoned that some were redeemable, and he was mostly proven right." I tossed the stirring stick into the flames. "Meeting my duty is what matters, with or without the judgment of others. I just hope I'm never called on to make a decision involving my family." There, I'd said it if only by implication.

A coyote howled. "Wish those critters would settle," Bode said, seemingly ignoring my comment. "We ought to turn in. Got another long ride ahead tomorrow." He looked up at what seemed like a billion stars spread across the night sky. He knew I was on to him.

The heat lay like a heavy blanket of damp burlap across the vastness of the Nueces Strip, as we plodded northward. I hadn't brought up the vigilante question again, though it was obviously weighing heavily upon me.

I began humming to myself, occasionally delivering lyrics in a near whisper. "Rest tired eyes a while...sweet is thy baby's smile."

Bode smiled as the melody flowed back toward him.

"Angels are guarding and they watch o'er thee," I continued. The unforgettable lullaby my mother used to sing each night to me and my siblings brought a certain peacefulness to my soul. "Sleep, sleep, *grah mo chree*...here on your mamma's knee." I abruptly stopped and stood high in the saddle. Something was out there that caught my senses.

Bode pulled up short. He knew better than to ask.

I motioned Bode to pull up alongside. "Something isn't right," I whispered. "Let's spread out a bit."

The retired lawman waited for me to ride off to his left about fifty yards before we both proceeded north on high alert. Whatever lurked ahead among the grasses wasn't making a sound. A buzzard up ahead took flight.

Buzzards? I felt a sense of relief. Whatever lay ahead was likely not alive.

As we crested a slight rise, a grisly sight revealed itself. The stench was near overwhelming, causing both of us to tie bandanas over our noses.

I pulled up. "Thought this ended years ago."

"Hiders! I'll be damned," observed Bode. "What a waste!"

Strewn before them were at least a dozen cattle carcasses stripped of their hides. There was nothing salvageable, nothing to do but ride on through and eventually report the abhorrent find.

We rode on through the killing field on now skittish horses. "Keep an eye out for any brands, Mr. McCully." I knew it was a most unlikely task, especially as hindered by eyes watered by the pungent aroma and the hides bearing the brands long since gone. "I'm reckoning this couldn't have happened more than a day ago. Whoever did this might not be so far off. Better keep an eye out."

Bode and I rode among the carcasses. "Somebody's missing a few head. Dang, but I don't figure there's a market for hides these days. The slaughterhouses cornered the market long ago."

"Look over yonder, Junior." Bode pointed to a spot off to their right. "Looks like they spent enough time to camp. Maybe there'll be some clues as to who did this."

By the time we reached the campsite, much of the odor had dissipated. I climbed from the saddle to begin nosing around. A shiny object attracted me. I bent to pick it up, then held it aloft for Bode to see. "Not often you find a broken spur." I examined the engravings in the shaft. "Pretty fancy for a bunch of petty hiders." I kicked at the ashes of the campfire. "Looks like they had time to enjoy some roast beef." I smiled at the utter irony. "What could they have been up to?"

"Grudge," offered Bode.

"Grudge?"

"Might be a range war."

"A dozen head of beeves slaughtered and skinned makes for an interesting response to a grudge. Maybe we should be grateful there are no bodies..." I stopped myself. I'd walked just beyond the perimeter of the campsite and come upon a fresh grave. "Damn!" I strode over to Tornado and fetched my shovel.

"You really gonna dig up the body?"

"Looking for clues, Bode. Can't say as it's a pleasant task, but I'll find my clues wherever they might be…buried or not." The digging in the sandy soil was easy, and I didn't have to dig very deep.

"Watch you don't bust any stitches." Bode shook his head at my stubborn drive for clues.

"You want to dig?" I held the shovel up to Bode.

"I think it's a fool effort." Bode stayed in his saddle.

"Suit yourself." I turned back to digging. "Surprised that buzzards or coyotes weren't at this before we arrived." Ignoring the pull on my stitches, I knelt beside the grave and dusted off the body. "Look at this, Bode." I pointed to a bullet wound in the chest and another between the dead victim's eyes. I began the distasteful task of groping the body for any pockets that might contain identifying items. All of a sudden, I pulled back, fully aghast. "Oh my god!"

My reaction caused Bode to dismount and hustle over to me. He peered down at the body. "Dang, Junior. It's a woman!" My search had exposed a woman's breast.

"Who could she be?" My sense of respect for the sanctity of a woman's body, especially one other than my wife, caused me to hesitate. I glanced at Bode, shrugged resignedly, and continued my search. Far as I could tell by her dark hair, she was young. But for the bullet wound and discolorations from bruising, she might have been a quite attractive woman. There was no jewelry to be found. "Mr. McCully, look at this." Upon rolling the body over, I'd found a burned area on the woman's buttocks. "Danged if she's not been branded. The bastards tortured her before the killing." I held back an involuntary retch.

Bode hunkered down beside me. "What sort of hate would…"

I forced myself to examine the brand. "Looks like the Bar A." I found myself confronted by a difficult choice. Was I to rebury the woman or wrap her body and transport it to Corpus Christi? A decomposing body, even one wrapped in a blanket, was about as undesirable a task as I could imagine. "You have anything to mark her grave?" I'd made my choice. Once back in Corpus, they'd likely learn whether a woman had gone missing and investigate the Bar A ranch. Sheriff Tyler would surely need to be told in addition to Captain Hughes. I turned to Bode as though for approval.

Bode had already found a couple of partially burned pieces of wood from the campfire and lashed them together in the form of a cross. "This should do it." He handed it to me. "See that lonely mesquite motte yonder? That ought to help anyone who's interested locate the grave." Clusters of trees and vagaries of landscape served as navigation beacons for folks traveling vast open spaces as found on the Nueces Strip, so the mesquite motte would indeed be important if anyone sought the woman's remains.

I stuck the makeshift cross at the head of the grave, stood, and doffed my hat. "Lord bless the soul of whoever this woman is. Amen." I walked back to Tornado. A broken spur, a dozen skinned beeves, and the deceased woman bearing the Bar A brand were the only clues to whatever was going on here in the vastness of the Nueces Strip. "Let's go, Bode." A heavy, solemn feeling one might experience upon leaving a funeral took possession of my demeanor, as I slowly led the way back to the narrow trail toward Corpus Christi. I resumed singing the lullaby. *Angels are guarding and they watch o'er thee*, filled my thoughts. It brought a sense of peace to calm the troubles that roiled through my mind.

"It's the danged barbed wire, Junior." They'd ridden several miles before Bode broke the silence.

"Possibly," I rejoined.

"Your cousin raises beeves out on the island, doesn't he?"

That brought an involuntary chuckle from me, as though breaking the barrier of solemnity. "No fences necessary on Padre Island." I laughed. I reflected a moment on the skinned carcasses and dead woman. "No telling what folks will do when fighting over land. Could be fences blocking access to water."

"Wonder why they killed the woman?" reflected Bode.

The question lingered in my mind as well. "Maybe we'll find out when we learn whose beeves are missing."

I was tempted to push on. We were a half-day's ride from home, but I had a bit of a premonition that one more night camped under the stars was fitting given the long journey with Bode. Questions still lingered. I'd been chewing on them like taffy, sticking to my thoughts but not nearly so sweet.

We finished the last of the roasted coyote, not nearly so savory as deer or even javelina but better than squirrel. Bode looked up from his feeding a piece of driftwood on the fire. "You got something heavy on your mind, Junior?" Retirement from the Texas Rangers after thirty years of pursuing lawbreakers couldn't erase the habit of reading faces and frames of mind.

I sighed. "Might say," I offered with a hushed tone.

Bode well knew what was on my mind. "You thinking it's me, ain't you?"

I gave him a penetrating gaze that would have sent a rattlesnake back to its lair. It said, *prove me wrong.*

"Some tough desperadoes have met their fate lately. Whomever the vigilante is, he seems to be doing the good citizens of South Texas a favor."

I shook my head. I'd have been totally stunned had Bode owned up to the bushwhacking. There was no point in even asking the question. Bode McCully had the skills, the state of mind, the weapon, and the opportunities, but it was next to impossible to prove he was the vigilante I was hunting and Bode knew it. "I expect so. Except it's murder. This vigilante is no better than the lawbreakers he's killing." I laid out my bedroll.

"Looks as though your wound is healing up right fine." Bode offered a weak attempt to change the subject.

"Wonder how Cassie would feel if she knew?"

Silence. My implication hit Bode like he'd been struck up the side of the head with the butt end of a rifle.

I didn't expect an answer but crawled into my bedroll. "See you in the morning." I figured to let Bode chew on his final comment. It was heavy-handed to bring his granddaughter into consideration, but it served as a sort of ace-in-the-hole for me. Short of a confession, the only way I'd catch the vigilante would be to catch him in the act. I hoped against hope that I might embarrass Bode into confession...if, in fact, my suspicions were correct. It hung like a dark cloud over me. I couldn't help but wonder whether it was a forewarning of an approaching storm.

TWELVE
RANGE WARS & POLITICS

STEPHEN POWERS LEANED back in the leather-upholstered chair with his boots nestled on top of the ornate mahogany desk. His boots squeaked as he recrossed his legs, striving to avoid damaging the finish with his spurs. The spurs were a sort of fashion statement for the political boss, as he rarely took to the saddle these days. Mostly, he traveled by carriage with a couple of well-dressed hired guns that served as bodyguards. With power came risk, and he couldn't be too careful. He took a long drag on his cigar and blew a couple of smoke rings aloft. "Wells says this Texas Ranger made it sound like y'all were right tight, Archie."

Archie Parr smiled, as he, in turn, took a long pull on his cigar. "I knew his daddy. Damn good Texas Ranger. Folks call him a legend." He stood and poured himself a drink from the ample supply of liquors nestled in the sideboard. "You know the Dunns have considerable holdings west of Alice. I believe the young 'un that Jim met up with has a respectable spread of his own. Right fine wife, too."

Powers's boots thudded against the floor as he dropped his legs from the desk and leaned toward Parr. He waved his cigar about like a pointer to emphasize what he was about to say.

"There's some bad feelings brewing down past Los Olmos Creek, Archie." He took a pull before once again pointing at Parr with the cigar. "You go talk with Tyler about staying clear of that business. Folks are tangling a tad about that damned barbed wire. Dang fencing causes nothing but trouble anyway."

Parr was already an established political power and wasn't about to do any squirming in the face of Powers's cigar. "Tyler's in your backyard, Stephen. You got something against taking care of your own housekeeping?" Parr preferred to stay clear of Corpus Christi.

Powers's cigar found its way to a large ceramic ashtray. As he twisted it into the colorful designs, he eased back in his chair. He didn't like being challenged but admired Parr's spunk. Neither man took well to being ordered to do anything. "Tell you what, Archie. How about you suggest to Hughes that he not mess with local wranglings, and I'll take care of Tyler."

Parr smiled. He liked at least the appearance of having had his way. He poured a second drink and promptly quaffed it. "You do need to come visit my spread up north of Alice, Stephen. It's not so big as King's holdings, but we might do a bit of hunting."

The conversation around the campfire, such as it was, had not set well with Bode McCully. He knew that I had fingered him as the vigilante. He was relieved that I hadn't made any outright accusation. That would have been embarrassing to deal with. It was clear that I was sensitive to Cassie's feelings and was in a considerable quandary. His own choices were decidedly straightforward. He could confess or stop bush-whacking fugitives. If he continued, it would force my hand.

We'd said nary a word since breaking camp that morning. The air hung pregnant with the mystery surrounding our grisly find a couple of days back and the question of Bode's likely overstepping of the law. Those considerations tended to offset what should have been some degree of elation at having disposed of William Riordan.

As we approached the city limits of Corpus Christi, I pulled up. "How about you go your way, Mr. McCully."

Bode knew that I didn't want to have to explain his presence to Captain Hughes. He nodded. "Been a pleasure working with you, Junior." He wasn't about to offer the relief that a confession would bring. "Figure that wound of yours should heal up right well." He paused. "I am deeply sorry about that." He gently poked his heels into his horse's sides and rode easy-like up the road.

I reckoned to give the retired Ranger a head start before resuming my ride to Corpus. I tried to think on whom I knew at the Bar A. In any case, I'd have to see Sheriff Tyler and wouldn't be doing anything without orders from Captain Hughes. I finally gave a gentle spur to Tornado and rode on to Corpus. I felt incentivized to take care of business and get on home to Cassie.

"Will you look at that! Yellow paper!" Bode exclaimed. It was next to impossible to miss the wanted poster plastered on the weathered old bulletin board out front of the post office. Jim Bigcrow had flown the reservation and was conducting his own brand of vengeance on his White oppressors. According to the poster, he'd already randomly slain at least a dozen farmers and ranchers ranging from Fort Sill to Victoria.

Bode fought the temptation to grab the poster and stuff it in his pocket. "Yellow paper," he mumbled, then whistled. Three thousand dollars was a heap sight of money. The yellow paper was likely intended to stand out as a special warning to place folks on alert, and the size of the reward aimed to make short work of bringing the Apache to justice. He felt a nearly impossible-to-suppress yearning to hunt down Bigcrow despite the risks. He read the description again. Bigcrow had ridden with Geronimo, so had gained plenty of experience accompanying the Apache chief on his predations. He'd been primarily associated with the Chiricahua Apache, but that was no matter here. This wanted savage was described as physically on the smaller side of average. The poster described a jagged scar that stretched from Bigcrow's left ear to his nose and noted that his left hand was partially crippled and missing a couple of fingers.

The retired Ranger sighed. He was determined to keep a low profile for now. He sighed and began to ride away. He couldn't resist. He brought his horse to a halt, dismounted, and glanced around to see whether anyone was lingering about that might see him. The street was devoid of human life. Bode strode up and tore the poster from the bulletin board. He folded it quickly and stuffed it in his hip pocket.

"Howdy, Sheriff." I had dismounted and draped Tornado's reins over the hitching rail. I'd caught Tyler just as he emerged from his office. "Brought a bit of news you might be interested in."

Tyler threw a wary glance to the left and right as though fearful of eavesdroppers. He turned and faced me. "What might that be?" he said in a near whisper.

I was rather taken aback at Tyler's furtive behavior. What could the sheriff be so concerned about? It was as though he didn't want to hear my news. "Expect you heard that I brought Riordan to justice. Delivered his body to Sheriff Forto."

"I heard," responded a decidedly impatient Tyler. It was as though he wanted to get this little meetup over as quickly as possible.

I strove to ignore the sheriff's reaction. "You aware of some goings on south of here near the Bar A?"

Tyler blinked.

"Came upon a spot where a dozen head of beeves had been slaughtered and skinned. Poked around and found a fresh grave."

Tyler blinked again, and his jaw dropped a tad. "Maybe you ought to come inside, Ranger Dunn." He darted inside and hastily sat behind his desk with his hands uncharacteristically fidgeting.

I followed the sheriff into his office and straddled a chair opposite. "I dug up the body. Turned out to be a woman." I caught the sheriff's squinty-eyed but concerned expression. "There was no identification on her. Dark hair. Slim. She'd been shot twice, likely the one between the eyes finished her."

"My god. Who coulda..." Tyler began shaking his head in dismay.

"You know who she might be, Sheriff?"

Tyler simply stared at his still fidgeting hands.

"Would it help if I mentioned that the Bar A brand was burned into her buttocks?"

My words broke Tyler like a sledgehammer on eggs. "Sally Corrigan. Had to be Sally." The sheriff leaned into me and spoke in a low voice. "Stay clear of this, Junior. Trust me. It's far bigger than you or me. Important folks are involved."

"I'll be reporting the incident to Captain Hughes."

"Do as you must, but he'll tell you to leave it alone."

"So...you're telling me there's something big going on, and we're to ignore any murder and mayhem."

"Don't get involved, Junior. You might as well dive into a rattlesnake nest. You'll die and not have proven a thing by it." Tyler had stopped fidgeting and sought to change the conversation. "Go find that vigilante."

I wanted to mention that his suspected vigilante had placed an errant bullet through my own side. I resignedly shook my head. "Thanks for the warning, Sheriff. Oh, and I think I'm close to finding that vigilante." I exited the jail and headed to the post office.

I reckoned that Hughes was prowling the Rio Grande and would have to be reached by telegram. The captain had already been dubbed The Border Boss for his successes in quelling trouble with restless Apache and troublesome Mexican banditos. I entered the post office and hailed the owner. "I need to get a telegram to Captain Hughes down in Brownsville, Slim." I was curious as to whether Hughes would, in fact, tell me to lay off the Bar A matter. Meanwhile, I had a wife that I longed to see. For the next day or so, I figured to get reacquainted with Cassie and not concern myself with whatever shenanigans I was being warned to stay clear of. I made certain the telegram was sent, then mounted Tornado and headed toward home. The more than two weeks I'd spent bringing Riordan to justice would soon fade, especially in Cassie's welcome embrace. I still would have to reveal the still-healing wound to my side. I hated to lie about how I got it, but was determined to protect her veneration of her grandfather. It surely wouldn't do to confess that Bode had shot me or that I was even with him on the hunt for Riordan.

Jim Bigcrow had acquired an 1895 Winchester rifle and was already proving quite adept at using it. The road south from Victoria to the Nueces Bay was well-traveled. He decided to hang out in the area, as it afforded him a wealth of targets. He knew he was a wanted man but possessed a near-suicidal urge to deliver his message of vengeance as often as he could. He'd avoided a posse north of San Antonio, but had seen no further sign of anyone on his trail. It served to frustrate him that he wasn't being hunted by Texas's best lawmen. He'd have let that inept posse catch him and gone down fighting, except he hadn't yet delivered enough carnage to satisfy his rage against the White man.

He sat under a live oak about fifty yards from the road and gnawed on some venison jerky. His horse grazed lazily nearby. From his vantage point, he had a wide view of traffic. The target would have to be isolated. He didn't want to be having to endure another posse just yet. The jingle of harness and creaking of a wagon being driven across hard-baked ruts soon came to his ears. He readied the Winchester.

A buckboard soon came into sight. A man drove the rig with a woman beside him and a shotgun leaned against the seat beside them.

Bigcrow decided to change his modus operandi of bush-whacking victims. He chambered a round, as he stepped into the road ahead of the buckboard. "Halt!" It was one of the few White man words that he knew. He aimed the rifle menacingly toward the couple.

The sight of an armed Indian with angry eyes and warpaint barely concealing an ugly facial scar took the startled couple by surprise. The apparition before them reeked of evil. The man desperately tried to brake the rig while reaching for the shot-gun. He likely never felt the bullet blow his head apart in a spray of brain and bone. The woman let loose a blood-curdling scream and clambered over the side of the wagon. She'd gone barely twenty feet before Bigcrow was upon her. He might not have been a big man, but held a wiry sort of strength that made him far stronger than she. With a knife to her throat, he tore at her dress and was quick to have his way with her. Her struggles were met with Bigcrow's ever-increasing pressure behind the blade. Blood flowed from superficial cuts as he sat astride her, pinned her arms beneath his knees, and tortured her viciously as though driven by some demonic passion. He was filled with a hateful venom, injecting his victim as if to make reparation for the cultural poisoning of his people. It was not enough to violate her. She represented all the White women he'd come to hate for their condescending treatment hidden beneath feigned compassion. Ignoring her pleadings, he made ever-deeper slices into her flesh. Blood covered his hands and stained the ground. She had nearly lost consciousness when the Apache savage heard the distant sound of horses approaching. His gunshot had apparently been overheard. It was time to finish his work and be quick about it. He grabbed her hair and pulled her upright. With a guttural snarl and a single motion, Bigcrow took her scalp. He held it triumphantly aloft. No matter that it was the scalp of a weak and wounded woman. No matter that his ancestors would have wept at so cowardly a deed. As she was about to scream, he ended her pain by plunging his knife deep into her chest. He glanced at the dead driver slumped in the buckboard seat. There was no time for taking what remained of the man's scalp. He ran to his horse, leaped on its back, and galloped off before whoever was approaching would arrive.

He heard the shouts behind him as he drove his horse west toward the shell road that would take him southward across the bay toward Nuecestown. He reckoned that the grisly killing of the couple might finally get some serious lawmen on his trail. It was time to find peace with his troubled mind. Peace in death.

Sheriff Brad Tyler was not a happy lawman. He waved the telegram in front of his face as much from exasperation at the seemingly endless lawlessness as relief from the damp heat. The vigilante was still roaming the region, Big Bill Riordan had been disposed of thanks to that wet-behind-the-ears Texas Ranger, and political pots were boiling to establish a civilized society by fair means or foul. Now, a rogue Apache was on the loose. The telegram from the sheriff up north in Victoria said the murderous savage was last seen heading south.

Tyler wasn't getting any younger. Stephen Powers and Archer Parr were driving him nuts with demands ranging from serving summonses to evicting homesteaders, all while delivering justice. Through it all, his top priority was simply staying alive. A rogue Apache? He'd be right pleased to let the Texas Rangers handle it. He was confident Hughes would tell Texas Ranger Dunn to lay off the Bar A matter. It made Tyler uncomfortable. In fact, he felt just a tad soiled.

A wall of humidity hit him as he stood. He'd already begun making plans upon retirement to head north, perhaps to Wyoming and raise horses and beeves. It would be a welcome relief from the Texas heat, both the weather and the lawless culture. He headed to the post office to get a telegram off to Captain Hughes before Wells and Parr could climb all over him about the Apache renegade.

As the night sky laid its blanket of stars across the landscape, I sat back easy-like in my favorite spot on the gallery spanning the front of the big house. Cassie nestled beside me on the bench. My arm curved around her shoulders offered both warmth from the evening chill and the sense of security she'd been missing.

I hadn't been able to hide my wound from Cassie. In fact, my wincing reaction to her initial welcoming hug had quickly let that cat out of the bag. Telling her that it was from Riordan was a sort of bent truth. That was a stretch, considering that I'd received the wound from the outlaw by way of an errant bullet fired by Cassie's grandfather that had ricocheted off the outlaw's manacles. Cassie's initial reaction to the wound had surprised me. She insisted on tending to it right away, though I suspected she wanted to see for herself just how serious it was. Once she had gently applied a fresh dressing to the nearly healed wound, two weeks of bottled-up passions had taken over.

I reckoned I'd dodged a bullet of sorts. The wound had been a wake-up call. I had already begun to have my own doubts as to his lawman role, and those qualms mixed with deep anxieties had fully captured my thoughts. My relaxed appearance as I sat beside Cassie belied my concerns.

Cassie had poured each of us a glass of wine, fruits from the vineyard we'd planted a couple of years back. The first crop had been terrible owing to drought, but we managed to ferment enough to bottle a passing fair, if not bitter vintage. After what seemed like a forever of silence punctuated by an occasional owl hoot or coyote howl, she looked up and studied my contemplative expression. She wondered what could be causing the faraway look in my eyes. "Are you going to share?"

"I'm thinking I might prefer tangling with cattle rather than lawbreakers, sweetheart."

Cassie pulled back. "Say, what?" My surprise revelation brought her both hope and concern. I always had exhibited an abiding desire to ensure justice, to strive to ensure a safe world free of manmade evils. It was in my blood, wasn't it?

"Is it worth it, sweetheart? Is it worth the risk?" I sighed as though longing for something elusive, like an answer.

Cassie wasn't sure what to think of my quandary. She'd been horrified at the ugly, still-healing scar in my side. Had it been a couple of inches...well, she'd have been a widow, a pregnant widow. "It's not for me to say, Lucas." She forced herself to play the dutiful supportive role of a lawman's spouse.

"I think we can yet squeeze a living from the ranch," I ventured.

"What about the vigilante? Do you feel led to finish the job?"

I stroked my chin. I wasn't one to not finish a job.

Cassie smiled, as she recalled my father similarly stroking his mustache when mired in deep thought.

"The vigilante? It's a tough case, Cassie," I finally blurted. I yearned to share that I was increasingly certain that the vigilante was her very own beloved grandfather. "There's not much hard evidence. Could be most anybody with an 1895 Winchester. Hunting him holds a lot of risk." I locked eyes with her to be sure she was grasping the weightiness of the task. "I'd have to catch him in the act. He mostly works at night, making it especially tricky. My dad always said evil folks prefer darkness to hide their sins, and murder headed his list of sins." I reflected a moment on my dad's advice. On top of my concern with the vigilante, I had yet to deal with the murder I'd uncovered on the ride back from Brownsville and its apparent connection with the Bar A. I'd keep that under wraps for now.

"You up to it?" she asked.

"I likely am." I didn't sound especially confident. "Like I said, sweetheart, hunting anything in darkness can be a treacherous business. I'm of a mind that the only way to catch this bushwhacker is to trap him. I don't think kindly of me being the bait in the trap."

It was the first time I had so fully expressed to Cassie my fears, concerns, and frustrations over the assignment. Had she also known what roiled around in my thoughts as to her beloved grandfather, she likely would have found deep distress added to her own anxieties. "I...I had no idea, Lucas." She knew I was no coward and that I held a strong aversion to injustice, so this doubt lingering in her lawman husband's mind weighed especially heavy upon her. She turned thoughtfully from my gaze and took a sip of wine. She stood pensively, leaned into the gallery railing, and stared out into the far reaches of the ranch. "I'll support whatever you decide, Lucas, come what may."

"What of our child? Does he or she support me putting our future in such peril?"

Cassie gently stroked her belly. She'd be giving birth in a couple of months. She turned to me and smiled. "Our child would surely be proud to know that his or her father was a brave lawman delivering justice." With that, she felt a kick from deep inside. She took my hand and placed it on her stomach. "Feel that?"

Startled by the kick, I pulled back my hand. I smiled and looked up at her loving eyes. "Seems the vote is in. Guess I've got a vigilante to catch."

We both laughed, though Cassie felt a momentary pang of doubt as to the assurances of support she'd given me. Widowhood was a nonstarter. A long kiss sealed my decision.

Bode McCully took a slow, savoring sip of beer. They eased back from the bar to take in the familiar aroma of sawdust, urine, sweat, and booze that lingered in the very floorboards of Taberna Bandana. He once again glanced over the now quite worn and torn yellow wanted poster. Jim Bigcrow, by now, must have every bounty hunter and lawman in the territory on his trail. It was obvious to the retired Texas Ranger that the Apache harbored a death wish. He'd heard about desperate folks giving up hope and wreaking violence with the aim of dying at the hands of the law. Bigcrow was fitting the pattern.

Now, it had become a question of how he would beat out all those hunters hopeful of cashing in on the reward. Bigcrow was playing a game, lingering to life, luring his pursuers along until he decided it was time to die. Bode reckoned the Apache shouldn't be that hard to find but was just crafty enough to delay the inevitable. It would test Bode's own tracking skills. He quaffed the rest of his beer and threw a couple of coins on the bar as he headed out. Where to begin? He had an inkling that upon escaping from his latest killings south of Victoria and purportedly headed west, the Apache renegade would likely avail himself of the shell road across Nueces Bay. The road was actually a reef that had been formed by accumulated oyster shells and was located just barely beneath the water's surface. It served for centuries as a secret route for local tribes.

He stepped from the saloon and scanned the street in both directions. It was a lawman thing. Not much to see other than a smattering of folks tending to daily chores, loading or unloading goods from wagons, and avoiding occasional mud puddles. Satisfied, he walked over to his horse and paused. He was certain that I was on to him. Was he pushing his luck, my hand? He patted the polished stock of the 1895 Winchester rifle nestled in the scabbard hanging from his saddle horn. He leaned his head against the saddle for a moment, then resolutely pulled back, checked that the cinch was tight, and mounted. He shook off the lingering uncertainty. Justice must prevail. The hunt was on.

Bode was unaware of the eyes watching him from the alley across from Taberna Bandana. The old lawman had missed one interloper. Buffalo Watts had felt the same suspicions as me ever since the Carlos Diaz incident. The old army scout and trapper had kept an eye on Bode McCully ever since, though he'd lost him for a couple of weeks. When he learned of the Big Bill Riordan matter, he intuitively held doubts as to Bode's role. He was determined not to lose the old Ranger again. He calculated that an hour's head start would likely allow plenty of space between hunter and prey. He assumed that Sheriff Tyler had been alerted as to Jim Bigcrow, but wondered whether the Texas Rangers would assign me to the case.

"Damn!" What else was there for a Texas Ranger Captain hundreds of miles from a problem to say? Hughes stared at the telegram. His lawman intuition told him that Tyler wanted no part of the Bigcrow manhunt. There wasn't much he could do about it from Brownsville. He'd relied on me for the Diaz matter and again in bringing Riordan to justice. Given the reward Tyler mentioned, every bounty hunter in Texas would likely be converging on the region around Corpus Christi. Innocent folks might be hurt or worse by some greedy, loose-triggered, wannabe hero.

He sighed heavily as he realized it was likely that Jim Wells would be on his doorstep soon enough with urgent pleadings to dispose of the rogue savage. The Ranger captain had no choice. He slammed his fist on the desk. "Damn!" he uttered again as he began to scribble a message to me. There was an irony to it all in a sense, as he'd hoped I could finally join up with the Texas Ranger company in Brownsville. The Border Boss was just a tad frustrated, but in a good way. It was reassuring that he could rely on me to represent the Rangers even though separated by a couple of hundred miles.

Still lingering in his brain were thoughts as to the murder connected with the Bar A and wondering why Archie Parr and his ilk were advising to keep hands off.

★★

Cassie happened to have stepped out onto the gallery to shake breakfast crumbs from the tablecloth so was first to hear hoof-beats approaching up the trail to the big house. Visitors these days generally posed no danger, but caution was always in order. She ducked inside and alerted me as I was just savoring the last drops of the morning brew. "Rider approaching, Lucas."

I stuffed one of my 38 caliber Colt revolvers into my waist-band and strode out onto the gallery to investigate. I didn't have to wait long, and the revolver would be unnecessary. "¿Carlos, qué pasa?"

Carlos was a hired clerk at the Nuecestown general store and doubled as assistant to the postmaster who owned the store and handled telegraph duties. It was typical of most small towns, as folks held multiple duties to make a living. He rode up to within arm's reach of me. "Good morning, Mr. Dunn. I bring an important telegram." He stood in his saddle and stretched to hand the message to me.

Cassie slipped in behind me. "*Buenos días, Carlos.*"

"My pleasure, Mrs. Dunn." He sat expectantly in his saddle.

I had begun to open the telegram when I realized Carlos was still there. I fished a coin from my pocket and began to hand it to the courier.

"Oh, no, Mr. Dunn. I must wait for an answer."

I disconcertedly unfolded the telegram and began reading. I absorbed the contents for a moment before handing it to Cassie then turned to Carlos. "Send a message to Captain Hughes that says I will take care of the problem."

Carlos responded with a nod and smile before galloping off.

I turned to Cassie. "Guess getting the vigilante isn't enough."

As we turned to go back inside, a voice stopped them.

Buffalo Watts appeared as if from thin air. He'd watched the courier ride off and observed my reaction. "That's how it began with yer dad, Junior. First, one outlaw, then another. Seems there's no way to quit. Wagh!" He let his all-too-prescient words sink in. Was that to be my fate? Would my life mirror that of my legendary father, leaving his wife alone far too often to hunt lawbreakers while she managed a ranch and raised ten children?

"Buffalo, you up for coffee?"

Cassie had already moved inside and grabbed the coffee pot.

"Thanks, but I'll pass on yer fine coffee for now." Watts

looked around sort of furtively. "Let's mosey on down to the barn an' pow-wow a bit." He hitched his horse to the rail and headed toward the barn.

I poked his head inside. "Gonna do some man talk, sweetheart. Be back shortly." I followed Watts. Man talk would be an understatement.

Watts squatted with his back against a stall and picked up a piece of straw that he waved about. His fringed buckskin leggings and blue cotton shirt might have been enough to peg him as a mountain man throwback, but the well-worn wide-brimmed hat, Bowie knife in its beaded scabbard, and the old 1861 Army Colt revolver confirmed that he was every bit the tough hombre he appeared to be. "Grab some straw, Junior." He pointed to the hay bale across from him.

I sat. My curiosity was fully aroused.

"Recall Bode McCully's wild-hair show with Carlos Diaz at Los Olmos Creek?"

I nodded.

"Was in Alice yesterday and spotted him starin' with lovesick eyes mostly all day at the poster for Jim Bigcrow."

I pretty much guessed what was coming next.

"He rode out armed to the teeth with that wild-hair expression across his face like he had at Los Olmos."

"Every bounty hunter within a day's ride from here and then some, will be slobbering to grab the reward for hunting down Bigcrow," I said matter-of-factly. "Dang, but they'll even kill the man that gets that Apache just to cash in."

"Figured yuh oughta know, Junior." Watts waved the piece of straw as he spoke. "I expect that telegram is tellin' yuh to bring the renegade Apache to justice." He pointed the straw at me. "Recall how when we hunted deer with yer brothers and dad. Safety was top priority. We always kept line of sight. Didn't want no accidents." He locked eyes with me. "Well, yuh an' I both know...and Bode should...that there's bound to be accidents out there hunting down that fool Injun'." He stood and looked up at the house. Cassie was standing at the gallery railing sipping coffee and likely curious at what he and I were talking about. "And keep in mind, they won't all be accidents. Wagh!"

I knew from years past with Watts that he never opined on anything that he hadn't given plenty of thought to. Likely owing to his many years in the mountains ranging from Wyoming to New Mexico, Watts was known to not mince words. As the saying went, he didn't use up all his kindling to start a fire. "What are you suggesting?" I arose from the hay bale and stood beside Watts.

Watts turned to face me. "Lay back. No point in gettin' yerself killed." He looked back up at Cassie. "Don't go makin' her a widah, son."

"But..." I protested.

"No buts, Junior. Get it into yer hide that it's about to become unfit for us out there until this Bigcrow renegade is disposed of. Damned Apache has a death wish for sure, but it best not be by yer bullets. Yuh don't want to be fendin' off bounty hunters, much less dealing with Bode McCully."

Concern spread over my face. "Sort of feel obliged to look out for him."

"He's a big boy, Junior. Bode's older but not necessarily so wise as he once was."

"Do you know?"

Watts smiled. "Know he's the vigilante?" I watched the piece of straw fall to the ground. "Pretty much."

"What are you going to do?"

"Same as you. Gonna hang back and watch the thing unfold." Watts chuckled. "I'd like to think the hunt will be like a pack of wolves chasin' down deer. Thing is, these wolves don't hunt in a pack. They'll be sneaky like mountain lions, lookin' out fer themselves."

I sighed resignedly. "Care for company?"

"Thought you'd never ask. Better enjoy some goodbyes

with Cassie there. I'll be waitin' at the gate." He hesitated. "Shouldn't be hard to pick up Bode's trail."

I headed back to the house. Deep within lingered thoughts of the possibility of dealing with the Apache and the vigilante simultaneously.

Watts called out as he trailed behind to retrieve his horse. "Have Cassie pack some of that cornbread, if it's not too much trouble. We're gonna be a day or two out there. Don't reckon it'll take all that long."

Archie Parr kicked back from his desk. Life sure could get ugly. How much would folks tolerate before insisting on justice? He pivoted in his chair and gazed from his office window. He reflected on the modest ranch he owned near Benavides, where he was learning about irrigation farming. Water was part and parcel to his life. There was more land to be had, but patience wasn't his forte. Serving as a county judge sort of helped his ambitions along. His momentary idle wasn't to endure. Heavy footsteps echoed from the hallway outside his office. Parr instinctively checked for his revolver, even though he'd never used it on a human. It offered perceived security.

His door was kicked open with a crash that seemed to shake the building's foundation. "Damn it, Archer Parr! That's the last straw! You promised there'd be no killin'!"

Parr fought to remain calm. Cal Pardoe was a burly man with a scruffy red beard and shoulders wider than a Hereford bull. "Killing?" responded Parr as calmly as possible. But it was with a certain intensity, like a mountain lion stalking its prey. He knew Pardoe had lost his wife but two years before to yellow fever. Now, with the death of his daughter, the man had every reason to be distraught.

"You don't know?! My daughter is murdered by those

bastards, and you don't know?! Or don't care?!" Pardoe was livid. His Bar A ranch adjoined Parr's spread. "Not enough to cut my barb' wire and kill my beeves, but they murder my flesh and blood!"

Parr's security hand, Johnnie, poked his head in. "Everything all right, boss?"

"At ease, Johnnie. Close the door, if you would." He calculated that it might calm Pardoe a little not to worry about Johnnie barging in.

Pardoe's anger still breathed white hot.

Parr persisted in maintaining a calm outward demeanor. "We'll look into it, Cal. I'm truly sorry for your loss." Parr boiled inside that his hired hands had carried the pseudo-range war too far by murdering his neighbor's daughter. "Amanda was such a sweet young lady." Inside, he reminded himself that he was happily married to his Elizabeth and shouldn't have been surprised that Amanda spurned his advances. She was a very attractive young lady, and he held hopes of eventually winning her to his bed. The men he'd hired had been sloppy, and he was determined that they'd pay a price. He stood, adjusted his tie, and tugged at his vest so as to project an air of calm power over the situation. "I don't blame you for being angry, Cal. I'll get the law on it right away." He tried to read Pardoe's body posture. The man had vented his rage and seemed to be calming down.

"Where's your precious sheriff, Archie?" Pardoe grumbled. He still seethed beneath a feigned calm. Like pretty much everyone else, he was sure Sheriff Tyler was on Parr's payroll.

Parr decided to keep the desk between him and Pardoe. He glanced at the drawer that held his Colt Peacemaker. With confidence born of power and a loaded gun in his desk, he responded as reassuringly as possible. "You aren't solving anything here today, Cal. Again, I'm sorry. I promise that we'll get the men who took your daughter's life."

Pardoe's furrowed eyebrows were evidence enough that he

wasn't mollified by Parr's promise. His right hand rested on the butt of the gun in his holster, though he made no motion to grip the weapon.

Parr simply looked as calm and compassionately as possible at the man. The silence had become deafening.

Pardoe finally had enough. "Damn!" He shook his fist, turned, and stomped away up the hall.

Archer Parr returned to his seat and smiled. He calculated that he'd yet have the Bar A under his thumb.

Bode slowly trod the trail along the south bank of the Nueces River. He'd dismounted a ways back. He was all eyes and ears, as he sought sign of Jim Bigcrow. He was likely one of the few men on the Apache's trail that knew of the shell road and expected the savage to follow the southern shore of Nueces Bay. If he were to encounter Bigcrow, it would likely be close quarters where his Winchester rifle wouldn't serve him so well. Thus, he kept his revolver close at hand. Very close at hand.

A puff of smoke off toward the river caught his attention. Could it be a bounty hunter? Might it be the Apache himself? Checking it out seemed appropriate, but he stopped abruptly. He sensed that he was being watched, and it wasn't from the smoke up ahead. Bode decided to backtrack before investigating the smoke. He much preferred being the hunter rather than the hunted.

Bode began to stealthily walk back from whence he'd come. All was quiet save for the sound of the swirling waters of the river and an occasional bullfrog. He'd backtracked about a hundred yards. He stopped and searched for any sign, anything that might reveal a human presence. An eerie feeling coursed through him. He'd expected by now to have run into men hunting for Bigcrow. The pursuit of the wanted Apache was more about greed than any sense of justice. Even the lingering prejudice against the Redman wasn't at issue. Despite even this small corner of the Nueces Strip offering a vast landscape in which to hide, he instinctively knew there should be some sign. Instead, there remained an unearthly quiet. It was just a tad unnerving, even for a man with Bode's experience.

He studied the area again and cupped his ears as if to better hear any threat. Nothing. He turned his attention back to the smoke.

I nudged Watts and rolled my eyes. "Close," he mouthed. The pecan tree along the southern bank of the Nueces River had offered barely sufficient shelter from Bode's practiced surveillance. Had he just gone a few yards further, they'd surely have been discovered. We waited for the retired Ranger to nearly disappear from our sight before resuming the shadowing of his trail. We used sign from now on, as our voices would tend to carry.

Watts stopped and signaled to me to be especially wary, as a suspicious Bode might be extra cautious and lie in ambush to catch whoever might be following him.

Soon enough, Watts's well-placed wariness proved prescient.

Despite the blued matte finish of Bode's rifle barrel, there was just enough polish to the rifle's receiver to catch a shard of sunlight.

Watts and I dropped into the tall grass. Had we been seen? Seconds ticked by. We heard a feint noise ahead, and I doffed my hat and peeked above the grass. I could see Bode beginning to resume his hunt for Bigcrow. Bode swiped his hand across his brow as a gesture of relief.

THIRTEEN
DEATH WISH

NAKED, save for a breechcloth, Bigcrow sat cross-legged on his blanket. A faint column of smoke still swirled skyward from what remained of his small campfire. He stared into the embers, then lifted his chin skyward and closed his eyes. His communion with the Great Spirit had assured him that this was to be the day his dreams had brought him to. His anger would be released to the spirit world, and he'd be forever at peace. With eyes closed and forearms resting on his knees, he breathed in the morning air and felt the sun's rays paint their warmth across his face. He'd been awake the entire night, trancelike, unmoving. He'd made no attempt to conceal himself, as he sat in the open mere yards from a live oak that could have sheltered him.

The Apache had summoned dreamlike images from his past. From his time with the great chief Geronimo to the here and now, his way of life had been constantly threatened by the White man. Rage, vengeance, indignation, and bitterness swirled within him, belying his trancelike state of the moment. Death would be his release from the pain.

"What could the sonofabitch be thinking?" inaudibly escaped Bode's lips. He was incredulous. After having backtracked and then waited to be certain no one was following him, the retired Ranger had set his sights on the smoke sign ahead. He'd slowly, silently, crawled with his rifle to within fifty yards of his prey. Halting at a slightly raised vantage point, he parted the grasses to get a better view of his quarry. There was no doubt as to whom it was. But Bigcrow simply sat there, apparently meditating. Bode reckoned the murderous renegade was communicating with his spirit world, if the savage had one. It was as though...then, it hit him. The Apache wanted to die. He was waiting to be killed. Bode figured to oblige, to send Bigcrow to whatever spirit world he sought.

He silently slid the Winchester up to firing position. One shot should do it. The Apache's back was to him. Bode aimed a few inches below Bigcrow's neck, right about where the long swirls of the savage's black hair ended. The renegade's skin glistened with sweat in the dampness of the morning. Bode could see his chest expand and contract with each breath. One more breath would be his last. The government's reward would be a small price to pay for Bode's providing this service to the good citizens of Texas.

Jim Bigcrow heard the metallic clicking of a round chambered into a rifle. He kept his eyes closed. It would be the last sound he would hear.

Bode McCully squeezed the trigger. The bullet flew true, burrowing into the Apache's back and exploded out his chest.

A second shot rang out just as Bode started to rise to confirm his kill. A bullet whizzed by his head. A second blast sent a dose of lead clean through his hat. He dove face first, eating Nueces Strip dirt. Another shot from beyond where the first two had come bellowed its deadly message into the morning air. Startled birds squawked and flew off helter-skelter. It was a big gun, likely a Sharps buffalo gun from the sound of it. There was a pained grunt from behind a stand of live oak not twenty yards from Bode's position.

Silence.

"Bode? You all right?" My voice was all-too-familiar.

Another boom roared from the Sharps.

A desperate voice sounded off in the distance, "Oh my God, I'm kilt!"

More silence.

I dropped to one knee and looked around to be sure the coast was clear before striding toward Bode. I finally stood over the disheveled former Ranger. "Damn, Mr. McCully! You're a mess." I fought off the urge to smile.

Bode sat up. He was covered with dirt and smeared with horse droppings thanks to his life-saving dive.

I extended my hand and helped him stand. I looked at Bode grim-lipped. "Thought you were done with this, Bode," I commented ironically. The situation had taken a quite serious turn.

Buffalo Watts emerged upon the scene with his Sharps rifle cradled under his arm and two horses in tow. "Bagged two, Junior." He looked askance at Bode. His broad grin was accentuated by the deep crevices that years in the Rocky Mountain weather had carved into his face. The grin belied his seriousness.

"Much obliged, Buffalo." Not said was having saved Bode's life. I reached down and rolled Bigcrow onto his back. The single shot from Bode's Winchester had destroyed the Apache's heart, though I reflected that the savage's life had likely been lost years back. I turned to Bode. "Guess Bigcrow got his wish," I offered solemnly.

Bode found himself shaking. He tried to control it but couldn't, as he realized how foolish he'd been, how close he'd come to meeting his Maker. He finally found his voice. "Th... thanks, Junior. How did y'all find me?"

Watts shook his head. "I've hunted bull moose that left less trail, McCully."

"We figured what you were up to right easy," I added.

"Does Cassie know?"

My eyes bored into Bode's very soul. "She's going learn about it if you do this one more time, Mr. McCully. This ends it. Am I clear?"

"How you going to explain it to Captain Hughes?" Bode was getting his thoughts together, as he finished dusting himself off.

I was ahead of him. "Hughes has other problems to deal with. Besides, if there are no more vigilante killings, that problem will disappear."

Bode shuffled his feet as he sought to phrase his next question. "But if I get the reward, they'll know. What about that?"

I turned to Watts. "Buffalo, haven't you been looking to improve that cabin of yours up in yonder hills?"

Watts scratched his head. "Now that yuh mention it."

Bode's draw dropped. "Wait a cotton-pickin' minute..."

I cut him off. "One word to Cassie, and her heart will be broken."

Bode shook his head more in disappointment than contrition. He'd more than subverted the law, he'd eviscerated it. The thought of the slow-moving wheels of justice ever stood as an abomination to him. Maybe, if he explained to Cassie...but he had no choice. "I surrender, Junior. No more killing."

"Let's get out of here afore we attract more hunters," interjected Watts. "The gunfire will bring 'em all runnin'." There was no point in tempting fate any further.

As we hoisted Bigcrow's blanket-wrapped body over the Apache's own pony, Bode took a deep breath and delivered what was big on his mind. "How'd you figure I was the vigilante?"

I paused my tying of the body into place. "I'll give you

credit. The evidence was pretty much what they call circumstantial. There are quite a few 1895 Winchesters around here, so that didn't narrow my suspicions much. But a hunch crept into my thinking a couple months back in Alice, when Trey Bolton was ambushed. The busted heel of your boot was an early clue. The vigilante left footprints with a busted boot heel behind."

Bode shook his head. "How sloppy of me." He paused. "But that wasn't much to go on."

"Your obsessive action in killing Carlos Diaz and then Big Bill Riordan, along with your expressed rationale of saving the government the time and expense of trials, began to bring the pieces of the puzzle together." I ruefully shook my head. Obsessive was indeed the operative word. I resumed tightening the knots holding Bigcrow's body over the horse's back. "It didn't take much to figure you'd be chasing after this renegade."

"So, you're not telling Captain Hughes...or Cassie?"

"Can you stop?"

Bode sighed deeply. "I'll try."

Watts snickered. "Should I keep an eye on him, Junior?" He opened one eye wide and stared hard on Bode.

Bode flushed. "Don't you dare, you mangy frontier piece of horse..."

I put a finger to my lips. "That'll be enough." I mounted Tornado. "Let's get to Corpus Christi and collect Buffalo's reward."

Bode snorted and mounted up. "I'm goin' home. Y'all don't need me none in Corpus." He turned his horse, but pulled up. He turned to me and took a big swallow of pride. "Thanks for keeping this under wraps. You're a hell of a good Texas Ranger, son."

"You going to make an offer to Cal Pardoe?"

Archie Parr leaned back in his chair. "I think the writing is on the wall, Johnnie. Hell, he ought to be coming to me begging to buy his spread."

"What about his daughter?"

"Unfortunate. She was collateral damage, as they say. She shouldn't have poked her nose into the rustling in the first place." Parr chuckled diabolically. "Hell of a loss, damn it. She had a sweet body that was to die for." It hadn't been for a lack of pursuing that body that Parr regretted her loss.

"You think Tyler or Hughes gonna do anything, Mr. Parr?"

Parr guffawed. "You know where Tyler gets his orders. As to the good Texas Ranger Captain Hughes, he gets his orders from Austin. Nobody there is going to tell him to lay a finger on any local matter."

"What about Junior Dunn?"

"He won't do anything on his own. I judge him as a by-the-book lawman. He's capable enough, but he's got other things on his plate like that renegade Apache and the vigilante. Plus his wife is pregnant. That can change a man's perspective."

Johnnie thought a moment. "Didn't stop his father," he reminded Parr.

"Not of quite the same cloth, Johnnie." Parr was quick to toss off the possibility.

"I wouldn't be too sure," said Johnnie.

"If it'll make you feel better, keep an eye on the Ranger. I've got other game to hunt." Parr lit up a cigar to close the door on the conversation. He watched Johnnie walk out and close the door behind him. Parr smiled and pulled deeply on the cigar. He blew a smoke ring.

FOURTEEN
RANGE WAR IMPLODES

THE TELEGRAM from Captain Hughes told me to stay clear of the range war for now and to report as soon as possible to the company in Brownsville. With Cassie ever nearer to giving birth to our first child, Brownsville wasn't exactly in my immediate plans. Duty called but something political or worse was at play with the Bar A business. I hoped the vigilante business was over. It was a right big hope, almost like sitting in front of an angry rattler and fancying that it might not strike.

I decided that a ride out onto the rolling hills of Heaven's Gate Ranch might shake some mental cobwebs loose. I needed time to think this all out. Given the power associated with land ownership and the associated political wrangling, I reckoned that Archer Parr, Jim Wells, and Stephen Powers surely had something to do with this range war that I was told to ignore.

The Dunn ranch had grown quite a bit since the few hundred acres me and Cassie were given as a wedding present. While my folks were overseeing a hundred thousand or so acres to the west as partners with Edward Thorpe, Cassie and I had managed to acquire about 20,000 acres ourselves. In fact, if my theory about the underbelly of the brooding range war was right, I figured that Archer Parr should eventually come knocking.

About two miles from the big house, I pulled up atop a grassy knoll. Three riders were headed west at a leisurely trot. The first question that came to mind was what were they doing on my land? The second was what fence had they cut? Last but hardly least was where were they heading in such an all-fired hurry? Naturally, I had to find out.

I knew the ranch like the backside of my hand, so it didn't require any special effort from Tornado to arrive at an arroyo ahead of where the trio of strangers would have to pass. I pinned on my Texas Ranger badge, held my rifle across the pommel, and guardedly awaited their arrival.

They were noisy travelers. The sound of their voices, hoofbeats, jingling of spurs, and startled birds hailed their arrival. Upon seeing me, they pulled up. They instinctively made a move for their sidearms.

"Don't y'all be touching those guns, gentlemen."

They paused at the commanding sound of my voice.

"I'm Texas Ranger, Lucas Dunn. You raise your hands easy-like to where I can see them."

The rider in front, the largest and most heavily armed of the three, spoke up. "What cause you got fer stoppin' us, Ranger?"

"I'll be asking the questions. You answer. Understand?" I chambered a round in my rifle as punctuation.

The men glanced furtively at each other. It was three against one. Was taking me on worth a try?

"I know what you're thinking." I turned Tornado such that the muzzle of my rifle was pointed toward the men. "You have to ask yourselves how many of you I'd shoot before you got me? Is it a good day for you to die?"

The men nodded. Their hands remained at shoulder level.

"Now, what were you doing on this ranch?"

"Passing through. What's it to you, Ranger?"

"Passing through to where?"

The lead man snickered as he challenged me. "None of yer business."

"Trust me, gentlemen, it's very much my business. I'm not sure I should arrest you or shoot you for trespassing." I paused for effect. "Trespassing on my land."

The men looked at each other concernedly. "Your land?" one of the men said.

"Did you cut my fence?"

The big man knew that fence cutting for trespass was a felony. He squirmed a bit in his saddle. "Not exactly. The fence was down, and we jumped our horses across." He looked to his companions for corroboration. They nodded.

"I can still take you in for trespassing. Sheriff Tyler keeps a right nice jail." I was beginning to enjoy the situation, but was curious as to what business these men had. I laid a hard gaze upon the big man. "What's your name?"

"Plug, Plug Nichols."

I had the urge to laugh. I wanted to ask the man's real name not a description of the plug nag he rode. "You still haven't told me where y'all are headed?" The implication was that they could avoid arrest by revealing their destination.

Plug sighed. "Alice. We're headed to Alice."

"Business there?"

"Hiring on as ranch hands."

I had already come to the conclusion that this trio was more into gunplay than ranching. They featured plenty of fire-power, and there was nothing in their rigs to give even the slightest hint of wrangling beeves. "Archer Parr's place by any chance?"

A hint of guilt begrudgingly swept across the men's faces. "Seems like," offered Plug. "Is that a problem?"

I shook my head resignedly. It didn't seem worth the effort to arrest these men for trespass, and I'd gotten the answers I'd sought. "Tell you what I'm going to do, gentlemen. Since you've been cooperative, I'm not going to arrest you." I noted the relief revealed in the men's eyes. "We are going to take a little ride to the north boundary of my ranch, and I'm going to set y'all on the road to Alice."

By now, Plug had lost any combative urge he might have harbored. Combined with the heat of the day, the idea of being cooped up in the county jail held no attraction whatsoever. "Much obliged, Ranger Dunn," he responded contritely.

"Y'all ride on ahead gentle-like, and I'll follow along." As the trio turned northward, I shook my head. It was becoming crystal clear that Parr was involved in the range war, if not a direct cause of it. I had plenty of time to think on Parr's apparent treachery, as I rode slowly along, escorting the three gunmen off my ranch. Would it be appropriate to confront Parr? What trouble might that put me in for disobeying an order? I was already testing Captain Hughes's patience by not having immediately departed for Brownsville. What to do? I struggled with where my true duties lay.

They finally reached the road to Alice.

"When you gentlemen reach Mr. Parr's ranch, please send him my regards." I thought a moment. "And y'all be careful about crossing fences and short-cutting spreads without permission." I slid the rifle back in its scabbard. "Some folks may not be so accommodating as me." I delivered my warning but figured that last bit of advice would likely go unheeded.

The trio nodded and nudged their horses on their way.

Then, it hit me. I would ask Hughes for a furlough to take care of personal business. I figured the captain would be agreeable, given that my performance had been remarkable. I'd delayed Carlos Diaz, brought Big Bill Riordan to justice, and seen to the demise of Jim Bigcrow. It was also likely that I'd solved the vigilante problem. I reckoned to have earned a bit of a respite. I gave Tornado his head toward the big house. The big Appaloosa didn't need much urging.

I had ridden barely a mile when I happened upon a buck

with a fairly sizable set of antlers not a hundred yards ahead. A venison dinner sure seemed good about now. It would be a fitting reward for some successful sleuthing. I halted Tornado and eased the Winchester from its scabbard. Chambering a round, I took careful aim and squeezed the trigger. Tornado flinched slightly at the booming report, then moved toward the deer at my urging. I dismounted and began field-dressing the buck. Indeed, venison would be right tasty and the rack was worthy of mounting and gracing the wall in my office.

As I approached the house, I spotted a familiar horse hitched to the post out front. Perhaps, we'd be having a guest join for dinner.

Buffalo Watts sat on the gallery steps sporting a broad, partly toothless grin. "Howdy Ranger. I see yuh bagged that trophy buck." He let out a chuckle. "Passed him coming in here and figured to leave him fer yuh."

I rode up and dismounted. Seemed I had beaten Watts to the prey, and the old frontiersman wasn't about to admit it. "You old reprobate," I said with a knowing smile. "Come help me skin this beast so Cassie can cook us all a venison steak dinner."

"You think she's got some of yer mother's cornbread?" He returned the smile and followed me to the skinning rig alongside the barn.

Upon reaching the barn, I hung the deer carcass and tended to unsaddling Tornado. "What brings you to Heaven's Gate today, my friend?"

"After that business with Bigcrow, I headed west for 'bout a day. I liked yer idea of fixin' up my cabin up in the hills."

"But?"

"I got itchy." Itchy was Watts's euphemism for curious.

"I'm okay, if that's what's worrying you."

"When we was finishin' up with the Apache, I had a sense that something else was stuck in yer craw."

I shook my head. The old hunter knew me all too well.

"You gonna tell yer old friend?" Watts persisted.

"Range war. It's gotten hot between here and Los Olmos Creek."

"Klebergs involved?" Watts wondered whether the King Ranch folks might be stirring things up.

"Don't think so. It's not their style," I mused. "Shoot, they're already sitting on a million acres."

Watts smiled knowingly. "So, old Archie's at work," he ventured.

"Sure seems probable. I don't think he'd stoop to murder, though. Amanda Pardoe's been killed. Don't know by who, but I found what was left of her among a bunch of skinned beeves in the middle of nowhere. That means the Bar A is involved."

"Just ain't been the same 'round these parts since that barb' wire craze divvied up folks' ranches. Dang, takes me twice as long to git anywheres fer havin' to skirt 'round fences."

"Pretty much." I had nearly skinned the buck and was butchering the recently departed king of the herd for its meat.

Cassie appeared at the railing to the gallery. She'd seen me ride in with the deer. "Lucas, you fixing to have that buck ready to be cooked up for dinner or are you two going to lollygag all afternoon?" She laughed. "You expecting cornbread, I suppose, Mr. Watts," she added.

I laughed and waved. "Be up there in a minute, sweetheart."

"You've got it pretty good, Junior."

"Couldn't agree more. You were hitched once weren't you?" I didn't catch myself spouting the question in time. It had been a hurtful part of Watts's life. "Sorry, my friend."

"It's okay, Junior. Blue Feather lives in my soul every day."

"So, I'm thinking of paying a visit to Archer Parr," I said as I quickly shifted the conversation back to the range war.

"Gonna stir things up a tad," reflected Watts.

"Something akin to that." I picked up a couple of fresh-cut

venison steaks. "Let's get these to Cassie. My mouth's watering just thinking about chowing down. Figure the buck must have been four or five years old. Can't believe I never saw him before." I began to walk back to the big house with Watts alongside.

"Maybe I took a pass on him a few times," Watts guffawed.

I caught the message. "Maybe," I acknowledged.

Dining with Buffalo Watts had been entertaining. He seemed to never run out of tales of his days on the frontier, as his travels took him from the headwaters of the Yellowstone River to the Platte River and on to the beauty of the Brazos and Frio in Texas. He'd hunted, trapped, and taken on his share of warriors as allies and enemies, including Sioux, Pawnee, Kiowa, Comanche, Apache, and more. Watts was sought out whenever a serious hunt was afoot, and I had soaked up as much of Watt's know-how as I could. The frontiersman had a special sense for tracking down mountain lions and lynx but was drawn to the ocelots around South Texas. It was said that he'd wrestled a gator or two and stared down a few rattlers, but he only seemed to share those adventures with the Dunn children. Enough said. Buffalo Watts was as tough as they came even without embellished stories.

Watts had headed out after dinner, citing unspecified plans. I had a sense that he'd be hovering around like some sort of guardian angel. Cassie had developed a heart for the man and had a mind to find him a woman, not to replace Blue Feather but to draw out the softer side she felt lurked within the frontier-hardened man.

Dawn brought another day and—most importantly—a home-cooked breakfast. A heaping plate of eggs, bacon, and biscuits seemed to magically disappear about the time Cassie had turned to pour more coffee. "There'll be more where that came from, Lucas." She placed two cups of coffee on the table, eased herself behind me, and kissed the back of my neck. It nearly had the desired effect as I pulled her around into my lap and met her lips with far more ardor than she'd expected. "Why Lukas, darlin'," she cooed provocatively. She knew it was all a tease, as he was determined to leave early for Alice. She reluctantly arose from my lap with a loving caress of my cheek. "Do you think Mr. Parr will offer answers?"

"Won't know until I ask," I replied while still savoring the kiss of but a moment before.

"What about that vigilante?"

I prayed that she'd never ask whom I thought the vigilante was. Better to let the matter's resolution hang like an empty noose for now. "Haven't been any killings lately. Maybe he felt too much heat around here and high-tailed it."

Cassie didn't push for more. My answer seemed plausible for now.

She felt me sidle up behind her as she washed the breakfast dishes.

"Can I dry?"

"You know you're anxious to ride out, Lucas. Go ahead down to the barn and saddle up Tornado. I'll pull some things together here." She paused. "I hear some rain is expected. Better take your slicker."

I mustered a satisfied smile as I turned and headed for the barn. Cassie was already acting like a mother.

She was waiting for me, as I led the big Appaloosa up from the barn.

I mounted up and took the saddlebags she handed to me. "Be gone but a day or two, sweetheart." I leaned down and kissed Cassie, patted the saddlebags now packed with scrumptious homemade victuals, and put my heels gently to Tornado. I was determined to meet with Archie Parr, mano-a-mano. For me, killing cattle for no purpose was a terrible thing, but the killing of Amanda Pardoe was not something to be ignored. With any luck, I'd be in Alice by late afternoon.

I wondered about the three strangers who were headed for Parr's ranch. What, indeed, was Archer Parr up to?

A strange sort of air of foreboding lingered in the air at Taberna Bandana. Bode sensed it, but that didn't stop him from numbing his tonsils with another splash of rotgut whiskey. He gave half a thought to yielding to this intuitive feeling, but shrugged it off. He motioned to the barkeep to refill his glass. He surveilled the room. There were a couple of cowboys bellied up to the bar, slow-sipping beer while carrying on some sort of talk about barbed wire and water rights.

The barkeep ambled over and poured another shot of whiskey.

"Leave the bottle, if you would," requested Bode. He continued his scan of the salon patrons. Power-hungry Archer Parr sat at a back table nursing his whiskey and trademark cigar. That vision alone could incline a soul toward feelings of foreboding. There were six other tables, and four were occupied by a mix of cowboys and ne'er-do-wells most anyone would expect to see in the saloon this time of day. Card play was underway at two of the tables, and the casual observer might have noticed that the stakes were low. The heavier gambling action would take place in the evening. There was really nothing out of the ordinary. Oh, and Parr's gunman, Johnnie, stood at the saloon back door just behind his boss. Despite appearances, that premonition of foreboding still hung like a heavy fabric of darkness draped over the scene. Almost as a reflexive reaction to his surroundings, Bode's old lawman instincts kicked in, and he, as unobtrusively as possible, slid his Colt revolver from his holster and placed it gently within easy reach on the table beside the whiskey bottle. He glanced at the front door, at Parr, and back to the front door.

The drone of normal conversations, snap of cards laid on the table, occasional clink of bottle top against glass, and the ticking of the grandfather clock at the back wall, did nothing to dispel Bode's intuitive feeling that something wasn't quite right. He took another swig of whiskey and returned his gaze to the salon entrance.

I pulled up beside a saddled horse in front of the old boarding house that served as Archer Parr's place of business, dismounted, and threw Tornado's reins over the rail. I dusted myself off and looked up and down the street before stepping up onto the clapboard sidewalk that aimed to keep folks out of the mud during the rare times rain swept through the area. It hadn't rained in weeks. I noted the bronze plaque on the door engraved with Archer Parr, Patron. I knocked on the door.

There was no answer, so I knocked a second time before venturing to try the doorknob. The knob turned. Dang, but the office was unlocked. I had no idea that Parr was at this moment enjoying a taste of Texas whiskey and a smoke at Taberna Bandana.

I decided to wait for Parr to return from wherever he was or whatever he was doing. I stepped inside, grabbed a chair that was close at hand, and kicked back to relax from my ride.

Heavy boots pounding the wooden sidewalk outside Taberna Bandana caught the attention of Bode and a couple of other folks that had been enjoying a relaxing afternoon in the saloon. He observed the barkeep move his shotgun to within easy reach just beneath the bar top. He also heard the back door open, and his peripheral vision caught Archer Parr rising from his table. Imminent danger hung in the air. Odors of sweat, piss, leather, and booze suddenly seemed more pungent.

The batwing doors at the saloon entrance suddenly slammed open, and the entry was filled with the silhouette of a gun-toting monster of a man. Pardoe's first shotgun blast was sent in Parr's direction and just about obliterated the sconce on the wall behind him. The barkeep grabbed his shotgun from behind the bar and was swinging its muzzle toward Pardoe, only to be greeted by a second shotgun blast that hit him full-on, thrust him against the back wall, and sent his only shot harmlessly into the ceiling. The two cowboys at the bar dove for cover. Bode grabbed his gun and tried to discern a target through all the gunsmoke now filling the air. Parr had managed to dive out the back door. Other patrons had already hidden under upturned tables as best they could while looking to escape the madman with the shotgun.

In the momentary silence, Bode heard the shooter eject spent shells and slip two more rounds into the shotgun.

"Archer Parr! Where the hell did you go, you murdering, chicken-livered sonofabitch?! Damn your hide!"

Bode recognized the voice from years back. It was Cal Pardoe, and he was angrier than a stepped-on rattlesnake.

Pardoe's bulk turned toward the back door. "Where the hell did you go, Parr?! What hole did you slide into?!"

Johnnie stuck his face out from the doorjamb to have a look at the threat to his boss and cover Parr's backside as he dashed behind buildings to escape Pardoe's wrath.

Pardoe swung the shotgun around and leveled a blast at the doorjamb that sent wood splinters into the face that had appeared.

Johnnie fired his gun twice wildly as he fell into the room.

He dropped the guns as his hands clutched at his splinter-laden face and he screamed with pain. "My eyes! My eyes! I can't see!"

Pardoe showed no mercy. He aimed the shotgun at the wounded man. "You're part of him, you damn…" He pulled the trigger and sent Johnnie to Heaven's gate or to hell, as the case might have been. He inserted two more fresh shells.

Bode had ducked behind a table. He looked down the sights on the barrel of his Colt as it rested all-too-comfortably in his hand. He'd already pulled back the hammer. The gun was lined up on the middle of Pardoe's back. Bode needed only to squeeze the trigger. He paused. This was a serious quandary. If he were to shoot Pardoe, he'd be violating my order. He heard Pardoe shove two more fresh shells into the shotgun.

By this time, most everyone alive but Bode had hustled from Taverna Bandana. The barkeep still breathed but lay in a growing pool of blood behind the bar. The growing sounds from outside gave ready evidence that the town was riled up as to the situation. The deputy sheriff was miles away, so there was no lawman to turn to.

Pardoe turned and swept the business end of his shotgun around the saloon to ward off any threat as he backed toward the rear door. He stole a cautious glance out the door, but Parr was nowhere to be seen. He turned and took in the mayhem he'd wrought. His eyes came to rest on Bode, half hidden behind an upturned table.

"Drop the gun, Cal," Bode ordered with as strong a voice as he could muster in the acrid atmosphere. The muzzle of his Colt peeked out above the table and remained aimed dead on at Pardoe.

Pardoe looked in Bode's direction. "Bode? What the hell are you doin' here?"

"Just enjoying retirement, Cal," he said sarcastically but calmly. Remaining as eased back as possible was of paramount importance toward defusing Pardoe's outsized emotions. Just maybe, Pardoe might drop the shotgun.

Pardoe experienced a reality check despite his crazed condition. "You...you can't arrest me! You ain't the law no more." Pardoe stood waving the loaded shotgun threateningly toward Bode. Up to now, no one had returned fire.

Bode pressed the rancher. "No, but I can shoot your sorry ass from here to kingdom come. You done wrong, Cal, and you must pay. Now, drop the damned scattergun."

"I ain't finished, Bode," Pardoe hollered desperately, as he headed for the front door. It was clear that he was intent on chasing down Archer Parr come hell or high water. He fired one barrel in Bode's general direction and fled out the door.

Bode ducked in the nick of time, as splinters from the table rained over where his head had been.

Spectators outside the saloon fell back in near panic as a crazed Cal Pardoe bolted through the door and leaped from the wooden sidewalk. He'd left a thick blanket of gunsmoke behind, as he headed on a hell-bent run toward Parr's office.

Bode eased on over to where Johnnie lay in the sawdust and rolled him over. No question that the man was dead. He checked on the barkeep who was groaning in his misery. "I'll get you help," offered Bode. With the interior of the saloon apparently under control, he cautiously emerged from the Taberna Bandana with six-gun in hand. He gestured at the crowd of horrified but frozen-in-place onlookers. "Somebody fetch a doctor to tend to the barkeep." His old take charge Texas Ranger persona came through loud and clear. "Anybody got a gun? Where's the deputy? Damn it! Where the hell is the law?"

Panic-stricken faces stared back. Civilization had taken a toll on the good citizens of Alice, Texas. None were prepared to defend themselves.

Bode had no choice. He cussed again, as he chased after Pardoe as fast as his aging legs could carry him.

Upon hearing the gunfire, my first instinct was to head out to investigate. I had just taken a step toward the front door to check it out, when I heard footfalls from my rear. Archer Parr, on a dead run, crashed through the back door of his offices. He ignored me but went straight for his desk, pulled open a drawer, and drew out a Colt Peacemaker. It was at that moment that he realized he had company. "Dunn! Damnit, what the hell?!"

Just as I turned to face Parr, Pardoe tore the front door from its hinges as he charged in with shotgun held waist high.

Seeing both Parr and me pointing guns in his direction, the angry rancher hesitated. It would be a fateful pause, as his anger cooled upon the sudden realization of what he was facing. Aggression necessarily turned to self-protection. A ruckus behind threw him into near panic.

"Give it up, Cal!" Bode called out from behind.

Pardoe's eyes widened with dread, as he spun around to face the new threat and fired blindly at Bode. The blast caught the old timer full in the shoulder. Pardoe whipped back around to face me and Parr, squeezed the trigger, and was aghast to find he'd already fired his only remaining shell. There wasn't a moment to reload. "Damn you all to hell!" He screamed. He grabbed the shotgun by the barrel and began swinging it like a club as he headed full tilt at Parr.

Mine and Parr's guns fired near simultaneously, both hitting Pardoe in the belly at point-blank range.

The shotgun left Pardoe's grip, sailed past my head, and wiped out curios on top of a bookcase behind Parr. Pardoe gasped with pain as he clutched his belly, doubled over, and snarled at Parr. "You killed my daughter and now you killed me, you sonofabitch!" He looked pleadingly at me before falling face down onto the floor. Only his final rasping breaths broke the silent aftermath, as he died in a growing puddle of his own blood.

I hopped over Pardoe's body and kneeled at Bode's side. "What were you thinking?"

Parr saw his chance to escape the scene and headed toward the back door.

I would have none of it. "Where you going, Parr? Go fetch the doctor!"

Parr wasn't used to receiving orders, but he wasn't about to argue. "I...I'll fetch the doc," he assured me and stumbled outside.

Doc was emerging from the saloon with an expression on his face that said the barkeep hadn't made it. He turned to a bystander. "Fred, gather some help and fetch a couple of coffins from behind the general store. Don't know about next of kin of Parr's man, but I think the barkeep had a woman. See she gets word of his passing." He ruefully shook his head and began trudging toward his office.

Parr ran up to him. "Doc, we've got a wounded man down at my office."

"Another one?"

"Bode McCulley."

Lost in the chaotic aftermath and gaggle of onlookers at Taberna Bandana had been the sound of more gunfire up the street. The doc sighed and headed to Parr's offices.

Having alerted the doctor as I'd ordered, Parr headed for his horse and was quickly mounted and riding at a gallop for his ranch outside of town. He found himself finally experiencing relief at not having been killed or even wounded. With the intense situation with Pardoe having subsided, he became aware of the dampness in his trousers. He'd soiled himself during the gunplay.

"Take it easy, Bode. The doctor is on his way." I was doing my best to staunch the blood oozing from Bode's shoulder as the doctor arrived.

Bode struggled for breath. "Damn shotgun. Shoulda got him back at the saloon," Bode struggled to get the words out.

"What the hell is going on with this town?" Nonplussed by now, the doctor had greeted me with a rhetorical question. He ignored Pardoe's inert body and nudged me aside to better examine Bode. "Step aside, son, and let me assess the damage."

Bode was still struggling to breathe and was feeling ever fainter from loss of blood.

The doctor shook his head gravely and looked up at me. "If we're going to save him, we must get him to my office," entreated the doctor. "I've got a lot of work to do."

I lifted Bode and followed the doctor from Parr's offices and up the street. By now the crowd of spectators had dissipated, and most oglers barely gave notice to us moving swiftly up the street. The horror of three men killed in less than five minutes seemed to have had a numbing effect. It wasn't that violence was acceptable or that morality was at issue so much as the sheer terror of deadly mayhem had been wrought from time to time and left to ferment on the minds of the citizens of Alice, Texas. Paramount in the minds of the good citizens of Alice and most any town was the reality, if not the perception, of being civilized.

I feared the worst. I strove to tote Bode as gently as possible so as not to worsen the damage. We finally reached the doctor's office. I laid the old Ranger on the table in the doctor's office. The groans ceased as Bode passed out.

"Is he going to make it, Doc?"

"He's a tough old bird, Ranger Dunn," he responded while removing Bode's shirt. "I could sure use your help. I think half the town is hunting for coffins."

I was a bit torn as to my duty, given that I was apparently the only lawman in Alice at that moment. I mulled that over for but a moment. "I think the shooting's over. What can I do, Doc?"

★ ★

Parr rode straight to the barn. He was determined to get to the big house and change his pants before his wife or any hands might view his embarrassing condition. Like a controlled prairie burn that blew up out of control, his strategy to acquire additional land had gotten out of hand.

He let his mount loose in the adjoining corral and headed to the house. He figured to come back later to see to his horse. Getting cleaned up was his priority.

"Are you Mr. Parr?"

Parr froze. He'd gone perhaps a dozen steps from the barn. Even in the dim late afternoon light, the dark stain spread across his crotch was pretty obvious. He cursed at not having grabbed a saddle blanket to hide his predicament. "Who the hell wants to know?" he said irritably.

"Name's Plug Nichols, Mr. Parr. You have some sort of work for me and my two friends."

Parr was understandably impatient. "Gather at the bunkhouse over yonder. I'll be with you in a few minutes," he said while trying to hide a decided testiness at the situation.

The men hesitated.

"Go! Go!" He shooed them along and resumed his awkward shuffle toward the big house.

The men rode over to the bunkhouse with heads down to hide their faces. Their smirks were revealing to say the least. "You see the man's pants, Plug?"

Plug stifled a full-blown laugh. He glanced back at the retreating form of Parr to be sure they were out of earshot. "Guess he had an accident," he guffawed.

"Must have been in a fix. His hoss over yonder is lathered a bit."

The three men dismounted to await Parr's return.

Plug rolled a smoke. "Something ain't quite right, boys."

He lit up and looked over at the big house. "I'm of a mind that there's a stink in the air."

"Maybe we shoulda stopped in Alice, Plug."

"Expect we'll find out soon enough," Plug said, as he took a drag on his smoke. "He shouldn't take long to clean hisself up."

"Mighta shit hisself. Could take a tad longer."

"Now, now, boys, if we're gonna work fer the man, let's show some respect," Plug chided. He sat on a log bench along the front of the bunkhouse. "Might take a load off, boys." He was still fighting the urge to laugh, though his curiosity had been raised as to what had led to Parr's situation.

"Don't that Ranger fella stick in yer craw, Plug?"

Plug chewed on that for about a full minute. "Naw. We was crossin' his land."

"Bothered me," said one of Plug's companions named Jasper.

"He treated us fair," said Plug.

"If he gets crossways with us again, it'll be..."

"Don't go makin' threats you can't keep, Jasper."

Jasper stroked the butt of the Colt Peacemaker in his holster. "Just sayin'."

FIFTEEN
HEALING

THE MORNING SUN shot its first rays of the day through the cabin's only window. It caught Buffalo Watts full in the face as he lay on the hay-filled tick that served as a mattress. He swiveled to an upright position, shook his boots of any critters, and slipped them on. He eased on over to the stove and stoked the fire under the coffee pot. Reckoning it would be a few minutes before the coffee heated up, he decided to tend to his horse and mule.

Watts opened the heavy oak plank door and stopped cold at the sound of heavy breathing. He gazed down to his left from where the dulcet snores were emanating. "Damn!" he exploded with surprise.

One Arrow awakened with a start.

"How long yuh been sleepin' there, by damn?" Watts extended his hand to help the aging

Comanche chief to get up.

The warrior smiled sheepishly. "Moon still high. Not want to bother."

"Well, come have some coffee." Watts showed the Indian inside his humble cabin. He hadn't seen One Arrow since years earlier, when they had hunted with the Dunns. The chief had headed back to the reservation soon after the hunt to care for his people. "Thought yuh was still in Injun Territory...er, Oklahoma Territory."

One Arrow had shaken off the sleep cobwebs and taken his first sip of coffee. "Miss old friends," he said and smiled. "Good coffee."

Watts laughed. "Yeah, I mix mule piss in it."

The Comanche's mouthful of hot coffee exploded at Watts's claim. He looked incredulously at the frontiersman.

"Just jokin', my friend."

One Arrow scowled menacingly and made a slicing motion across his forehead.

Watts reared back, unsure as to the chief's humor.

"Just joking." One Arrow laughed. He had one-upped Watts's humor.

Watts smiled. "You hungry?"

The chief needed no further encouragement. "Travel many days. Wire make slow."

"Guess yuh ran into some barbed-wire fences. Dang things make it tough to get to places," pined Watts. "You're sure a long way from home."

"See plenty White man. White man never see One Arrow," he said as he pointed his finger proudly to his chest.

"Yep," said Watts. It touched a nerve, as it made him realize that the open frontier was disappearing. One Arrow's visit was serving to bring that home like the tips of the arrows the chief carried. "A hunt sounds like a great idea, Chief."

"We find Ghost-Who-Rides." One Arrow referred to my father by the name the Comanche had given him.

"We can try. He's been a tad gimpy from what I've heard. A longhorn nabbed him in the leg, and it ain't healin' right."

"Junior hunt."

"Junior's a Texas Ranger these days. Pretty danged good one, too," offered Watts. "I'm sure he'd hunt with us."

"Like father."

"Pretty much. I've helped when I could. Got his own ranch and married a sweetheart of a woman. They gonna have a child soon."

One Arrow offered a satisfied smile. "Is good. One Arrow have one woman now." He held up one finger for emphasis. "Sons good warriors. Have one woman and plenty horses." He caressed the cross hanging from the bone necklace that he still wore, a gift from my mother. He'd been raised in the Comanche spirit world, but leaned toward the Christian faith that my father had shared with him. It had been part of his seeking to understand the White man's ways. He'd rejected polygamy and hedged his meditations by including the White man's all-knowing Great Spirit. "Me go see Luke, hunt with Junior."

"Well, I was figurin' on headin' out to find Junior later this mornin'. Join me," said Watts. "Maybe we can find some eatin' better than that jerky I served up fer breakfast."

One Arrow nodded and smiled. "Jerky not bad. We hunt together."

"What day is it?" Bode awakened in the softest, plushest bed he'd ever lain in.

"Thursday, Grandpa." Cassie smiled. "You been sleeping for three days."

He became painfully aware of his left shoulder. "What hit me?"

"You were shot up in Alice."

"Must have been bad."

"Lucas asked me to fetch him when you woke up. He's out at the barn." She drew back the window curtain to let life-giving light into the room. "I'll be right back. I'll get Lucas and then get you some soup I made special."

Bode smiled and relaxed his head on the pillow. He

vaguely recalled the gunplay in Alice, up to the point when he'd been shot.

The sound of my spurs preceded me as I strode into the bedroom. "Glad to see you're awake, Mr. McCully."

Bode brought his eyes into focus on my lanky frame. "How'd I wind up here?"

"Had to wait a day after the doctor patched you up, then hauled your sorry ass here to the ranch. You took a full blast from Cal Pardoe's scattergun," I said, shaking my head. "Tore up your shoulder something fierce."

Bode forced a smile. "Hurts like hell."

"Gonna be that way for a while. Doc said you can likely get around okay in a couple of weeks."

"I should have shot him back at the saloon."

"Maybe."

"You told me not to take the law into my own hands," groused Bode. "So, I hesitated."

"Three men died, Bode, but it wasn't your fault," I offered consolingly. "Mr. Parr and I disposed of Pardoe."

"Pardoe was hotter than a nest of angry rattlers. He was shouting that Parr had crossed him."

"No surprise at that, Bode. Something's stirring up south of Alice."

"Even Parr wouldn't stoop to killing." Bode closed his eyes for a moment as much from fatigue as concentrating on the issue at hand. "He likes to control."

"I caught three strangers crossing Heaven's Gate the other day. They said Parr had hired them. From the weapons they carried, I didn't reckon them to be ranch hands."

"It's not like Parr to up the ante when it comes to violence," offered Bode. "Leastways, I don't figure him to hire guns. Betcha Parr has had enough for now and sends them away."

I rubbed my chin. "I think you may be right, Bode."

"So, what are you doing next, Junior?"

I stepped back distractedly as Cassie walked in with a bowl of soup.

Bode saw the steam rising from the bowl and didn't feature adding a burned tongue to his shoulder pain. "Thanks, Cassie. Just set it down on yonder table and let it cool just a tad."

"But…" She caught herself. No point in arguing with her grandfather. She set the bowl down and turned to me. "Let Grandpa get some rest, Lucas."

I nodded, then paused and turned back to Bode. "I feel led to find the men that killed Pardoe's daughter."

Bode gave up a tired sigh. "Sheriff Tyler won't touch it."

"That's what I figured," I reflected. "We'll talk tomorrow, Bode. You get some rest." I followed Cassie from the room.

"Mr. Nichols, I'm pleased to pay you and your companions for your trouble, but it turns out I won't be needing your services." Parr stood before the trio. He extended three sacks of coins to the men.

Plug had just put a fresh smoke to his lips and taken a drag. He coughed and inadvertently dropped the smoke. "Damn, Mr. Parr. We was lookin' forward to helpin' you." He looked down at Parr's crotch and smiled now that the man had dry pants.

"Well, the situation has changed. A bit too much heat got stirred up," insisted Parr.

Plug was pleased to accept the payment. He figured that whatever heat had caused Parr to soil himself likely contributed to the change of plans. The fact that they weren't being sent off empty-handed took the edge off their disappointment. "Much obliged, Mr. Parr."

"If the need arises, I will call you, Mr. Nichols," assured Parr. He smiled reassuringly, pivoted, and began to head back to the big house.

"Mind if we bunk down here and head out in the morning?"

Parr paused in mid-stride. He didn't even look back. "Just be sure you're gone before sunup."

Plug shrugged. "Damn! Talk about easy money." He handed a sack to each of his companions.

"Shoot, Plug. Why hang around here? Let's head up to Alice tonight."

Plug was about to say that it was dark.

"Plenty of moon an' a decent road," interjected Jasper. He'd anticipated Plug's protest. "Rather be drinkin' an' beddin' a soiled dove."

★★

I sat on the gallery, weighing my options. I'd taken up paper and pen and scrawled a note to Captain Hughes describing the shootout in Alice. I didn't include my suspicions of Archer Parr inciting a range war for personal gain. There seemed no point in poking that bear. I did request some time off, though I didn't mention my intentions of investigating the murder of Amanda Pardoe. Something about the circumstances nagged at me. It didn't seem right to let her death be forgotten.

"You want hunt?"

I started at the voice.

Buffalo Watts and One Arrow both wore broad grins as they eased around the corner of the gallery and stood facing up to me.

"One Arrow?!" I leaped from the bench. "Cassie, we've got guests," I hollered over my shoulder. "Come on in." I waved my hand for them to join us. "Dang, it's great to see you!" I grabbed both One Arrow's and Watts's hands. "And yes, I could use a good hunt."

One Arrow hesitated at the door.

Cassie was quick to recall the Indians not liking the claustrophobic feeling of buildings. "I was just fixing breakfast," she smiled. "It's such a pretty morning. Let's eat out on the gallery."

Sand and dust kicked high, created a thick blanket that could be seen for miles across the grassy prairie just west of Laguna Larga. Prolonged drought had parched the soil and tended to add to the earthen grit. Nearly sixty head of Bar A-branded beeves had been rounded up, though ownership was decidedly uncertain. Four cowpunchers of anonymous employer origin had been ordered to round up the livestock remaining on Cal Pardoe's ranch before the state or the bank moved in to seize the ranch assets. Anonymous employer? In this case, it loosely translated to Archer Parr. Far as anyone knew, Pardoe had no heirs and owed the bank a passel of money.

"Turn 'em, Hank!" one of the punchers called out, as a barbed-wire fence loomed a mere quarter mile ahead.

Hank whipped his throw rope around to distract the cattle. "The hell you say! Critters smellin' water!" Swinging the lasso high overhead wasn't doing the trick. The drover was half-tempted to fire a round but feared starting a stampede.

The herd careened into an arroyo carved through the soil just shy of the fence, as they instinctively headed toward the water. To the surprise of the cowboys the span of wire over the arroyo had been cut. The lead longhorn plowed through the opening, and the remaining beeves funneled through.

"Damn, Hank! Can yuh believe that?"

Not a hundred yards beyond the cut, the herd rumbled past Plug Nichols and his companions. Not but another hundred yards, and the beeves were enjoying the waters of a creek feeding into Laguna Larga. Two of the cowboys rode on to the creek to gather in any strays while Hank and another cowpoke pulled up to where Plug had halted.

Hank couldn't help but notice that the three men were heavily armed. "Much obliged for cutting the fence. Where y'all headed?" He kept his hands clear of the Colt Peacemaker nestled in his own holster. He'd only had to point it at humans a couple of times, and this wasn't going to be one of those situations if he could help it.

"Passing through," responded Plug. He looked at Jasper, smiled, and continued. "Headed to Corpus Christi. Looking for some work."

Considering the trio's armament, Hank wondered what sort of work the three sought but was not inclined to inquire. "Name's Hank Johnson. We're temporarily gathering these beeves at Mr. Archer Parr's place until folks decide who owns them." He'd likely revealed too much, but the guns made him uneasy. To his judgment, the men likely knew that fence cutting was a felonious offense, though not enforced so much anymore.

"Well, I'll be! We just departed Mr. Parr's ranch a few hours back. My name is Plug Nichols." Plug laughed at the coincidental Parr connection. "Parr seems like a straight shooter."

Hank nodded. "And powerful Mr. Nichols. Archer Parr's not one to be messed with." He stroked the butt of his revolver for emphasis. "I gather y'all know what I mean."

"Somethin' we should be aware of, Mr. Johnson?"

"Been a range war goin' on over fences and water rights. Mr. Parr hired us to encourage some ranchers to open the range a bit."

"Mr. Parr seems like a no-nonsense sort of man," responded Plug. He had begun to realize that these four were more than cowboys. They were Archer Parr's enforcers.

Hank was warming to the conversation, as it bordered on a sort of professional courtesy. "We had to get rough a time or two," he boasted. There was no point in delving into specifics, as he'd let Plug's imagination fill in any blanks.

"Well, we'll be headin' on to Corpus. Y'all stay clear of that barbed wire," Plug offered friendly like. He reckoned that Corpus might afford him a chance to relax and think on Archer Parr. He had fast reached the conclusion that it wasn't to his advantage to spend time with Parr's men.

Hank tipped his hat. "Well, we've got beeves to tend to. Y'all enjoy Corpus." He turned and rode off to join his compadres.

As Hank rode out of earshot, Jasper leaned into Plug. "Damn, but it looks like Mr. Parr was raising an army."

Plug smiled. "And we'd have been his soldiers. Let's go get drunk on in Corpus," he said as he gently spurred his horse and turned it in the direction of the city.

"You're acting feisty, Grandpa," observed Cassie. "You might try getting loose of that bed a time or two each day like the doctor said."

"I'm not gettin' any younger, darlin'. Just hope I can get around like my old self."

Cassie smiled lovingly, as she straightened the bedcovers and removed the dirty breakfast dishes from the nightstand. "You get your rest, now," she said and left the room.

Bode stared out the window. It had been two weeks since Cal Pardoe's shotgun had nearly wrecked his shoulder. The wound was healing up well, and he was anxious to see whether he was up to target shooting. I had been kind enough to bring his saddlebags and the coveted rifle up from the barn. The Winchester leaned against a chair in the corner of the bedroom. The sun's rays reflected from it in the morning as though casting out a challenge that said, "Come chamber a round, squeeze my trigger…" It was insanely tempting. Just as he was giving serious consideration to rising from the bed, there was a knock at the door.

"You decent, Mr. McCully."

I insisted on addressing him formally this morning despite being his wife's grandfather. Bode found that he actually preferred it. "Come on in, Junior."

I strode in. It was obvious that I was outfitted for a day or so on the trail. "Figured I'd stop in before I head out."

"Captain Hughes callin' you back?"

"Captain gave me a month off, though Cassie's getting close to delivering."

"So, what are you up to that pulls you away from the ranch."

I lowered my voice. "Seems like the worry about the vigilante has died down," I said with a confidential tone. "I've been catching up with ranch chores and looking in on you, but I've got a hankering to find out who killed Amanda Pardoe."

"Didn't the powers that be tell you to stay clear of that range war?" said Bode with a touch of concern.

"I'm not investigating a range war. Besides, it seems to have cooled a tad with Archer Parr calling off his dogs."

"What dogs you talking about, Junior."

"When I was headed to Alice a couple of weeks back, I chased three heavily armed men from Heaven's Gate. They said that they had been hired by Mr. Parr. I heard that after the shootout in Alice, Parr decided he didn't need them. He paid them and sent them on their way."

Bode's curiosity was aroused. "Where'd they go?"

"Took up residence at the Longhorn Saloon in Corpus. That's how I learned of Parr's doings. Liquor tends to open mouths."

"They have anything to do with the range war?"

"Not that I can figure," I responded. "Just them being around is a concern. I figure to have a chat. Maybe they know something."

Bode recognized that three unemployed gunmen generally spelled trouble. He longed for his lawman days. "Wish I was a fly on the Longhorn wall, Junior."

"I'll bet you do, Mr. McCully." I laughed.

"Promise you'll fill me in on what you find out. I feel so danged worthless waitin' for this danged shoulder to heal."

"Might be just as well." I chuckled knowingly.

Bode glanced at the Winchester propped in the corner.

I caught the distraction. "It's not loaded." I locked onto Bode's eyes. "Take your time and heal up good, Bode."

"Happy hunting, Junior."

"Hunting? I'm heading out in a couple of days with Buffalo Watts and my old friend One Arrow to do a bit of hunting."

"Good luck. Can't say the critters will have any." Bode laughed. He winced at a twinge of pain in his still-healing shoulder.

★★

"Howdy, gentlemen. Been a while." I had strolled over to the table occupied by Plug and his companions. The Longhorn still reeked of odors of its storied past—of booze, sweat, piss, leather, and horse droppings.

Plug recognized me immediately. "Er, you on duty, Mr. Ranger?"

I smiled friendly-like. "I like to stop in here at the Longhorn, when I get to Corpus. Can I buy y'all a drink?"

Plug did a double take. What and why was I making a social call? He glanced at Jasper and his third hand, Gordo. They nodded. "Pull up a chair, Mr. Ranger. It's Texas Ranger Dunn, ain't it?"

I motioned to the barkeep to bring a round as I pulled up a chair and sat. "Hear tell, Archer Parr didn't take you boys on."

"You heard right. He was good for it, though. Paid us for our trouble."

"That was right generous of him," I responded.

Plug took a swig of beer. "You have a lingerin' interest in us?"

"Not especially. I do have concerns about some lawbreaking…not that y'all were involved. Been a range war of sorts."

"We heard 'bout that. Met some cowpunchers movin' beeves a few days back. Saw the Bar A brand on their hindquarters. Claimed to work for Mr. Parr."

"Moving beeves, you say?" I quickly added in a piece of the puzzle over the aftermath of Cal Pardoe's demise.

"I gather Mr. Parr was goin' to keep a watch over them," added Plug.

"Well, I appreciate knowing that, Mr. Nichols."

Plug nodded, then lit up at recalling a detail. "They were heavily armed for cowpunchers. The head man, fella named Hank Johnson, I recall, said they had to get rough with that range war business."

My jaw slacked just a tad before I regathered myself. "Thanks right kindly. Y'all have been most helpful." I motioned to the barkeep to give the three another round. "I must be on my way, but it's been a pleasure seeing you boys." I arose, touched the brim of my hat, and departed. I left the Longhorn mulling over a visit to Parr's spread and a conversation with Hank Johnson.

The buck stood tall on full alert. The scar on his rump, compliments of a mountain lion's failed hunt, gave testament to the results of letting down his guard. His majestic rack gave further evidence of having sustained a long life among the hills and valleys of the northern reaches of the Nueces Strip. Many bucks had taken a whipping for attempting to have their way with this master's harem of does. He was indeed master of the herd. Now, he stood in the sights of Buffalo Watts's Sharps rifle.

Watts hesitated. "Dang. I just can't bring myself to do it," he whispered, barely audible to his companions. Respect for the buck had overtaken his instinct for the kill.

At Watt's whisper, the buck turned his head toward the hunters.

Watts stood and waved his arms. I smiled at Watts's antics, and One Arrow shook his head in dismay. We'd spent five hours stalking the buck.

"Let's call it a day," I suggested.

We'd make camp for the night with plans to enjoy one more day of hunting before heading home. I set to work unsaddling and hobbling horses and mules, while One Arrow built a cooking fire. We had plenty of meat from an antelope kill earlier in the day. It was just as well that we feasted on the antelope, as it tended to spoil quickly.

The sky was clear and big as ever. The moon would show its full self, much to the delight of howling coyotes and hooting owls.

"One Arrow full," belched the chief unceremoniously.

Antelope, coffee, and the last of Cassie's cornbread had fully met our culinary desires.

"You still figuring to try and figure who killed the Pardoe woman?" Aside from natural curiosity that had been gnawing at them, Watts figured to broach the topic before our hunt ended. He'd already endured a good-natured ribbing for not shooting the buck, so he reckoned it was time to open a more serious subject.

One Arrow looked quizzically at Watts and then me as he rubbed his belly. "Woman kill?"

"Captain Hughes directed me to stay out of the range war, but that killing has stuck in my craw."

"Craw?" queried One Arrow.

"Tight in his stomach, Chief," offered Watts.

One Arrow nodded for me to continue. He was ever curious as to the speech of the White man, especially our habit of using strange metaphors and colloquialisms.

"On the journey home after disposing of that Riordan varmint, Bode McCully and I came upon about a dozen beeves that had been skinned. Looked like hiders, but it wasn't. I discovered a shallow grave in their midst. Upon digging up the remains, they turned out to be a woman I later learned was Amanda Pardoe. She was the daughter of the owner of the skinned beeves. Apparently, she was the unintended victim of a range war that was likely started by Archer Parr. Of course, it can't be tied to him directly. My suspicion is that his hired hands got carried away, rustling the cattle. Amanda came upon the scene and was murdered for her trouble."

"Any idea who?" asked Watts.

"I think I may have lucked out there. I inquired of some men whose guns Parr had decided not to hire. They shared that a Parr hired hand name of Hank Johnson boasted of resorting to violence."

One Arrow smiled. "You pow-wow with Johnson?"

"I'm not sure how to draw the man out. He or his men might have killed Amanda Pardoe, but I have no evidence. Hearsay doesn't count."

"You hunter. Set trap for prey."

Watts caught the drift of the chief's thinking. "A trap? You just might lure him out." He smiled. "Go up mano-a-mano, face-to-face, an' ask him 'bout the killin'. It be like baitin' a beaver trap. Takes a touch of castorum to attract 'em."

"Castorum?" I asked.

Watts smiled. "Forgot yuh ne'er had the pleasure of huntin' beaver up in the northwest. Castoreum's from the beaver's very own glands. Draws the furry beasts like bees to bluebonnets. Her name be like castoreum, if he killed her. It'll draw him out fer sure."

"That's a great idea, though it might get Mr. Parr stirred up. I expect he'd like to keep a respectful distance between himself and any skullduggery." I shook my head a bit resignedly. "He'll likely tell Captain Hughes."

One Arrow once again looked questioningly at me. "Skull-duggery?"

I chuckled. "It means playing tricks, deceiving, making things appear as they are not."

"Bait good idea." One Arrow nodded his agreement.

Buffalo Watts smiled broadly. "Solved that. Wagh!"

I actually felt a surge of peace sweep through me. I now had a plan toward possibly entrapping the murderer of Amanda Pardoe. I'd have to pick the right place to confront Hank Johnson, as Parr likely wouldn't cotton to questioning his hired hands on his ranch property. This hunt with Watts and One Arrow hunt was successful no matter how many critters we bagged. Confronting Hank Johnson just might draw out the killer I sought.

After dressing out a couple of deer and enjoying venison cooked to perfection over a modest fire, we settled in for a relaxing night under a starlit sky. I watched One Arrow and recalled the days when the Comanche chief visited my father and would regale me and my siblings with tales of buffalo hunts and triumphs against rival tribes. I admired the chief's seeking to better understand the ways of the White man with his powerful God, written laws, and ownership of property. My ancestors had driven out the Indians just as the Indians had driven out others before. The story of conquest endures through the ages. A cross still hung from the bone necklace around One Arrow's neck. It had been a gift from my mother to Three Toes, mentor to One Arrow.

One Arrow felt my weighty gaze. "Your God is powerful, son of Ghost-Who-Rides," he offered in a near whisper.

The Comanche's sudden response to a question not asked took me by surprise. I smiled and nodded.

"One Arrow have many horses," continued the chief. "Have one wife." He paused and smiled. "Chief in Washington give us land."

I laughed nervously. "Gave you your own land."

"Comanche not own land," responded One Arrow.

I could do naught but shake his head. There was nothing I could do about it. The powers in Washington had it in their heads that they knew what was best for the Indians.

"It okay," said the chief. "Peace is good...but need scalps." A deep belly laugh followed, as he took me in with his ironic joke.

I pulled the bedroll around me with a smile still on my face. The days of ducking arrows from Comanche seemed over.

"Me go home in morning," said One Arrow.

SIXTEEN
VIGILANTE URGES

"WHAT THE HELL IS THIS ABOUT?" Hank Johnson's face had turned beet red.

"Just what I heard in Alice, Hank. The Texas Rangers want to talk with yuh 'bout that Pardoe woman," said the cowpoke apologetically.

My ruse was working. Just took a dropping a few words in Corpus.

"Go tell Mr. Parr, Hank," suggested one of the other hired hands. "He'll take care of it."

"Don't need no damned Texas Rangers snoopin' in our business." Hank slammed his fist into the corral gate crossbar. "Damn!" he exclaimed, as pain shot up his arm. "Why can't them confounded Rangers just leave us be?" He tried to shake the pain from his bruised hand.

"What's stirring you boys up so this morning?" Archer Parr had decided to take his usual morning stroll and happened to pass within earshot of the commotion.

Hank sought to bring his anger under control, as he turned to face Parr. "Can't be legal, boss. The Rangers are accusin' me!"

Parr took a deep breath. "Accusing you of what?"

."The boys here say the Texas Rangers have put out word that they want to talk with me 'bout the Amanda Pardoe killin'." Hank spat into the dirt.

Parr maintained his calm. "Dang, Hank, but that is bold. The Texas Rangers could have come out here and..." he stopped himself. He laid a hard gaze on Hank. "I'll bet this is the work of one particular Texas Ranger, that Dunn fellow."

"What are the Texas Rangers doin'? This ain't their business," stammered Hank.

"I'll take care of it," assured Parr.

"I didn't mean to kill her, boss." In his distraught state, Hank blurted out a confession that even Archer Parr was unprepared for.

"You what?"

"Was accidental. She had no business bein' out on the range. She said she'd tell the sheriff 'bout us skinnin' Bar A beeves."

"And you shot her?" Parr was incredulous. He'd been oblivious to the dastardly deeds of these hired hands. Turned out, they were more like hired guns. Worse, he'd thought Cal Pardoe had been lying about his daughter being murdered by Parr's hired thugs. "Damn!"

"Sorry, Mr. Parr."

"Sorry? You've got me in a fine fix," said Parr, turning the air thick with sarcasm. "I can't cover for you, Hank. You're fired. You and your men pack your things and be gone." Parr shook his head, pivoted, and stalked on back to the big house.

"Not so easy as that, Mr. Parr."

Parr turned. A hideaway double-barreled derringer filled his hand. He pointed it dead-on at Hank's chest. "You threatening me, Johnson?"

Hank swallowed hard. He had underestimated Parr. "No sir. No sir, Mr. Parr," he pleaded. He had no desire to have a bullet added to his woes. "We be on our way peaceful like."

Parr watched the men turn to the bunkhouse to retrieve

their personal belongings. He resumed his walk to the big house, occasionally glancing over his shoulder out of an abundance of caution.

There was dead silence in the bunkhouse, as each of the four hands gathered their personal effects.

Finally, one of the hands spoke the question the others seemed reluctant to ask. "What now, Hank?"

"We're headin' to Alice to drink an' think."

"Smart move," said Bode, as Cassie shared the news with him. "Should draw this Johnson fellow out. He'll be pretty danged edgy, if he's the killer."

"Killing that poor young lady. Maybe we could use that vigilante about now," opined Cassie.

Bode swallowed hard. "Gotta let the law do its work, Cassie dear." He was concerned that I had stepped over the legal line. Laying accusations out in public did all but put a price on Hank's head. He reckoned that Archer Parr and Captain Hughes would be none too happy.

"I hope Lucas draws the man out, Grandpa."

Bode was distracted. He felt an old urge.

"Are you okay?" asked Cassie.

"I wonder if it's too early to do a bit of plinkin'?"

Cassie's facial expression turned apprehensive. "You might hurt your shoulder."

"Maybe you're right, Cassie darlin'." He stole a sideways glance at his beloved Winchester rifle leaning against the wall.

The four former Parr hands sat dejectedly around a corner table at the Taberna Bandana. A part of the table's edge still bore splinters thanks to Cal Pardoe's shotgun blast. A carpenter was busying himself repairing the rear door jamb. Blood had already been washed away and the remainder camouflaged by a few days of trail dust. "What we gonna do 'bout that Ranger, Hank?"

Hank swallowed hard. His anger hadn't cooled much since leaving Parr's spread. "Might need to move on, boys."

"What yuh got in mind, boss?"

"Hear tell, there's money to be made up north. Maybe Kansas."

As the words left his lips, his worst dream stepped through the swinging batwing doors. The image instantly threw cold water on any lingering anger. A new challenge was presenting itself, and the rifle in my hands may as well have been a cannon.

The new barkeep's eyes darted from me to the cowboys and back to my physically imposing heavily armed self. He reached under the bar to assure himself that the shotgun was near at hand.

My eyes scoured the room. As they became accustomed to the dim light, my gaze swept past card-playing cowboys and a drunk with his head planted on the table to focus on Hank Johnson. The cowboy was easy to distinguish from his companions by the way their body movements subtly distanced themselves. "You Hank Johnson?" I demanded.

Johnson's right hand slipped from the tabletop. "Who wants to know?"

"I'm Texas Ranger Dunn," I responded, as I judged Hank's reaction. "You get that hand back on top of the table, Mr. Johnson," I said as firmly as possible but with an implied threat should the cowboy call me out. "Just looking to have a conversation."

Hank realized that his companions' body language spoke loudly that they weren't up for any gunplay. "What you wanna talk 'bout?"

"Mind if I pull up a chair?"

Hank motioned at a nearby chair. "Pull up a chair."

I grabbed the chair and sat opposite Hank taking care to keep the rifle muzzle aimed in his general direction.

"You wanna drink?" Hank pretended to be sociable, as he felt less threatened.

I waved off the drink offer. "Permit me to get right to the point, Mr. Johnson. You have anything to do with the killing and skinning of a few Bar A beeves a couple of weeks back?"

"Hiders?"

I shook his head. "Please, Mr. Johnson. Answer my question," I responded with a lawman's somber tone. This wasn't going to be a friendly conversation.

One of Hank's companions nervously broke off one of the splinters along the edge of the table. Guilt swept across his face, a sure sign of his having borne witness to the incident in question.

"Might have been there," responded Hank.

"You ought to know, Mr. Johnson. You were either there or you weren't."

Hank's fingers began drumming nervously on the table. He blinked, as he diverted his eyes from me. There seemed no escape. Tension ramped up.

"Did any of you men see who shot Amanda Pardoe?"

With that, Hank swiftly lifted the heavy oak table and pushed it full force at me.

Taken completely by surprise, I found myself on my back and struggling with the weight of the table while Hank and his men ran from the saloon. By the time I'd managed to escape the table, my suspects were mounted and galloping out of Alice as fast as they could.

I staggered to the front door and helplessly watched the escape. There were too many folks around to resort to any gunplay. I immediately thought of raising a posse, but that would take too much time. I didn't cotton to pursuing the four men by himself, especially having proven to my own satisfaction that they were likely guilty of the sort of violence that led to the Pardoe woman's death. I reckoned it was time to inform Captain Hughes of my having confirmed my suspicions about the murder and its link to the range war. I'd have to be politic and avoid mentioning that the fugitives were Archer Parr's men, and that the rancher was likely the cause of the incident. Once Hughes was informed, I could go about getting a wanted poster issued for Hank Johnson.

The barkeep helped me with the table. "Pleased to help, Ranger. My name's Sam. I heard them fellas talkin' 'bout Mr. Parr. They was angry at his tellin' them to pack their belongings an' leave his ranch."

"Appreciate that, Sam," I said, thinking how Parr was showing some good sense though still guilty by way of having inspired the men to violence in the first place.

"They were talkin' 'bout headin' to Kansas."

That news grabbed my attention. I needed to catch the fugitives before they left Texas. To my thinking, I couldn't wait for a poster or posse or even a telegram to Captain Hughes. Then, I took a deep breath. I thought back to what he'd learned from my dad and Buffalo Watts about tracking bandits and Indians. Unless hard-pressed, the pursued rarely did what was expected. This was especially true of human prey with enough savvy to know the tricks of the hunt like misdirecting and backtracking. I asked myself just how savvy Hank might be? I decided to send the telegram to Captain Hughes after all as well as one to Cassie. I didn't want to worry her, but had to let her know that I might be gone for more than a couple of days.

"Why we headin' east, boss?"

"Figure the barkeep heard us talk 'bout headin' to north to Kansas," responded Hank. "We gotta keep that damned Ranger off our trail."

"You think he can track us?"

"If he be fool enough to chase us. We be four agin' one."

"But, he's a Texas Ranger, Hank."

"He still only be one man," insisted Hank. "We'll head toward Nuecestown then head north to Victoria." He recognized the doubt written across the faces of his companions. "Y'all with me?"

The men looked at each other. They hadn't reckoned on the possibility of engaging in gunplay with a Texas Ranger intent on bringing them to justice. So far as they were concerned, the Ranger only wanted Hank. The situation had come down to a question of loyalty balanced against a justifiable fear for their own welfare.

"Y'all with me?" reiterated Hank.

"Yeah, boss. We're with yuh." There was a lingering sense that they might not be relied upon in any gun battle. It had been one thing to rustle and skin a few cattle and been witness to murder, but quite another to be looking down the barrel of a Texas Ranger's guns—especially mine—even at four to one odds.

"We'll rest soon, boys. We don't want to run these cayuses down."

"What we gonna eat, Hank?"

"Plenty of game. We'll cook us a deer or somethin'," promised Hank. He figured a gunshot wouldn't matter a hoot in this part of Texas. He turned his mount eastward and gave him enough spur to quickly put distance between him and his men.

For their parts, the men watched Hank for a moment. They looked at the thick mix of mesquite, wiregrass, and cacti before them, shrugged resignedly, and followed him.

★★

"You say he's chasin' after those four cowpokes by himself?" Bode was aghast at the news, though he tried to contain his concern so as not to upset Cassie.

"Here's the telegram, Grandpa," said Cassie, thrusting the telegram at Bode. She studied his face. "You look worried."

"Junior's a big boy," said Bode. He unfolded the telegram. "Not to worry. He wouldn't take undue risk." He read the message twice as though looking for some secret code buried within the lines. "Dang telegrams always too short," he lamented.

"Do you think he knows where they're headed, Grandpa?"

"Pretty much gotta figure he has a sense for it. Unlikely they'll head south and run afoul of Archer Parr or the Kleberg folks." Bode's brain had spun into high gear. "They'd be expected to go north, so they won't. That leaves east or west."

"Does he just guess, Grandpa?" Cassie was trying to rivet in on Bode's line of reasoning. It all seemed so uncertain.

Bode smiled. "He'll find some sign that'll point him in the right direction, darlin'." He knew I had plenty enough tracking savvy to spot any change of direction that Hank and his boys may have made. He felt reasonably certain that the amateurish outlaws weren't experienced enough to cover their tracks. What he'd seen at the cattle kill with Amanda Pardoe's shallow grave put him to thinking they were sloppy as desperadoes go. He stole a glance at his Winchester, propped in the corner in all its lethal glory. The urge to shoot was striking him with ever-greater frequency, as was his craving for efficiently and effectively delivering justice. He looked up at Cassie and feigned tiredness. "I'm thinkin' it's time for a nap, darlin'," he murmured.

Cassie twisted the tie of her apron, smiled tentatively, kissed Bode on the forehead, and exited the room. Such was the life of a lawman's wife. She found herself wrestling with the conversation she'd had with me about ranching and raising our family. Was this to be a regular talk within herself? Would it always be this way?

Bode listened intently as the sound of Cassie's footsteps faded down the hall. He sat up and swung himself to the edge of the bed, all the while with his eyes focused on the Winchester. He experienced no pain from his shoulder, as he stood and eased on over to his prized possession. If the rifle could sense any feelings, it would be reveling in the familiar grasp of Bode McCully. He caressed the stock lovingly. Bullets? Where did I hide the ammunition?

Tornado sensed my intensity, as I pushed the big stallion on at an easy lope. Johnson and his boys had a head start, so I felt driven to close ground while looking for any sign that they changed direction. All the while, I took what I knew of Johnson and tried to work my way into the fugitive's head. What might the cowpoke be thinking? If he were to head to Kansas, what route might he take? How hard would the man push his horses? How loyal were his men?

Roughly two miles north of Alice, I happened upon a clear sign that four horses had halted, turned from the road, and headed eastward. The country was rough enough to challenge man and beast quite considerably. "That's slow going, Tornado," I said. "I'm thinking we can head them off. Do you have it in you, big fella?" With that, I continued north. My instincts told me that they were likely headed to Nuecestown before turning northward to Victoria. I figured to head north and catch a road eastward that would enable me to outdistance and head off the four lawbreakers.

All was quiet, as Bode tiptoed in his socks easy-like from the big house. He sat down on the edge of the gallery and slipped on his boots with nary a twitch of discomfort from his shoulder. He'd pulled together some jerky for the ride ahead, though not so much as to weigh him down. Importantly, he'd found the ammunition for his rifle after searching through only two drawers. It was clear that no one was expecting him to be doing any shooting, much less heading out on the trail. He wore a self-satisfied smile, as he cradled the Winchester in the crook of his arm on his walk down to the barn.

Saddling one of the family's fine stallions was no problem, and Bode soon found himself heading up the road to Nuecestown. Like me, he had a sense that the fugitives would head east, obtain supplies, and then head north. Assuming the lawbreakers would make camp rather than risk travel at night in the rough terrain, Bode seized the advantage the road afforded him by enabling him to travel at night. A full moon and plenty of stars lit his way like a bold invitation to deliver justice on his terms.

Moving at a fast walk so as not to overly tax his mount, Bode chewed on an early breakfast of venison jerky. It brought back memories of doggedly hunting lawbreakers back in his days as a Texas Ranger. The hunts were nearly always successful, but too often ended in disappointment, when they'd bring in a fugitive only to have him escape captivity or get a lenient sentencing at trial. Every time that thinking danced through his mind, it served to fortify his commitment to delivering justice on his terms. He hardly noticed when he'd ridden through Nuecestown. Wasn't much of a town these days. He paused to study the eastern horizon. There were the beginning hints of the pink glow that would signal the sunrise.

It occurred to Bode that he had no physical description of the man he sought. He reckoned they wouldn't be too difficult to identify, as men on the run had a certain aura about them. The same would likely be said of their leader, Hank Johnson.

This bushwhacking might go down a bit differently from his previous encounters. Killing the wrong man would place him much too far on the wrong side of the law. By his reckoning, I could very well be lurking in the vicinity. After his promise to stop taking the law into his own hands, he dared not run afoul of his granddaughter's husband. He'd need to complete his work and disappear, perhaps even return to Heaven's Gate before any suspicions grew. He could always say that he'd gone plinking. The thrill of delivering justice ran strong in his veins, so much so that his shoulder offered not a twinge of discomfort.

Hank roused his men. "Come on, we can't be more than an hour's ride from Nuecestown."

They'd finally given in to the fatigue of their horses which bore scratches and cuts from the prairie's torture-inflicting foliage. They'd bedded down as best they could, not realizing that they were within shouting distance of the road to Nuecestown. The men's shredded leggings and their own assortment of wounds were the least of their worries as hunger began to dictate their reasoning. "We gotta eat, boss." Discomfort reigned supreme.

Being called boss had a right nice ring to Hank's way of thinking. The cold reality of not feeding his gang had yet to seep through his growing ego. Just maybe, he had the beginnings of a business of sorts. What with squabbles over water and fences, there were likely ranchers looking to hire some firepower. A flashback to the dime novels of his misspent youth lent a bit of color to the idea of being hired guns.

"Damn, Hank! You listenin'?"

Hank snapped out of the dreamlike fantasy world he was concocting. "Yeah, Nuecestown ain't far." He gave his mount an extra touch of his spurs, and the beast reluctantly plodded forward.

"That Texas Ranger can't prove nothin', boss."

Hank found himself a tad exasperated. He sensed a weakening loyalty among his men. It seemed ever more likely that they'd break and run when confronted with a gun battle. Still, they were all he had. "Our runnin' gave him what he needed, boys."

"Runnin' ain't evidence," protested one of the men.

"Just do as I say, an' we'll be oughta this," insisted Hank, as the four men emerged onto the road to Nuecestown.

No sign. I pulled up just shy of Nuecestown. Stroking my chin, I pondered what might have become of Hank Johnson. I'd seen no sign of the fugitives having returned to the road. I took my new binoculars from my saddlebag and scanned the dusty streets and aging buildings. In the dim pre-dawn light, nothing seemed to be moving. I decided to investigate more closely, so I put a light spur to Tornado and headed the big Appaloosa into town.

From his hidden vantage point among the pecan trees along the south bank of the Nueces River, Bode had been watching me pause and surveil Nuecestown. "He hasn't a clue either," Bode mumbled to himself. He had long ago learned the value of patience. If his hunch was correct, Hank Johnson and his gang should be along eventually. He smiled as I rode on into Nuecestown. He'd have to remember to make his escape by skirting around the town to avoid detection.

Bode had found himself a comfortable spot and was well camouflaged in the pre-sunrise shadows. His trusty Winchester rifle lay snuggled beside him as though begging to be put into action. The rising sun would be to his rear, sending its piercing rays into the faces of his prey. He'd hobbled his horse further eastward toward the town. If all went as he figured, he'd be quickly mounted up and back at Heaven's Gate Ranch before anyone was the wiser.

The sun had just poked above the horizon, when Bode heard the sound of several horses on the hard-packed road into Nuecestown. He slid the Winchester into firing position and sighted down the barrel toward whomever would come into sight. He hadn't long to wait.

The four men were riding two abreast, with one of the lead riders positioned perhaps a half horse length in front. Bode deduced that this was likely Hank Johnson. The body language of the others appeared deferential to him. He waited patiently, as they drew closer. He reckoned to get off no more than a single shot, so it needed to count. If Johnson's companions chose to fight, he'd still have the advantage, though it seemed likely they'd run. He stole a glance over his shoulder toward Nuecestown. I had not reappeared.

Hank finally rode within range. He had ducked his chin low to enable his hat to shield his eyes from the rising sun. "Nuecestown is just ahead, boys." Those would be his final words. He never heard the sound of the Winchester's lever, as Bode chambered a round, aimed, and squeezed the trigger. The rifle's booming report echoed in the morning air. The bullet? At less than a hundred yards, the slug tore through Hank's throat, severed his spinal column and carotid artery, and blew him clear of his saddle. He was a dead man before he hit the ground. His men were horrified. They panicked, turned about in a clamor of flying reins, squealing horses, and loud expletives, and spurred westward as fast as their fatigued mounts could carry them.

I had been walking the main street of Nuecestown. At the sound of the single shot, I paused in front of the general store. A couple of folks poked their heads from buildings out of curiosity at the apparent proximity of the gunfire. I swung onto Tornado's saddle, and cautiously headed up the street, turning west along the south bank of the river toward where the sound of the shot had come.

Out of my peripheral vision, I caught a glimpse of a rider camouflaged by the long shadows cast by the sun's rays well south of the town. Nevertheless, I was compelled to investigate the source of the gunshot. Pursuit of anyone must necessarily wait until he could determine whether any crime had been committed. I'd ridden about a quarter mile west of the town when I saw the body lying in the road with a riderless horse standing nervously nearby. "Damn!" I uttered under my breath. I didn't particularly like what I was suspecting. I rode up to where the body lay.

A shot sounded farther up the road. In the distance, I could see that a man had put his broken-down horse out of its misery. I needed a witness, so a man on foot would be handy. It didn't appear that his companions were returning for him.

Shaking my head resignedly, I stopped just short of the body lying lifelessly in the road dust of South Texas. There was no doubt that the dead man was Hank Johnson. Had the shooter aimed just a couple of inches higher, the man's head might have been decapitated. Was this, in fact, the murderer of Amanda Pardoe? Could anyone ever be certain?

I glanced up to see the man who'd mercy-killed his horse walking toward me. Apparently, the wannabe gunslinger had no stomach for a fight.

I kneeled down and removed Hank's revolver. I looked up toward the approaching outlaw before searching Hank's body for positive identification.

The outlaw strode within earshot. "You got him, Ranger. That's Hank Johnson. He's the one what killed the girl."

I stood and faced the man. "Stop right where you are, mister. Lay your rifle gentle like on the ground along with that saddle and do the same with that gun in your holster. Step away with your hands high where I can see them."

"No trouble from me, Ranger," he responded as he dutifully laid his weapons on the road and stepped away. "You're a hell of a shot."

"What's your name?"

"Brownie. Brownie Cullen," said the outlaw respectfully but with uncertainty etched across his face.

"Step away from those guns."

"Yes sir," responded Cullen as he took a half dozen hesitant steps toward me.

I towered over the man. "Well, Mr. Cullen, you're under arrest," I said as I grasped the outlaw's wrists in my strong hands and secured the manacles on his wrists.

Cullen offered no resistance.

"Just to be clear, I didn't shoot Mr. Johnson, here." I felt the need to clear the air of any doubt as to who shot Hank.

"Well, somebody did, Mr. Ranger, an' it weren't one of us."

I ignored the comment. "Did you see who shot and killed Amanda Pardoe?" I wanted to hear Cullen's admission again.

Cullen glanced down at the ground a moment as if contemplating his answer. "Guess it don't matter none now. Hank. It was Hank done it, Mr. Ranger. She done rode in all sassy-like an' threatenin' to turn us in. Hank shot her straight away."

"Soon enough you'll need to say that under oath, Mr. Cullen," I said as I began to lift Hank's body over the saddle of his horse. "You can ride behind the body," he directed Cullen. "I'll carry your guns and saddle, though you may not be needing them." I mounted Tornado. Once the outlaw had climbed up behind the dead man, I turned toward Corpus Christi. Me on the big Appaloosa with a manacled outlaw and corpse made for a sight traveling through the main street of Nuecestown and on to the city. I reckoned that Sheriff Tyler would likely be quite pleased, though roiling through my mind were thoughts of just who fired the shot that killed Hank Johnson and could it have been whom he suspected?

SEVENTEEN

JUSTICE DELIVERED

BODE ARRIVED at Heaven's Gate just as the rooster announced the day. Working feverishly, he managed to unsaddle his horse and let him loose in the corral. He studied the yard in front of the house. Not a soul was stirring. With Winchester in hand, he raced to the gallery steps, slipped off his boots, tiptoed into the house, and made it to the bedroom sight unseen. Incredible as it was, Bode had actually managed to sneak back into the big house undetected.

He carefully propped the Winchester in the corner of the bedroom, stripped down to his skivvies, and slid into bed. He'd barely caught his breath when there was a knock at the door.

"Grandpa? You decent?"

"Come on in, Cassie dear," managed Bode, trying to sound as though he'd only just awakened.

Cassie swept into the room carrying a tray heaped with breakfast fixings. Eggs, ham, grits, and biscuits were the menu of the day. She lay the tray on the nightstand. "Did you sleep well, Grandpa?" She felt a breeze and saw the open window. "Did you open the window? You must be feeling better," she said cluelessly.

Bode began to dig into the breakfast. "Maybe I'll take a walk outside this mornin' darlin'."

Cassie smiled. "Seems about right, Grandpa."

"Where's Junior?"

"Lucas hasn't returned from Alice yet. I hope he'll be home today, as there are a couple things in need of fixing, and my horse has lost a shoe."

"You ain't ridin' in your condition, are you?"

"I'm not some fragile piece of China, Grandpa," she responded with a laugh. "You finish up that breakfast. I've got chores to take care of. Let me know when you're ready to take that walk."

Bode smiled. "I figure I can walk on my own, Cassie darlin'. I don't break like China either." He paused. "Unless somebody shoots me with a shotgun," he said with a chuckle at his own humor.

★★

"Good to find you on duty, Sheriff." I dismounted and tossed Tornado's reins over the hitching rail. "Brought you some gifts."

Tyler's eyes spoke volumes that he recognized Archer Parr's hired hands. "What'd these men do, Ranger?"

I was momentarily taken aback. "Guess you didn't hear. Hank Johnson murdered Amanda Pardoe in a cattle rustling and skinning scheme that went wrong. Mr. Cullen here will testify to that."

Tyler glanced up at Cullen. "That right?"

Cullen nodded.

Tyler locked onto my eyes. "You have evidence?"

"Nothing hard, Sheriff. Johnson confessed and ran, and Mr. Cullen here bears witness to his deed. I got a lead from some men that Mr. Parr had decided not to hire. They said that Johnson all but confessed to the murder. I confronted

Johnson and his three men at the Taverna Bandana in Alice, but they managed to jump me and escape. The barkeep at the saloon gave me a heads-up as to where they were headed. I tracked them to Nuecestown. There were two more fugitives, but they escaped. Cullen might have escaped, too, but his cayuse failed him. He surrendered easy-like. I expect he'll give up the other names in exchange for some leniency."

The sheriff acknowledged the story with a nod. "Did you kill Johnson, Ranger Dunn?" Tyler wasn't wasting time gathering facts.

"No," I said with absolute finality. "Don't know who did, but I have a sneaking suspicion that our vigilante is back at work. The hole through Johnson's neck was likely from a Winchester slug."

"That make sense to you, Mr. Cullen?"

"Twern't us, Sheriff, an' ne'er saw the Ranger shoot." Cullen was twisting uncomfortably at still being seated behind an increasingly foul-smelling body.

"Guess y'all's word has got to stand for this. Climb down from that nag, Cullen." Tyler helped the man down. "We've just installed new bars and beds in the cells, so you'll be right comfortable."

"Happy to park Johnson's body in the usual place, Sheriff," I said, referring to a shed behind the jail. "It's getting a bit ripe. I expect selling his horse should pay for his funeral."

"I'd appreciate that. I'll send for a box and arrange for burial," responded the sheriff. "You going to hunt down that vigilante?"

"Expect I should, Sheriff," I acknowledged. Time was getting on, and I was anxious to get home and have a chat with Bode McCully. "Thought I had him nailed. I'll telegraph Captain Hughes about the situation." I wasn't especially looking forward to that task. I reckoned that the captain was not pleased at my delays toward joining him in Brownsville.

I rode ever-so-slowly up to the barn, slid from the saddle, and led Tornado inside. During the entire journey from Corpus Christi, I'd wrestled with how best to deal with Bode McCully. How was I to prove that a retired Texas Ranger recovering from a serious wound had roused from his sick bed, stolen away in the wee hours of the morning, bushwhacked a wanted man, and returned undetected? I unsaddled the big Appaloosa and took my sweet time currying him. There was no hurry. I finally closed the door to the stall and almost reluctantly headed toward the big house. There was no point in examining the other horses in the barn and corral, as plenty of time had passed since the early ambush. Any horse ridden early would have cooled down by now.

I paused at the first step and took a deep breath. I could hear Cassie bustling about in the kitchen. I finally walked up onto the gallery, paused again, and entered.

"Lucas! You're home!" exclaimed Cassie. She quickly moved into my waiting arms.

"Happy to be home, darling," I offered a bit distractedly.

Cassie sensed that I was unsettled and pulled away from my embrace. "Did all go well in Alice?"

"Mostly," was my truncated response.

"What's wrong, Lucas?"

"How's your grandfather?"

Cassie cocked her head inquisitively. "Getting feisty. Is that what's bothering you?"

"I think I'll go check in on him." Distraction and concern were written large across my face. "Has he left the house?"

Now, Cassie's concern increased significantly. "Not that I know of, Lucas," she offered curiously.

I turned toward the downstairs bedroom where Bode had been recovering over the past few weeks.

"Shall I join you? He might be sleeping."

"I must speak with him alone, Cassie." I gave her hand a squeeze, smiled at her, and placed my hand on the doorknob. I paused for a moment, weighing what I was about to do, turned the knob, and slowly swung the door open. Bode lay in the bed, apparently asleep. I glanced at the Winchester leaning in the corner and walked over to it. It had been turned around, since I'd last seen it. I lifted the rifle, drew out a small knife, and poked its tip into the muzzle.

"What you doin' with my Winchester, Mr. Ranger?" Bode was awake, after all.

"Good afternoon to you too, Mr. Bode McCully." My head turned, and my eyes locked onto Bode's. "You fire this rifle this morning, Mr. McCully?"

Bode groaned slightly, as he drew himself up to a sitting position. "Dang shoulder is still hurtin'."

"Got fresh residue. Anyone else shoot it?"

"I don't recall it bein' borrowed, Junior," said Bode suspiciously.

"Well, someone did."

Bode offered a questioning gaze.

"I left a small wad of cloth in the muzzle. Seems to be gone."

Bode's mind raced. "Is that what fell out when I cleaned it?" He felt a momentary sense of relief.

"Well, it sure needs cleaning again." My gaze fell on the boots lying beside the bed. A fresh patina of dust coated their soles. I shook my head apprehensively and shifted my weight uneasily. I leaned the Winchester against the bed and locked onto Bode's eyes. My patience was wearing thin. I strolled easy-like over to the dresser and opened the second drawer. The box of ammunition had been opened, and five bullets were missing.

Bode averted his eyes. He couldn't miss the foreboding signals I was giving off, and guilt rode a wild horse across his face. He sighed deeply enough to cause a twinge in his shoulder. "Laid the sonofabitch out cold, didn't I Junior?"

The unexpected confession hit me like a bucket of iced water. There'd be no more cat-and-mouse cogitations over the vigilante matter. What to do next?

"You're wonderin' what to do, ain't yuh?"

"Cassie's going to feel a world of hurt, Bode. And your old Texas Ranger buddies…well, I expect there'll be a mixed reaction." I sighed resignedly. "I'm not going to arrest you here in my own home. I've thought on this, and I'm going to let you turn yourself in to Sheriff Tyler."

Bode raised his eyebrows. "That's right noble of yuh, Junior."

"Not so easy on you, Bode," I cautioned. "You must explain yourself to Cassie before turning yourself in."

"Dang, Junior," replied Bode, already dreading the task.

"I gave you a chance to put this business behind us." I felt a surge of righteous indignation. "You're well aware that your self-serving obsession with taking the law into your own hands would have costly consequences, no matter your intentions. You broke the law every bit as much as the fugitives you bushwhacked. You've tarnished a stellar career by your actions."

There wasn't anything Bode could say. I had him dead to rights. He'd been offered the opportunity to desist from his vigilante ways, but the compulsion to deliver justice by the rifle had simply been too great.

"I'm going to go see to my horse, Bode." I turned and picked up the Winchester. "I'll hang onto this." I strode over to the door and paused. "I'll send Cassie in," I added and walked out.

Bode sighed deeply, swung his legs out, and sat on the edge of the bed to await his fate.

★★

"Grandpa, Lucas said you have something to tell me?" inquired Cassie.

Bode stood. Cassie's gentle manner didn't make this any easier. He was all-too-aware of her admiration for him, and what he was about to say was like a thousand daggers plunged into his heart. He beckoned her over and took both her hands in his. "I love you, dear granddaughter." It was all he could do to hold back a tear. Finally, he took a deep breath. "I have a confession."

"You're the vigilante Junior's been chasing," she blurted.

Bode stepped back incredulously. "You knew?"

"Well, I suspected it. Lucas held it back from me, but I can read him like a book."

"What you may not know is that he gave me a chance to go straight, but I couldn't do it. I went out afore dawn an' bushwhacked another lawbreaker. Junior caught me dead to rights." Now, a tear did make its way down Bode's cheek. "I must turn myself in, dear Cassie."

Cassie sat on the edge of the bed and gazed up at him. "It's the right thing, Grandpa," she said thoughtfully. "I don't admire what you've done. In fact, I condemn it." She stood and gave him a gentle hug. "I still love you, Grandpa. I'll always hold on to the memories that made me so proud of you. Now, I'm proud that you're turning yourself in."

"I'm so sorry, Cassie," lamented Bode, as he sat on the bed and wept. He'd given up his reputation for a deadly obsession. He'd enslaved himself to it, and it had been so very wrong.

Cassie placed her hand gently on his shoulder. The sorrowful, aged shadow of a Texas Ranger sobbing before her was not an image she expected to carry in her memories. She urged him to stand. "Pull yourself together, Grandpa."

Bode struggled but stood in his helplessness.

"Sheriff Tyler is close to retirement. He's not looking to stir up any nests of rattlers. He might not even put you in a cell, Grandpa," offered Cassie tenderly as deference to Bode's age.

"I expect he won't be giving you back any guns," she said with a smile.

Bode wiped away the tears.

"Maybe he'll order what they're calling house arrest," she encouraged.

"Guess I'd best get on with it," responded Bode resignedly.

Cassie gave him a kiss on the cheek, turned and left the room.

Bode slipped the Colt revolver from under the pillow. He fondled the cold steel in his hands. Would it bring peace? Would it be right? No, doing this would surely kill the very soul of his beloved granddaughter. He laid the gun on the table. It was time to make himself presentable for the sheriff.

I curried Tornado with so much passion that the big Appaloosa neighed and snorted, as though readying for some new adventure. The stallion had been washed, had his shoes checked, and been fed an apple in addition to a bucket of oats. Life was good.

"Yur gonna wear that cayuse's hide out, Junior," said Buffalo Watts.

Startled, I dropped the brush and swept my hand to the gun that wasn't there. It hung uselessly in its holster nearby rather than on my hip. "Dang it, Buffalo. Don't do that!"

"What's eatin' at yuh, son? Yer jittery as a passel of prairie dogs."

"Mr. McCully confessed to being the vigilante."

Watts smiled. "Shucks, that's not news, Wagh!"

"But he finally owned up to it. Ambushed Hank Johnson early this morning," I responded. "He's turning himself in to Sheriff Tyler."

"That should bring a shine to that Ranger star," observed Watts.

"Cassie admired him. It'll hurt her."

Watts leaned against the side of Tornado's stall. The fringe on his buckskin jacket tossed in the breeze. He stroked his whiskers thoughtfully. "Dang shame. Guess McCully had his reasons. Remember that the version of the hunt told by the hunter is always different from that told by the hunted. McCully had his own reasons for what he did." He stroked Tornado's rump. "Ultimately, it's the hunter—you, Junior—that controls the story. You're doin' the right thing, far as I can tell. Wagh!"

"Guess we all knew early on."

"Seems you had what they call a dilemma, Junior," observed Watts. "It's tough to catch a lone operator. Like a good hunter, you found the signs an' stuck with it."

I rode beside Bode. Not a word was spoken as we followed the road to Corpus Christi. Nothing need be said. We pulled up in front of the jail.

Bode dismounted. He glanced up at the sky as gathering dark clouds told of storms soon to come. "You comin' inside, Junior?"

I shook my head. "Nope. This is your play, Mr. McCully." I nodded toward the front door, as the sound of Sheriff Tyler's boots could be heard approaching the door. "I'll be taking your horse back to Heaven's Gate." I paused, set my jaw, and offered a grim smile. "You're doing the right thing, Mr. McCully. Cassie and I are respectful of that." With that, I touched my fingers to the brim of my hat and began to turn away just as Tyler emerged from the jail.

"What do we have here?" asked the sheriff.

Bode set his jaw and looked up. "Just turnin' myself in, Sheriff."

"For what, Mr. McCully?" inquired Tyler.

"Bushwhacking outlaws. Yer lookin' at the vigilante."

"Damn!" exclaimed Tyler. He gathered his wits and motioned Bode into the jailhouse.

Bode held his head high as he strode past the sheriff.

"What brought this about?" asked Tyler.

"Texas Ranger Dunn convinced me of the error of my ways," confessed Bode.

"Caught you red-handed, aye?" He eased over behind his desk.

"Pretty much," admitted Bode.

Tyler stood for a moment debating with himself as to how to proceed. Standing before him was a retired Texas Ranger of some repute who had apparently taken the law into his own hands. Locals regaled in the exploits of Bode McCully. "I expect we'll need some sort of written confession, Mr. McCully," he finally stammered and pulled a pencil and blank sheet of paper from his desk drawer. He pushed it toward Bode. "If you'd be so kind."

Bode was nothing if not thorough, as he listed the names of each of the outlaws to whom he'd delivered his vigilante justice. Beside the name of Carlos Diaz, he made a note to the effect that he had been helping me with a Texas Ranger assignment. Upon completing the confession, he held it up and scanned what he'd written. He placed it back on the desk, signed it, and pushed it over to the sheriff.

"Guess it'd be right to at least lock you up overnight, Mr. McCully," said Tyler with a regretful tone. He motioned toward the stairs leading to the cells on the second floor. "Anything I can get you?"

Bode conjured up a sheepish smile and a sigh. "Guess I'm a tad hungry, Sheriff."

★★

"Lucas! Come quick," called Cassie. She'd drawn back the drapery at the front window to let in the morning sunshine and found herself greeted by a most fearsome sight.

I bolted down the stairs, stuffing my shirt in my pants and grabbing the Henry rifle in one swift motion. I passed Cassie as she stood with one hand over her mouth and the other pointing to the front yard. I barged through the front door with rifle at the ready to find myself staring into the faces of Texas Ranger Captain John Hughes and two dozen heavily armed, tough-looking Rangers. I pulled up short.

"Why Ranger Dunn," drawled Hughes calmly. "Hope we're not inconveniencing you."

Silence.

Cassie joined me on the gallery.

Awkward silence.

"Y'all care for some coffee?" ventured Cassie.

Hughes finally broke the silence with a hearty laugh and dismounted. He looked up at me and then over his shoulder as his company. He smiled at Cassie. "Ma'am, if you have a couple of dozen cups of coffee, we're pleased to oblige."

"I better boil up some water," interjected Cassie uncomfortably, as she pivoted with a rustle of skirt to go back into the house.

"Sorry ma'am, just joking," called out Hughes.

Cassie paused.

I simply looked on with mouth agape.

"Wouldn't want to put y'all out," continued Hughes. "Ranger Dunn here and me do need to have a conversation, and we'd sure be delighted to have it over some of your coffee."

Cassie smiled. "Does the good captain like cornbread?"

"Yes ma'am, Mrs. Dunn," said the captain as he climbed the gallery steps and extended his hand to me. "By dang, Ranger Dunn, but you've caused quite a stir among the folks in Austin. Bringing Big Bill Riordan to justice, stopping Carlos

Diaz, putting a range war to rest, and now ending a reign of vigilante terror...it's all put quite a shine on the Texas Ranger badge."

I couldn't suppress a blush.

The entire Texas Ranger company dismounted. It was a tough ragtag bunch, but they set about easing saddle cinches and looking for shady spots to rest.

I caught myself as I shook Hughes's hand and invited him into the house. I paused at the door and looked out at the company. "Y'all feel free to water your horses," was offered up as an afterthought.

Hughes hustled me inside. "Come on, Ranger."

We pulled up chairs at the kitchen table as Cassie delivered two cups of coffee and a platter stacked with cornbread dripping with melted butter. She poured herself a piping hot cup of coffee, and without a second of hesitation, joined us at the table.

I smiled nervously at her and looked at Hughes.

Hughes balked a tad. He wasn't used to a woman thrusting herself into what he saw as a man's business.

"Cassie is part of this conversation, Captain," I assured him.

Hughes shrugged and was right quick to favor himself with a piece of cornbread. He wiped a bit of melted butter from his chin. "By golly, Mrs. Dunn. You do make some fine cornbread." He'd recovered from his momentary faltering.

I was becoming ever more curious as to the true purpose of the Ranger captain's visit and was having a tough time keeping my metaphorical powder dry.

Cassie smiled at Hughes. "Why, thank you, Captain. It's Ranger Dunn's mother's recipe." The demure smile accompanying her gratitude didn't cause her to pause from boldly asking Hughes's business. "What brings you to Heaven's Gate today, Captain?"

I sat just a tad chagrined at Cassie's boldness, but silence can be a blessing when someone else has something to say.

"Folks in Austin have asked me about forming another Ranger company under your leadership, Ranger Dunn." He took another bite of cornbread and savored a sip of coffee. "Seems success does have its rewards," added Hughes.

Cassie's and my eyes locked on each other. There was a choice to be made. I recalled my dad juggling roles of lawman, rancher, and husband. Each of those roles demanded great effort. Moreover, at least one placed his dad's very life at risk. With Cassie about to give birth to our first child, was it right to stay the course with the Texas Rangers?

"Expect you might have to think on that a bit, son," offered Hughes, as his practiced senses honed on years of interrogating fugitives noted our hesitancy.

"I appreciate that, Captain," I said, stroking my chin thoughtfully. "It's sure an honor, and we'll think seriously on it." I tacitly acknowledged the doubt that lingered in my mind. I'd been operating alone and had found it challenging but rewarding. I hadn't even been afforded the opportunity to work with Captain Hughes as part of a company of lawmen. To lead a company of tough men, many of less-than-honorable backgrounds, seemed a tall order. Was I a leader?

"We'll be in Corpus for a few days, Ranger Dunn," advised Hughes. "Please let me know by week's end." He sipped the last of his coffee and turned toward Cassie. "Thanks kindly, Mrs. Dunn, for the fine cornbread. Can't say as I've ever enjoyed better." With that, he arose, tipped his hat to Cassie, and walked to the door.

I escorted the captain to his horse. "I'll be back with you right promptly, Captain." I looked out at the company of Texas Rangers now preparing to mount up and move out. "Sorry, we didn't have enough coffee and cornbread for everyone." I chuckled nervously at my own humor.

"You take care, Ranger," said Hughes. "Don't be making

any rash decisions. If you decide to accept the offer, you're likely to be a Texas Ranger for a long time to come." With that, he mounted and led his company out.

★★

The Texas Ranger offer swam around in my mind over the next couple of days. Whether wrangling beeves on the outer reaches of Heaven's Gate Ranch, plinking at rabbits and groundhogs, or tending to fixing a loose horseshoe or two, I found myself torn. I thought hard on the conversation with Cassie a few weeks back. There would be no justice in her becoming a young widow. Certainly, there was all manner of threats. Death could be reaching for my horse's reins at any time. Being a Texas Ranger just brought a higher risk of just such an eventuality. It seemed that there would always be lawlessness, but there was also a critically important need for solid, productive citizens to bring civilization to pass. Someone had to deliver justice.

I sipped my morning coffee with my feet propped on the gallery railing in the very worn notch fashioned by my dad. It was near time to inform Captain Hughes of my decision, of *our* decision. Cassie was certainly part of that choice. I closed my eyes.

"Lucas!" cried Cassie.

My eyes opened wide.

"Lucas! Come quick! It's time!"

There was no time to fetch Cassie's mother. I dashed inside and followed her upstairs. I paused at the top of the stairs and gathered my wits as best I could. I ran back downstairs and filled a bowl with warm water, grabbed a handful of towels, and headed back to join Cassie.

"Oh my, Lucas! Oh, it hurts! Hold me...hold me."

"Breath, Cassie," I urged, recalling what her mother had shared. "Push, sweetheart."

Soon enough, the crown of a little head began to emerge. "The baby's coming," I exhorted. "Push...push." I held her hand tightly and wiped the perspiration from her brow.

Cassie mustered all the energy she had left, and a new life met the light of the world.

"A boy! We've a son, Cassie!" I fully surprised myself, as my newborn son took his first breath and wailed a loud plaintive Dunn wail. I washed my son, knotted and cut the umbilical, wrapped him in a warm towel, and gently placed him on Cassie's chest.

Cassie's face was flushed with the love that only a mother to a newborn can know. "He's got your eyes, Lucas," she cooed. She turned her gaze to me. "The name we agreed on?"

"Sean," I whispered. "Sean Michael Dunn...after my lost brother."

"It's a manly name, Lucas," said Cassie lovingly. "A strong Irish name it is."

I sat beside Cassie and looked upon mother and child. The time seemed frozen in forever. "I love you, Cassie Dunn." I watched in the amazement that only the father of a first child can cherish, as Sean slipped to his mother's breast.

Cassie looked down at our child, then back up at me.

"I think I have Captain Hughes's answer, sweetheart."

"The judge sure must like something about you, Mr. McCully," said Sheriff Tyler as he led Bode from the jail to the stable. "You heard him clear as day. You'll be under house arrest at your granddaughter's place until trial. If it were up to me, they'd be trying you for murder, Mr. McCully. The judge is calling your vigilante goings on voluntary manslaughter. Guess he's cutting a fine line legal-wise." He shook his head in mock amazement. "You do seem to lead a charmed life."

Tyler was obliged to escort his charge to Heaven's Gate.

"Guess there's no point in putting the danged manacles on you, Mr. McCully. Just don't be shooting any lawbreakers between here and the ranch," said the sheriff with a wry smile.

Bode didn't miss the humor. He was relieved at not having to spend a second night in the roach-infested Corpus Christi jail with its odors of sweat and urine ever permeating its very walls. "They took my Winchester, Sheriff. I expect everyone's safe from me."

Soon enough, they'd headed their cayuses toward Heaven's Gate at an easy walk.

Bode sat on the gallery, taking in the cast of the sun's morning rays on the gently rolling hills of the ranch. He'd walked up from the cabin near the barn that would house him for the next few weeks, poured himself a cup of coffee, and inadvertently grabbed a seat in the very spot that I habitually occupied. He was just about to savor a sip, when I emerged with a cup of coffee in one hand and newborn son in the crook of my other arm.

I smiled. "Don't get carried away with this house arrest thing, Bode. Move your sorry posterior over a bit."

Bode obediently slid over.

I sat beside him. "Your great-grandson says good morning." I chuckled as I turned baby Sean so Bode could better see the new addition to the Dunn household. Bode swallowed hard as he gazed at the tiny bundle nestled in my well-muscled arm. It brought back long-lost memories of the birth and lives of his own children. Most had been lost to disease and violence, though Cassie's father had survived to bear a daughter that now had born a great-grandchild.

"Here...hold him, Bode," I urged and offered little Sean to Bode.

Bode gently took the fragile bundle from my arm. He couldn't hold back tears, as he held Sean to his chest.

"I expect my son will have a touch of you in his bones, Bode. Hope it's all the good parts."

Bode smiled.

Just then, Cassie appeared in the doorway. We weren't aware of her at first, as she took in the three men, three generations of men basking in the peace of the moment. She sighed lovingly. "Y'all mind some company?"

Sean seized the moment to fuss just enough for Bode to hand him over to Cassie. He reflexively averted his eyes, as she, as demurely as possible, bared her breast and fed her son.

"I'm heading to Corpus Christi this morning, sweetheart," I reminded her. "I figure to give my answer to Captain Hughes face-to-face."

"Answer?" queried Bode.

I stood. "They've offered me the command of a Texas Ranger company, Bode."

"That's wonderful news, Junior. You acceptin'?"

I smiled. I kissed Cassie and looked lovingly upon my son. "I'll be back before dinner, sweetheart. Bode, you watch over the place while I'm gone." I winked at Cassie and headed for the barn. Tornado was already neighing at the distant sound of my approach.

"What's he gonna do, Cassie?" asked Bode.

She smiled mischievously, covered her breast, and held Sean to her shoulder. "You'll be finding out later, Grandpa."

Bode was like a dog with a bone as he kept his eyes peeled for my return. He finally moseyed down to the barn as though that would hasten the anticipated arrival. He was dying to learn what the father of his great-grandson had decided.

His mouth turned dry, and his breathing became labored

as he approached the barn. The water trough was near at hand. He kneeled beside it, cupped his hand, and bent over the trough to more fully enjoy the warm but much appreciated water. Of a sudden, Bode felt as though a bronc had kicked him in the chest. He couldn't breathe. He clung to the side of the trough but dropped to his knees. He fought for air before releasing his hold and slowly lying back in the soft grasses. He tried to cry out to no avail. He fought for air. His hand stretched out toward the house, then fell limply to the ground.

It wasn't but moments before I trotted up the road from the entrance to Heaven's Gate. I leaped from Tornado at first sight of Bode lying beside the trough. The elder man's skin already had turned to the pallor of death, and his lips had turned blue. I remained calm. I had seen death before. I placed my hand on the old Ranger's chest. There were no heartbeats. I touched my ear to Bode's mouth. There were no breaths to be detected. Bode McCully had peacefully gone to meet his Maker. I doffed my hat and stood silently for a moment, out of love and heartfelt respect. Bode wouldn't be enduring the embarrassment of a trial or any punishment.

I led Tornado into his stall. "Be back shortly, big fella."

I hefted Bode over my shoulder. As I strode slowly up to the house, I reflected on how a life was won as another was lost. I had a son, but had now lost my son's great-grandfather. I climbed the stairs to the gallery and laid Bode in the rocking chair he loved. I looked again at the dead man before entering the house. The old Texas Ranger was at peace.

Cassie was fixing dinner, oblivious to anything happening outside the house. It was hard to believe she'd given birth just two days before. She turned toward me. "You're back earl..." She paused as she took in my somber expression.

"Bode has passed, sweetheart."

She dropped the soup ladle. Her hands rushed to her mouth. She'd have fainted had I not caught her. Her body racked with uncontrollable sobs, as I sought to comfort her. Suddenly, she pushed away. "Where? Where is he?"

"I laid him in the rocker on the gallery, sweetheart."

Cassie ran out and knelt beside her ever-beloved grandfather.

"He's at peace now, Cassie. No one save a handful of us will ever know his torments." I tried my best to comfort her. "Soon enough, we'll be telling our children tales of Bode's strong sense of justice and his good deeds as a lawman."

Cassie stood up beside me, and we quietly gazed at her beloved grandfather. I put my arm around her. "I'm at peace, Lucas," she offered softly. A plaintive cry from inside brought a motherly smile. "Somebody's hungry," came out as a whisper out of respect for Bode.

"I'll ride into Nuecestown in the morning and make arrangements, sweetheart."

Cassie sighed and went inside to feed Sean, while I gently lifted Bode from the chair and respectfully carried his body back to the cabin. It would serve to keep his remains sheltered from varmints.

I took my time rubbing down and talking to Tornado before returning to the big house.

Cassie greeted me at the door with baby Sean in her arms. "Did you see Captain Hughes?" She laid our newborn son in a cradle by the kitchen table.

"Yep," I responded with a nod and a smile.

"And?"

"I gave him our answer." I led her over to the chest against the wall of what served as an entry foyer and ceremoniously pulled open the top drawer. I drew the polished silver Texas Ranger badge from my pocket, buffed it on my shirt, and gently placed it in the drawer.

With that, Cassie—flushed with a sense of relief—wrapped her arms tightly around me.

Feeling her against me, combined with the adrenaline rush

of having made a final decision on our future, caused me serious arousal.

"Not just yet, cowboy." Cassie smiled provocatively. *Men,* she thought. Two days after childbirth, and her man was roused to passion.

I looked down into her crystal blue eyes and figured what she was thinking. I kissed her long and hard. "They shouldn't make new mothers so danged sexy," I whispered.

"Let's fill your other appetite, Lucas Dunn. Dinner's just about ready." She pulled away and pushed me toward the dining table.

Captain John Hughes sat tall in the saddle, as he led his men by a column of twos, south from Corpus Christi. They were headed back to the Rio Grande to deal with some threatening stirrings by a troublemaker named Pancho Villa.

His lieutenant pulled alongside. "If I may, Captain?"

"What's on your mind, John?"

"Will Lucas Dunn be joining us?"

Hughes cracked a broad grin. "One of these days, John. One of these days." He looked off into the distant horizon. "Texas Rangers never give up the badge." He gave an extra nudge to his horse and pulled ahead of the lieutenant. "Never give up the badge," he said softly to himself.

EPILOGUE

THE NUECES STRIP of 1896 was still mostly a vast prairie of tall grasses and loamy sands stretching as far as the eye could see and beyond. Grasses tended to grow high enough to reach a horse's withers, though stands of live oak, mesquite, and prickly pear cactus brought to the prairie from the south mostly by seed-carrying birds and by cattle droppings had already begun to proliferate. Winds blowing through the wiregrass created their own special music. Brush proliferated, often creating nearly impenetrable barriers owing to the density and occasional thorniness. The Nueces Strip, called "Wild Horse Desert" by some, reached south from the lazily flowing Nueces River all the way to the meandering Rio Grande along Texas's southern border. Its eastern extremity enjoyed the sea breezes wafting in off the Gulf of Mexico from Corpus Christi all the way to Brownsville. Nestled in hills at its northern extreme was the little town of Uvalde, while the semi-arid rolling terrain of Laredo was generally regarded as its far western reach. Rough but serviceable roads were being carved out of the Strip and mostly paralleled the railroads.

A form of creative destruction was in full flower. While telephones were supplanting telegraph, railroads had made huge strides in reaching their tentacles across the frontier toward expanding the transport of goods heretofore limited to boats on meandering waterways and wagons on ill-kept trails. Towns were often made or destroyed by the routes chosen by the railroads.

Despite its uninviting environment, the Nueces Strip drew opportunists like moths to a light bulb. Texas remained a prime destination for second chancers, folks who'd met with rough times and looked to restart their lives. Towns, farms, and ranches sprung up at record pace. They were pressed to conquer a challenging terrain. Mottes or small clusters of live oak or mesquite offered occasional shade relief on the sunbaked prairies. The often-dry creek beds and arroyos eventually filled with rainwater and emptied into Nueces Bay and...farther to the east...Corpus Christi Bay. Flash flooding was an ongoing fear. Summers? Well, they tended to be hot and humid. Weather was pretty much whatever you wanted, if you waited long enough.

The abundant animal life on the Nueces Strip featured deer, javelina, fox, coyote, lynx, black bear, and mountain lion. Armadillos and prairie dogs competed for prairie real estate. At one point, horses were more numerous on the Strip than any animal, including humans. Occasionally, spotted ocelots and even wolves could be sighted by the practiced eye. Owls, hawks, eagles, buzzards...they abounded. Come spring, wildflowers swept across much of the landscape painted like a huge rainbow, with scarlet sage, hibiscus, daisies, poppies, lilies, and the ubiquitous bluebonnets. Groves of cypress, juniper, and palmetto could be found. Pecan trees drew their sustenance from rich soil along the Nueces River. The very name "Nueces" was Spanish for nuts. Cactus, along with yucca and agave, abounded. The Nueces Strip surely served as God's canvas.

If you were on foot, it was advisable to keep an eye and ear peeled for rattlesnakes. They tended to blend in fairly well with their surroundings, so their rattle was often folks first and only warning of an impending attack. The rattlesnake spawned many a "Texas-ism" like "he's so bad he has rattlesnake fangs and twice the venom" or "he's so tough, he cuddles with rattlesnakes."

Much of Texas history centers around the Nueces Strip. No discussion of it can ever be complete without mention that much of the most significant fighting of the Texas War for Independence was fought on and just north of the Nueces Strip back in 1835 and 1836. It was also scene to the first skirmishes of the Mexican-American War of 1846. The Strip was officially ceded to the United States by the Treaty of Guadalupe Hidalgo in 1848, though Texas had already laid claim.

While the "Cast of Historical Characters" provides some helpful true-to-life framework to the life and times on the Nueces Strip, woven into *Lone Star Vigilante*, are actual settlers of the frontier as drawn from my own extensive Texas family ancestry. Such real-life characters coupled with actual events have served to reinforce the fictional setting with a strong dose of reality. I have also tossed in an affectation undertaken by one of my characters. Mountain man, scout, and buffalo hunter, Buffalo Watts occasionally punctuates his statements with "Wagh!" It loosely translates to "Need I say more, it's all plain as day."

My poet/novelist cousin, Mary Maude Dunn Wright—pseud. Lilith Lorraine)—in writing the preface to her father "Red John" Dunn's biography *Perilous Trails of Texas* back in 1932, posed a convicting question: "Not in the spirit of judging their actions by artificial standards which in their day had no existence, but by asking ourselves if we were in their places, should we have acquitted ourselves as well, and by putting to ourselves the still more potent question: how well have we kept the birthright that thy have given us, how well have we safeguarded the liberties that they purchased through untold privations, how courageously are we meeting the problems that confront us today, in short when we stand before the tribunal of remote posterity, to whom shall the laurel be awarded?" Y'all might think on that.

The plentiful and accessible longhorn were for years the "low-hanging-fruit" of the Nueces Strip economy. They were a hardy breed that could withstand the South Texas heat, fend off disease-carrying pests, and carry just enough meat on their bones to make them reasonably profitable to raise. Originally brought from the Iberian Peninsula by early Spanish priests, the longhorns eventually escaped the mostly failing missionaries, proliferated, and roamed wild and free across the prairies. Millions of the beasts soon covered Texas and especially the excellent grazing lands of the Nueces Strip. They competed with those wild mustangs that had also been introduced by the Spaniards. Ranchers were increasingly importing and breeding meatier, shorter-horned breeds like Brahmans, Angus, Herefords, and even Richard King's Santa Gertrudis. Of course, there had been the indigenous buffalo, millions of the beasts. They'd been a staple of the indigenous people's way of life until their hides were taken in wholesale slaughters to enrich eastern merchants and scions of fashion. The Texas prairies nevertheless provided plenty of feed for all.

The factor that would ultimately win the west was the family—the larger, the better as children grew up in the face of all manner of lurking dangers. Families established the ranches and farms popping up not only throughout the eastern portions of the Nueces Strip but across Texas as a whole. People sought fresh opportunities. The territory east of the 98th meridian, sliced through the very heart of Texas that was fast becoming an economic juggernaut, and the Strip was no exception. Its economy was based on growing cotton and raising cattle and horses. Cotton was bundled and hauled to port for transport to markets in Louisiana and points east while cattle were driven mostly to Texas slaughterhouses.

Indians were pushed ever westward, as tribes were overcome by a cocktail of socioeconomic forces and disease.

While the frontier grew ever westward, there was ongoing worry about the threats posed by Comanche, Kiowa, and Lipan Apache, as well as the rogue marauding bandits from south of the Rio Grande and lawbreaking opportunists from the east. This all served to keep early Texans on this wild and often lawless frontier ever vigilant. It was easy to make the case for calling up companies of Texas Rangers to patrol the Nueces Strip, as they took it upon themselves to go where the military found it politically undesirable. On the other hand, the legislators in the state capital in Austin often were unable to pull together the financial means to fund the necessary companies of Rangers. They had to rely on the US Army, which could be chancy at best, as it was subject to the politics of whomever was in power and the perceiving of real or imagined threats.

Thus, the setting for these later Tumbleweed Sagas is hardly any less challenging than mere decades before. Yet civilization marches inexorably onward, taming the remaining frontier.

A LOOK AT BOOK NINE
GUNS ON THE GUADALUPE

Blood runs hot beyond the Nueces Strip.

Texas Ranger Lucas Dunn, Jr. ("Junior") rides deep into the heart of South Texas in 1896, where the Guadalupe River hides more than just water beneath its surface. Five brutal murders in Kerrville bring Junior under the command of legendary Ranger Captain John Hughes—and into the crosshairs of killers with nothing to lose.

Land-hungry men. A vengeful hired gun. A seductive, scheming temptress. And the dark influence of powerful politicians. The closer Junior gets to the truth, the more tangled—and deadly—the trail becomes.

With the advice of famed U.S. Deputy Marshal Bass Reeves guiding him, Junior wages a quiet war against chaos. But when a threat strikes too close to home, he'll do whatever it takes to protect his wife, Cassie —even if it means meeting death face to face.

Justice rides fast in Texas. And in the shadows along the Guadalupe, it might not ride alone.

AVAILABLE JULY 2025

ACKNOWLEDGMENTS

Authoring books simply doesn't happen in a vacuum. The author provides the creative talent and crafts the stories, but there's so much more that demands acknowledgment. There's lots of folks and places that contribute to my authoring endeavors. So, it is with *Lone Star Vigilante: Justice Texas Style*. It takes place in 1895, ten years after my Tumbleweed Sagas series. The epic exploits of the legendary Texas Ranger Captain Luke Dunn were at the core of the Sagas, but this novel stands apart. Luke Dunn's son has pinned on the Texas Ranger badge. The Tumbleweed Sagas now become his story.

At its core, this tale is also about the taming of the Nueces Strip. Its protagonist symbolizes the lawman image, the pursuer of law and order in the person of a hero, protector, knight-errant sort of character. But there's much more to him. He embodies a family legacy of grit, tenacity, rugged individualism, and bravery nuanced with a masculine vulnerability and a search for redeeming values. He epitomizes the freedom of America's western frontier and represents a final bastion of honor in America. Hopefully, readers will find *Lone Star Vigilante* an adventure worthy of their time and emotional involvement.

I've been blessed with many friends and family who have supported my writings. My wife Carolyn's reviews and encouragement were a huge help, along with very important tech support from our sons Mike and Matt. Other supporters have included Cara Miller, Jim May, Ernie Angell, Chris Haug, and my dear cousins Johnny Dunn, Jim & Cindy Holmgreen, Francette Meaney, and Eddie and Nancy Thornton. Many more friends have contributed support at some level to the creation and publication of *Lone Star Vigilante: Justice Texas Style*, be it encouragement or advice.

Naturally, I am major grateful to the great folks at Wolfpack Publishing. The team they bring to publishing is first-rate, from editing to typeset to cover design and the myriad tasks that lead to successful book sales.

It's only right to acknowledge my ancestors who were actual settlers of the south Texas frontier. In addition to inspiring me, they provided a quite helpful true-to-life framework as to the life and times on the Texas Nueces Strip. It was appropriate to weave them into the tapestry of my western novels. Matthew Dunn (1809-1863) immigrated to Corpus Christi from County Kildare in 1845, established a homestead on Upriver Road in Nuecestown, and served as a sutler to General Zachary Taylor's Army in the Mexican-American War. Peter Dunn (1807-1890) immigrated from Ireland in 1850 and established a blacksmith shop in Corpus Christi, John Dunn (1803-1889) ranched and grew thousands of acres of cotton, Lawrence Dunn (1837-1864) fought and died with Captain Ware's Confederate cavalry, and my great-great-grandfather Nicholas Dunn (1835-1912) was a rancher, drover, livestock speculator, marksman, and Comanche fighter of some repute. My cousin John Beamond "Red John" Dunn (1851-1940) served as a Texas Ranger in the 1870s under Captain Bland Chamberlain (Company H), subsequently joined a "vigilance committee," became a farmer and merchant, and curated a museum of military weapons displayed to this day in the Corpus Christi Museum of Science & History. Red John Dunn's brother Matthew Dunn also served as a Texas Ranger, and another cousin, Rut Evans, served as a Texas Ranger in the 1890s—Company E, Frontier Battalion, Alice, TX. My cousin Patrick Dunn was quite successful at raising longhorns on

North Padre Island east of Corpus Christi from 1883 to 1937. John Hillard Dunn (1883-1958), whose personal narrative about his family and his own adventures drove my pursuit of my Texas family and inspired my own writings. Finally, my grandfather, Horace Charles Greathouse served as a Texas Ranger in 1920—Company C, Austin, TX. Such real-life characters coupled with actual events have served to reinforce the historical settings and aura for my writings.

Most of my authoring has occurred in my home office as decorated to channel my inner Texan, but my creative juices have often been inspired and imagination stoked in cafés and coffee houses across America. My favorites were Hester's Café & Coffee Bar in Corpus Christi, TX; Nueces Café in Robstown, TX; Java Ranch Espresso Bar & Café in Fredericksburg, TX; PAX Coffee & Goods in Kerrville, TX; Ragged Edge Coffee House and Bantam Coffee Roasters in Gettysburg, PA; 1889 Coffee House in Helena, MT; Dunn Brothers Coffee in Rapid City, SD; Postmasters Coffee & Bakery and Brio Coffeehouse in Waynesboro, PA; Birdie's Café and American Ice Co Café in Westminster, MD; and Baltimore Coffee & Tea Co., Frederick Coffee Company & Café, Deja Brew Coffee in New Oxford, PA and Deja Brew at Miney Branch in Carroll Valley, PA; and Dublin Roasters in Frederick, MD. The décors and easy-listening music in these fine establishments, combined with friendly clientele and savory cups of coffee, tended to set me in the right creative frame of mind.

Last but not least, I'm especially thankful for the many folks who have read and enjoyed my books.

I do believe it is important to acknowledge how the old west represents the brave pioneering spirit of settlers that met the challenges and transcended mere survival to enable America to achieve exceptional growth. The settling of the American west is replete with tales of leveraging freedom for individual achievement. I hope you will agree that reliving our past—even through history-based fiction—often has the effect of pointing the way to an ever-brighter future. Might we be up to it? I hope that the inspiration I have drawn from my having walked the very earth my characters have trodden, coupled with my extensive historical research, will enable readers to fully experience the grit, adventure, and passion of my characters while sensing aromas of gunsmoke, trail dust, leather, and bluebonnets.

Thanks kindly to all of you.

ABOUT THE AUTHOR

 Award-winning author Mark Greathouse's love for the Western genre draws upon his deep family roots and love of the outdoors, honed from teen years spent hiking the Appalachian Trail and family travels across America's frontier. He hopes his work reveals his passion for America's western history.

A member of Western Writers of America and the Wild West History Association, Mark also contributes articles on the history of America's west to Western-themed magazines. He was recognized as a 2024 Finalist in the Western genre by the American Literary Book Awards for his sixth Tumbleweed Saga, *Nueces Truth: Texans Face War's Realities*.

Mark began writing full time after a successful career as a business executive and later as an entrepreneurial investor and advisor. His service as president of several business and community nonprofits led to their extraordinary growth. He holds a BA in English and MBA in marketing.

Mark also donates time and books annually to support wounded military warriors. He was a Boy Scout leader (Eagle Scout) and served on a local school board earlier in life.